The Apothecary

The Apothecary

THE APOTHECARY

The City of Dreams
Book One

The Scottish novelist Joan Fallon, currently lives and works in the south of Spain. She writes both contemporary and historical fiction, and almost all her books have a strong female protagonist. She is the author of:

FICTION:
Spanish Lavender
The House on the Beach
Loving Harry
Santiago Tales
The Only Blue Door
Palette of Secrets
The Thread That Binds Us
Love Is All

The al-Andalus series:
The Shining City (Book 1)
The Eye of the Falcon (Book 2)
The Ring of Flames (Book 3)

NON-FICTION:
Daughters of Spain

(all are available in paperback and as ebooks)

www.joanfallon.co.uk

JOAN FALLON

THE APOTHECARY

SCOTT PUBLISHING

The Apothecary

© Copyright 2019
Joan Fallon

ISBN 978 0 9955834 8 1
First published in 2019
Scott Publishing
Windsor, England

ACKNOWLEDGMENTS

My sincere thanks to my editor Sara Starbuck for helping me to create an exciting novel out of a turbulent period in history, to Lawston Designs for the cover, and Angela Hagenow for going through my manuscript and removing all the typos. Their advice and support have been invaluable.

Thanks also to 'Falconaumanni' creator of the map of the taifas, displayed on the following page. Creative Commons Attribution-Share Alike 2.5 Spain

MAP OF SPAIN AND PORTUGAL IN 1031 AD

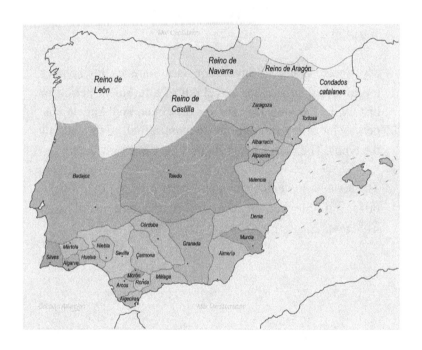

(published under licence Creative Commons Attribution-Share Alike 2.5 Spain Author Falconaumanni)

LIST OF MAIN CHARACTERS

The ruling class
Yahya ibn Ali ibn Hammud al Mutali, Khalifa of Malaqah
Fatima (his wife)
Hassan (his eldest son)
ben-Yahya (his youngest son)
Prince Idris ibn Ali ibn Hammud al Mutali (his brother)

The apothecary's family
Makoud ibn Ahmad
Basma and Abal (his wives)
Umar, Ibrahim and Dirar (his sons)
Aisha (his daughter)
Daud (his son-in-law, deceased)
Rafiq ibn Makoud, (his uncle)

Friends
Avi (a Jewish merchant)
Gideon (his son)
Rebekah (his wife)
Bakr ibn Assam (a shipwright)

The army
General Rashad
Talib (young soldier)

The court
Grand Vizier, Labib
Ibn Baqanna (new grand vizier)
Naja al-Siqlabi (tutor to the princes)
al-Azdi (servant to Yahya I)
Abu al-Jabir (royal physician)

Other rulers
Abbad I (ruler of Isbiliya)
Habbus al-Muzaffar (ruler of Garnata)
Samuel ibn Nagrilla (grand vizier of Garnata)
Muhammad ibn Abd Allah (ruler of Qarmuña)

MALAQAH

1035 AD

CHAPTER 1

When Aisha woke to the gentle cooing of the doves in the dovecot, the hurt was still there, on her left side, just beneath her heart. It was no longer the sharp pain that had taken her breath away when her dearest Daud had died in her arms. Now it was just a persistent ache that wouldn't leave her for a single moment.

She had cried that night as though her heart would break, and the next day and the next, and the next, until her father arrived and took her and the children back with him to his house, her old home.

How she missed her husband. When she'd looked at his wasted body, once so beautiful, now exhausted from his desperate struggle to live, she had wanted to die with him but the child within her body would not allow it. She knew she had to be strong for both the baby and his sister. She reached across and gently rocked his crib. Imran smiled in his sleep and rolled onto his side. Daud had never known he had a son; how proud he would have been and how pleased that she'd named him after Daud's father. Her daughter yawned and stretched her arms, but didn't wake.

She was a sturdy three-year old with a strong independent streak in her and loved sleeping up there on the roof in the summer; it was so much cooler for all of them than inside the house.

Aisha closed her eyes and thought of when she'd got married. It had been the most perfect day, one she had longed for since they had become betrothed. She and Daud had known each other since childhood—they were friends long before they became lovers—so it was only natural that when she reached puberty, her father spoke to Daud's parents about them getting married.

Tears filled her eyes as she thought back to those happy days, a time before the sickness came to Ardales. She wiped them away with the hem of her robe; there was no point dwelling on the past. She had to look forward; that's what Baba said. If not for herself then for the two sleeping children beside her.

A falcon lighted on the wall, his black eyes fixed on the dovecot. The doves had gone quiet now, sensing the danger. The bird remained motionless, waiting, watching for any movement. It was an adult male, white breasted and with a dark grey helmet; his eyes were ringed in yellow. He looked so quiet and gentle sitting there that you wouldn't think him capable of harming the doves, but she knew differently. She had seen peregrines chase pigeons, and other birds, relentlessly. Their prey would try in vain to outdistance them, weaving, swerving, diving, trying everything to get away from their predator, but nothing could shake off a falcon. Daud used to say that they were the fastest hunting birds there were and she believed him; she'd often seen a falcon dive on its prey like a streak of lightning and snatch it in its talons, then sit on the ground, tearing it limb from limb before devouring it. They loved the chase and pulled smaller birds from the sky as easily as picking olives; nothing was safe from them. This one wasn't a wild bird; she could see the jesses dangling from his legs. He probably belonged to her great-uncle who had a number of Barbary falcons and let her brother Umar take them out every evening to hunt. Aisha had often gone with him and Daud when she was younger, and before she was married. She heard a low whistle and the falcon flapped his long, pointed wings and soared into the air. He circled once, still with his eyes on the dovecot below him then flew off in the direction of the sound.

Today Umar was saying his farewells to the birds because the family was leaving for Malaqah. Today they were going to start a new life. Baba, as much as her, wanted to get away from Ardales and have a fresh start. They were the lucky ones, the ones who'd survived the sickness which had raged through the village and decimated the population. Not only had her dear husband died, but both her parents-in-law and her grandparents. Her great-uncle Qasim had done what he could to save them but all his physician's skill was useless; there was nothing he could do to cure them.

She stretched her arms and sat up. The sky was growing paler, a delicate pink creeping along the horizon; soon the sun would break upon the day, an orange-red ball of fire that would flood everything with its bright light. She ought to get up and rouse the children but her body felt heavy and lethargic. Baba had said they were to leave straight after prayers; it was a long walk to Malaqah. The lonely call of the imam began, ringing out across the valley. Below her she could hear her family stirring inside the house. Aisha sighed. If only Daud had been here then this would be an adventure filled with promise and excitement, but instead she was filled with dread. She had no choice in the matter; she was a widow and she was back living with her parents. She had to do as Baba wanted.

*

The road to Malaqah was long and dusty but she hardly noticed it; her heart was too full. At first she had believed Baba when he said that leaving Ardales was a good thing for her and the children, but now all she could think was that with every step she was moving further away from her beloved. She hoisted the baby onto her other shoulder, kissing his cheek absent-mindedly as she did so.

Maryam tugged at her skirt and whispered, 'Mama, when will we get there? I'm tired.'

'Soon, my little one. Soon.'

'Here, child, come and have a ride on the donkey,' said Makoud, taking his granddaughter's hand and swinging her onto its back.

Her father was smiling and looked happy to be on his way at last. Baba had been impatient to leave, but they had to wait out the period of mourning; by law Aisha should have remained in her mother-in-law's house until iddah was finished—four months and ten days—but the imam had allowed her to go back to her father because of the contagion. They had burnt all the bedding and most of the clothes that were in her mother-in-law's house—those had been Qasim's instructions. More people would have died if it hadn't been for his intervention; he set up a system of quarantine. He said it was the only way to stop the disease spreading. All the families who had the sickness in their houses were forbidden to go to the communal well, to the market and the mosque; instead people would take food and water to them and leave it outside their houses. The schools were closed and most people stayed within their own homes, frightened of infection. Aisha hadn't seen her parents for months, not until the dead had been buried and she'd been declared well and not contagious. Now all she had were her widow's robes: a white djubba, a veil, a grey djellaba and her wedding dress—she couldn't bring herself to burn it. But none of that mattered now. She tried to stop thinking about Daud; tried to remove those last images of him as she'd washed his emaciated body, closed his eyes and lips—lips that had once tasted so sweet—and wrapped him in his shroud. He now lay in the cemetery in a shallow grave so that he could continue to hear the imam calling the faithful to prayer, surrounded by the friends and family who'd suffered the same fate. She bit her lip in anguish; she should be there with him, not crossing the country in order to start a new life.

'What is it, daughter?' asked Abal, her mother. 'Why so sad?'

'It's nothing, Mama.'

'Would you like me to carry the baby for a while?'

Aisha gratefully handed little Imran to his grandmother. Her back ached. She stopped a moment to sit on a rock and remove a stone from her sandal. She must force herself to stop thinking of the past; she would never be able to move forward unless she did so. If this was to be a new beginning then she must put her children first and think of the future.

CHAPTER 2

The walls of Malaqah were now within sight. The city was like a jewel cast on the shores of the Middle Sea and surrounded by mountains. Makoud had been looking forward to this day for many long months. He had been born and bred in Qurtubah and it had pained him to leave the city, even though it was that or suffer at the hands of the Berber soldiers. His life in the small town of Ardales had been good; quiet and tranquil, and he and his family had been able to return to a normal life after two years of siege but despite that a restlessness had remained inside him. He had grown up with his nerves on edge, watching, waiting, never sure when the soldiers would come and terrorise Qurtuba; his mind was sharp to changes in his surroundings, his reactions fast. The young boy had become a warrior without realising it. And that warrior had remained inside him, always alert, forever restless.

Now he was a middle-aged married man, a family man, a respected apothecary. He had learned his trade in sleepy Ardales, following in his aunt's footsteps, but he was a hybrid—a man of peace who spent his days trying to cure people yet also a fighter, a man who could not shrug off his past. He longed for the excitement of living in a city once more. And now here he was, at the gates of Malaqah, the most important sea port along the southern coast. He could feel the quickening of his heart as he approached the high stone walls and looked up at the turrets of the alcazaba and its protective fortress looming above it.

His wives hadn't wanted to leave Ardales, especially his first wife, Abal, because she wanted to stay in the small country town where she'd been born. But he'd persuaded her that it would be good for Aisha to get away from the village and its memories, so she said no more. Makoud's three sons had been excited at the prospect of moving to a big city—they were still young, the eldest barely seventeen and full of the spirit of adventure—and, in the end, Basma, their mother, was happy as long as they were happy. Maybe he had been a bit manipulative but then that was his prerogative; he was the head of his family after all.

The little group of travellers stopped at the more northerly of the two bridges which crossed the sluggish Guadalmedina river. Ahead of them lay the Puerta de Antequera; their final stop along the mountainous road that had taken them from Ardales to Álora, across the Guadalhorce river to Almogía and along the winding valley of the Guadalmedina, with steep mountains on either side. Now they had arrived and once they went through that gate they would be in the city of Malaqah. He looked up and saw couple of soldiers walking along the ramparts; they stopped to study the travellers for a moment and then continued on their way, the sun glinting on their helmets.

'Is this it, then?' asked Abal, rather peevishly, as though she'd been expecting something altogether more grand than a fortified walled city.

'Yes, this is our new home,' replied Makoud, unable to keep his pleasure hidden. 'This is Malaqah.'

'It's very big,' said Dirar, his youngest son. 'And look at all those soldiers. Are they preparing for war?'

'War? You said it was safe here,' said Abal, instantly on her guard.

'It is safe here, wife. It is safe because the city is well protected. Come let me see a smile on your pretty face. Soon you'll be inspecting your new home. Avi sent word that he has found us a comfortable house within the city walls. He will take us to see it tomorrow.'

'So where are we staying tonight, Baba?' asked Aisha. She looked tired and worried; she had one small child in her arms and another hanging onto her robe.

'Don't worry daughter, Avi will look after us. He lives close by, in the alcalcería with the other cloth merchants. We can stay with him tonight.'

Avi was a friend he'd known as a child in Qurtubah. When the city had fallen to the Berber armies, Avi and his relatives had fled to Malaqah with other Jewish families. The Berbers had been indiscriminate in their killing but the Jews had fared far worse than most: Avi´s family had been lucky to escape.

'Had we better water the animals before we cross?' asked Basma. She was leading a brown faced donkey with large sad eyes, and a rather irritable mule with panniers on each side; behind them stood their camel, her jaw constantly in motion as she chewed the cud. All were heavily laden with the family's possessions: pots, pans, plates, jugs, clothing, bedding, plants that Abal would not leave behind—as though they couldn't find any new ones in Malaqah—cushions, oil lamps, rugs and a small cooking stove. Basma was his second wife and Abal had made sure that she always had the more menial jobs to do.

'Yes, you're right, wife. We will stop here for a while and let the animals rest.' In his haste to enter the city of his dreams he had forgotten that they had only stopped once since sunrise. No wonder his daughter was looking so exhausted.

'Tell us about your friend, Baba,' said Umar, his eldest son. 'How is it that you know someone living here? You told us that you'd never been to Malaqah before.'

'That's true; I haven't been here before but I had heard of it. As for Avi, I knew him when I was a boy; we went to the same school in Qurtubah and were close friends, even though he was Jewish and I was Muslim. The last time I saw him I must have been about your age. When the city fell we went our separate ways but then, a few years back, I heard about him again. It was quite by chance. You remember when your sister was getting married? She and Abal went to the souk to buy material for her wedding dress. Do you remember her dress? No, I don't expect you took much notice. Well it was made of the most exquisite white cotton.'

'I still have it, Baba,' said Aisha. 'I shall keep it for my own daughter's wedding.'

'Good. It cost me a small fortune.'

'What has this to do with Avi?' asked Umar, already losing interest.

'Well the merchant asked Abal if she knew of a man called Makoud ibn Ahmad, from Qurtubah. At first she wasn't sure what to say, but when he explained that he had bought the cotton from a Jewish merchant in Malaqah who said he was a friend of this Makoud, she remembered me speaking about Avi. So she told him where to find me.'

'And then you got in touch with your old friend again?' asked Dirar, who was hanging on every word. 'And that was Avi?'

'Yes, exactly. He has a thriving textile business now and he suggested I come here to live. He said there were great opportunities for young families.'

By now they'd found a wide stretch of river bank where the animals could reach the water with ease. A group of willow trees dragged their long branches in the river; it was a perfect place to rest out of the sun.

'Umar, Ibrahim take the panniers off the mule and Dirar, see to the donkey. I'll unload the camel,' said Makoud.

He set about loosening the ropes that tied their belongings to the animal's back and carefully slid them to the ground. He'd become fond of this camel over the past couple of days; she was quiet and even-tempered, not like some who could be quite vicious when they didn't know you, and difficult to control. She belonged to his uncle Rafiq who'd insisted they take her with them; but he knew that Makoud was not very good with animals and had chosen wisely.

They all stretched out on the river bank in the shade of the willows, while the animals drank their fill. Aisha closed her eyes and was soon asleep, leaving Abal to mind her grandchildren.

'The soldiers are watching us, Baba,' said Dirar, who was lying with his head propped up on his hands so that he could look across the river.

'It's just idle curiosity, son. I imagine it's a boring life standing guard all day. I expect they're glad of something new to talk about.'

The city wall was close to the Guadalmedina at this point and he could see the guards on the ramparts clearly. They all wore hauberks of linked mail that glittered in the westerly sun, and some of the guards were clearly bowmen, while others carried long lances. He had to admit that it looked more like a show of force than a routine guard, but he wasn't going to share his concern with Dirar. What was going on? Had something happened? Were they expecting an attack?

'I'm going to be a soldier,' said Umar, suddenly sitting up. 'I have decided. I will go straight to the Dar al-Jund and enlist.'

'What was that?' cried Basma, who had been dozing with her back against a tree. 'A soldier? No, Umar. Why on earth would you want to be a soldier?' She glowered at Makoud. 'This is your fault. You said we'd have a better life; the children would have a better education, but now your son wants to be a soldier.'

'So what if he wants to be a soldier? He's a man now. He can choose for himself,' Makoud said, irritably. If it wasn't one wife criticising him, it was the other. He was too soft with them.

'Maybe we all could be soldiers?' suggested Dirar, with a twinkle in his eyes. He knew how to tease his mother.

'That's enough Dirar. Don't upset your mother. Now go and see to the donkey. If they have all had their fill then we must get on our way. I want to get to Avi's house before nightfall.' The sight of the soldiers on the ramparts had unnerved him. The sooner he had his family safely inside the city walls, the happier he would be.

*

Avi was as good as his word. They found his house with little difficulty—everyone knew of Avi the merchant who lived in the barrio of the alcaiceria—and were greeted as long lost friends despite the fact that the two men hadn't seen each other for more than thirty years.

'As-salama alaykum, my old friend,' Avi said, hugging Makoud and kissing him on the cheeks. 'Welcome to my modest home. Welcome. As you will see, there is not a lot of space for you and your family here, but do not worry. Tomorrow I will take you to see the apothecary's shop I have found for you. The old man has died and he had no sons to take over his business, so his wives and daughters are selling it and moving back to the country. I'm sure you will find it perfect for your needs. But enough of that for now. Come in. Come in. Sit down. Take the weight off your feet and my daughter will bring you something cool to drink.'

One by one they removed their shoes and put on the slippers that were by the door, then trouped into Avi's rather splendid house and sat at the low table he indicated. Makoud was conscious of how weary and dusty they all looked from the journey in contrast to the gleaming tiled floor and the spotless silk cushions scattered across Persian rugs that seemed to be far too expensive to sit on.

'I need to see to the animals, first,' he said, hoping he'd get the chance to clean his face and hands before he sat down.

'No need. Joseph will attend to them. Come, sit down.' Avi clapped his hands lightly and a tall young man, with a fair complexion came into the room. 'Joseph, take ibn Ahmad's animals into the yard and give them some food and water.'

'Yes, Sayyad. What shall I do with their luggage?'

'Just unload it and store it in the same room for now. The sayeda will tell you what to do with it, later.'

For the first time Makoud became aware of the women, five of them, all standing by a flimsy dark curtain that separated the room where Avi conducted his business from the interior part of the house where his family lived. Five sets of round, black eyes were staring at him, identical in all aspects except for the amount of wrinkles around them. He made a guess: Avi's mother, his wife and his three daughters. Avi and his family were Sephardic Jews and today the womenfolk were all dressed in their local costume in honour of the visitors; the caps that each wore on their long hair were sewn with sequins and semi-precious stones and the hair itself covered by a brightly patterned scarf. The grandmother had an elaborately decorated shawl draped over her shoulders and they all wore wide silk sashes around their waists. They looked like five gaily coloured peacocks against the dust covered djubbahs of his own wives and daughter.

'Let me introduce you to my family,' Avi said, beckoning the women over.

Each in turn bowed politely to Makoud and his wives, then one of the daughters disappeared, only to return almost immediately with a tray of tiny glasses and a pot of mint tea.

Makoud was so thirsty that he could have drunk the entire pot himself but contented himself with sipping the sweet liquid politely. Gradually the women relaxed and began to chatter freely; they were eager to hear about their journey and whether they'd had any problems with bandits. A boy of about four-years-old looked shyly round the door and was soon playing with Aisha's daughter. Little by little he saw Aisha's face soften into the beautiful smile that he thought she'd lost forever and he felt a pang of guilt; he shouldn't have insisted that she move away from Ardales.

But it was done now and, in time, she would thank him for it.

*

Later that evening, after they'd all eaten and the women and children had gone to bed, the men sat together on the patio; they'd been joined by Avi's sons—all four of them and all working for their father. They were lively young men, who enjoyed talking about the family business, despite their father constantly trying to steer them on to other matters.

'So you had no problems on the journey?' one of them asked, reluctantly dropping the topic of how they could buy silk from Turkestan much cheaper than from Istanbul.

'No. But that's the second time I've been asked that today. Did you expect us to have problems?' Makoud asked, looking at his old friend.

'Well people have been on edge recently. We've lived in relative peace for the last ten years, ever since Malaqah became a taifa. But lately there have been so many rumours.'

'What kind of rumours?'

'There's always been a feud between the khalifa and the Abbadids. It goes back a long time, to when Abu al-Qasim ibn Abbad was nothing more than a local qadi in Isbiliya. One of the first things Yahya did when he became Khalifa of Qurtuba was appoint Abu al-Qasim as governor of Isbiliya but within a few months the turncoat had declared the city independent and established his own taifa. Quite a slap in the face for Yahya. The two families have been struggling for supremacy ever since.'

'Hence the rivalry between Malaqah and Isbiliya?' asked Makoud.

'Yes, it all comes down to two men trying to prove who's the stronger—a pissing competition in other words,' Avi said with a grin.

'But you said that's been the case for some years?'

'Yes, but now it seems that Yahya is on the attack. They've moved from who can piss the furthest, to war. There is talk that the khalifa's planning an offensive against Isbiliya. He won't win. He has to be mad if he thinks he can defeat Abbad.'

'Is it likely to happen?' asked Umar, suddenly much more interested in the conversation.

Avi shrugged. 'Who knows? One hears all the time of possible attacks from the Christian princes and threats from North Africa. When I came here I thought I was escaping war and famine. Now I'm not so sure.'

'There seemed to be a great many troops on the ramparts when we entered the city,' said Makoud.

'Just extra vigilance,' said Gideon, the older of Avi's sons, a tall, gangly youth with a typical Jewish cap set on his thick curly hair.

'So that's all there is to the rumours?' Makoud asked. 'No other problems that we should be aware of?'

'Well, only pirate attacks and bandits,' Avi said with a grin which reminded Makoud of their childhood—Avi was always trying to frighten him with some tall story or other.

'Oh, we country folk can cope with pirates and bandits,' he said, clapping Umar on the back. 'Isn't that right, son?'

Later that night, when he'd retired to his room, Makoud knelt to say his evening prayers. Tonight he would thank Allah, not just for his goodness but also for the gift of good friends and for bringing them all safely to this beautiful city.

CHAPTER 3

Yahya ibn Ali ibn Hammud al Mutali, Khalifa of Malaqah sat up, his head spinning, and clutched at the muslin coverings that hung over his bed. What was wrong with him? His heart was hammering away as if he were about to go into battle rather than waking from a night's refreshing sleep. But that was it, it hadn't been refreshing sleep at all. He, a man who could sleep in a tent on the battle field as soundly as if he were here in his own palace, had been beset with nightmares and hallucinations. He had dreamt that he was dead and roamed about the afterlife looking for a way into heaven; he had encountered men with horses' heads and sea serpents that spoke to him in a tongue he couldn't understand. And when he awoke he didn't know which way was up and which down, and he could swear that there was someone or something in his room. For a moment he thought it was his father, long dead these past seventeen years.

'Your Majesty, can I help you?' his servant asked, timidly.

'Yes, bring me a flask of water and pull those damned curtains back,' he snapped, struggling to regain his balance and escape from the enveloping muslin canopy.

The servant, a young lad, no more than ten-years-old, hesitated for a moment and then decided to deal with the curtains first before scampering off to bring his master the water.

Yahya put his head in his hands and waited for the dizziness to abate. Could he be ill? He wasn't even fifty yet; he was no age at all. He would send for his physician at once. No, he couldn't do that. If he spoke about his hallucinations they might think he was losing his mind. First he would go to the mosque and pray for Allah to help him. It was almost daybreak, soon the call of the imam would be echoing through the city.

'Hurry child,' he said, taking the delicately formed glass that the servant had just filled for him. 'Now run and tell al-Azdi to come and dress me. The sun is about to rise.'

And with its rays dispel the demons from my head, he finished the quote in his head. Yes, prayer would help him clear his mind. He could not afford to be ill, not now; not with Abbad's army at his door. This was the best chance they'd have to defeat that Abbadid traitor Abu al-Qasim; his own army looked strong and— insha'Allah—he would have the support of his neighbour Habbus al-Muzaffar from Garnata. This time Allah would grant them victory.

'Your Majesty,' said a tall, thin man, bowing low before the khalifa so that his flowing green robes swept the floor behind him. It was al-Azdi.

'Make haste and prepare me for morning prayers,' he told him, a little more harshly than he intended. He stood thinking of other things as his servant disrobed him and then followed him into his private bath area. He could see the steam rising from the hot pool as he tottered over to it. His masseur was already waiting for him.

'Your Majesty, would you like me to trim your beard?' the masseur asked. He had a huge razor in his hand and for a moment Yahya imagined it dripping in blood.

'No,' he barked. 'Not today.'

'But Your Majesty, you like to have your beard neat before you go to the mosque,' the masseur said. 'It is rather long today.'

Was he threatening him? The Nubian was smiling at him broadly, his big even teeth gleaming in the flickering light from the oil lamps.

'Is there something wrong with your ears?' Yahya demanded, angrily. Was this a conspiracy? Had someone hired this man to murder him? 'Leave me now, before I send for the Palace Guard.'

The masseur backed away quickly and allowed the khalifa to step into the hot water.

This was what he needed, to relax, to let his mind rest. He lay back so that his head was under the water and held his breath. He could see the lights from the oil lamps flickering on the surface of the water above him; it was quiet and peaceful lying there below the water. He could stay here forever. Suddenly the pressure in his chest was too much and he rose to the surface, gasping in the perfumed air greedily.

'Is everything all right, Your Majesty?' asked the masseur.

What was he still doing here? Was he going to drown him now?

'Azdi,' he called. 'Azdi, come here.'

'Yes, Your Majesty?'

'Who is that man? Get rid of him. I don't want to see him again. Ever,' he whispered to the servant.

'It's your masseur, Taofik, Your Majesty. He has been with you for many years,' al-Azdi replied.

'I don't care. Get rid of him. Call the guards. Throw him out. Now.'

'Of course, Your Majesty.'

He watched as the hapless masseur was led away by two burly palace guards and leaned back and closed his eyes. He was safe now. The hot bath was doing him good. His muscles were relaxing and he could feel his head clearing. It had been nothing, just the stress of the impending campaign playing tricks with his mind.

Now he could look to the future. Before the year was out Abbad I would be defeated and he, Yahya I, would rule Isbiliya; the taifa of Malaqah would be the greatest in al-Andalus and he would be its khalifa. It made his blood boil to think of how his enemy had betrayed him. And to think that he was the one who gave Isbiliya to Abbad in the first place. What a mistake that had been, but he hadn't known then what a treacherous man he could be.

Yahya had come a long way since being governor of Sebta—a role that he had now happily handed over to his brother Idris. Their father, Ali ibn Hammud, had been a good man and a great warrior; it was he who had founded the Hammudid dynasty and become Khalifa of Qurtubah. When he died, instead of inheriting what was rightfully his, Yahya had to fight for ten long years to gain the khalifa's throne. First his uncle Qasim had taken the crown, then that bastard son of his, Muhammad. At last the people of Qurtubah, tired of so many rebellions, asked Yahya to become their ruler. He'd been delighted to assume the title without having to fight for it—his uncle was dead and Muhammad had been deposed—and to be acknowledged as ibn Hammud's rightful successor. However when he went to Qurtubah he could see that the city was no longer the impenetrable stronghold that it had been in the days of the Omayyads and tension was rife, so he went back to Malaqah, leaving Qurtubah in the hands of his grand vizier. And he'd been right to do so. Within six months his grand vizier had been expelled and the people of Qurtubah had elected another khalifa.

They were turbulent times. But, as the wise man says, good may blossom from misfortune and that is exactly what happened to him. He was the rightful khalifa by birth, but he needed a kingdom. He decided to create the independent taifa of Malaqah for himself. This new taifa stretched from the frontier with Garnata in the east to the Pillars of Hercules in the west and included the smaller enclaves of al-Jazira and Sebta. This was his kingdom. Now he was about to make it even greater.

'Your Majesty, it's time to move into the cold pool,' said al-Azdi. 'It is almost dawn.'

Yahya stretched his lean, muscular body one last time in the warm bath and stood up. The water glistened on his dark Berber skin and formed a pool at his feet. He felt better already; his mind was no longer troubled and he could see his nightmares for what they were, simply bad dreams brought on by anxiety. He stepped into his slippers and made his way to the final bath, the cold one.

*

General Rashad waited for the grand vizier and leader of the Zirid army, Samuel ibn Nagrilla, in the reception room of the royal palace in Garnata. As he stood by the window, listening to the sound of running water in the palace gardens, he looked at the view with the eye of a seasoned soldier. The fortress had been built some two hundred years before, on the site of some Roman ruins. It was in a good position, on a hilltop above the city—the Romans had always chosen good defensive situations for their forts—with wide-ranging views over the surrounding land. It was fertile ground, planted with oranges, lemons, wheat, barley and sugarcane, plenty to sustain a besieging army. He could even see a grove of pomegranates. The fort itself was formed from the land around it, a reddish clay, which had created a small, ugly fortress that looked incapable of withstanding any sustained attack. Recently it had undergone extensive renovations and rebuilding, instigated he assumed, by ibn Nagrilla after the fall of the nearby Medina Elvira when the townspeople, many of them Jewish, had decided to make Garnata al-Yahud their new home. Its fortifications may have been improved but it was still possible that the city would benefit from strong allies; an alliance with Malaqah would be to their advantage.

'As-salama alaykum, General. Welcome to Garnata al-Yahud. It is indeed a pleasure to meet you in person. Your reputation precedes you,' said the tall, robed figure of ibn Nagrilla. 'I hope I have not kept you waiting long?'

'Ahlan wa sahlan. Not at all,' replied the General. He too had heard of Samuel ibn Nagrilla's reputation as the emir's right-hand man, a Jew who had risen to a position of power in Garnata that was only second to al-Muzaffar himself.

'Come inside and have some refreshment,' his host said, leading the way into a small room off a central patio. 'We can speak more freely in here.'

Rashid sat down on a low sofa covered in a fabric richly woven with peacocks and geometric designs; on the table before him were glasses, a pitcher of water, and a green and blue plate of figs. Simple fare.

Ibn Nagrilla poured out two glasses of water, saying, 'Would you prefer tea? I can call for some tea.'

The General shook his head. He knew they had to go through the traditional protocol of polite conversation but he just wanted to get down to business and he had the feeling that ibn Nagrilla felt the same.

'So, tell me, General Rashad, to what do we owe the honour of your visit?' the grand vizier of Garnata asked, after he had run through the usual etiquette of asking about his guest's journey, his family, and the health of the khalifa.

General Rashad sipped some of the water; it was deliciously cold as though it was fresh from a mountain spring, most likely from the snow-capped mountains he could see through the window.

'I have come, ibn Nagrilla, at the command of Khalifa Yahya I. He is planning an attack on Isbiliya and he would like your support. He believes that Abbad I has become too powerful and will continue to expand his kingdom unless he is stopped. He is sure that Abbad has eyes on the taifas of Malaqah and Garnata and he wants to stop him before it's too late.'

'I see.'

The general watched his host carefully, trying to read his thoughts.

Ibn Nagrilla lent back on the silk cushions and stroked his beard pensively. After a long period he sat up and said, 'This is not something that has escaped our attention. We know that Abbad has expansionist ambitions; he would dearly love to subjugate us to his rule and no doubt, Yahya I is correct in his assumptions about Malaqah as well. However, we must be realistic. Garnata does not have a large army and I assume neither does Malaqah, otherwise you would not be here. Even together we could not defeat Abbad I. Our combined strengths would not amount to half his troops. I believe it would be the greatest of follies to attack him without further allies. Has Yahya I considered joining forces with one of the Christian princes? Or employing mercenaries?'

General Rashad had been expecting this response; he knew he had come on a fool's errand. There was no way they could defeat Isbiliya, with or without the support of the Zirids, but the khalifa had been adamant.

'He doesn't want to ally himself to any of the Christian princes; he sees them as an enemy worse than Abbad and he hates Abbad with a passion. As for the independent mercenary armies, he doesn't trust them. He thinks the smaller Muslim taifas should band together in a show of combined force.'

'Well, I'm sorry, but I couldn't commit our army to such a reckless attack on Isbiliya,' said ibn Nagrilla. 'Not without more allies.'

So that was that. He'd come on a fruitless journey, just as he'd expected. The general rose and was about to wish the grand vizier a good day, when ibn Nagrilla motioned for him to sit down again.

'That does not mean we will not help the khalifa to weaken his enemy's dominance over al-Andalus. That would be to everyone's advantage. Be seated, my friend and we will discuss this further,' he said.

The general was intrigued. Maybe this wouldn't be a wasted visit after all.

'It is impossible for small taifas like us to tackle Isbiliya head on; they have too many allies,' the grand vizier continued. 'So what we must do is defeat Abbad's allies first, one by one. In that way we will become stronger and he will weaken. Then, and only then, can we attack him.'

The general stared at him. It was a clever plan. 'Where do we start?' he asked.

'I would suggest with Qarmuña. It lies right on the border between Malaqah and Isbiliya. If the khalifa defeats Qarmuña he will be able to move his troops right up to the frontier with Isbiliya.'

'And would your armies support us in this?' asked the general.

'Yes. That is something we'd be happy to do.'

'What will al-Muzaffar say about this idea?'

'That is not a problem. I have already suggested it as an alternative plan and he is in complete agreement,' replied ibn Nagrilla.

'Very well, I will put your proposal to the khalifa.'

'Good. Now that our business is concluded, may I offer you some more refreshment?'

*

When Yahya returned from the mosque, General Rashad was already waiting for him. He looked tired and dishevelled, as if he'd ridden all night

'What news from the Zirids, General?' he asked.

'As-salama alaykum, Your Majesty. I have just returned from Garnata this morning, and I have spoken with the grand vizier.'

'And? Will they help us to defeat Isbiliya?' Yahya asked, eager to hear their answer.

'No, Your Majesty. Forgive me, but ibn Nagrilla says it is foolhardy to take on Abbad's army; they are too strong. He says that even our combined forces won't be sufficient to defeat him.'

'The man's a coward. What did al-Muzaffar say?'

'I did not speak with the emir, but I know that he holds his grand vizier in high esteem. He will heed his advice.'

'The advice of a Jew?'

'He may be a Jew, Your Majesty, but he is a very powerful man,' replied the General.

'So that's it. We will fight the bastard alone,' said Yahya, the rage building up in his chest. He was not afraid to tackle the armies of Isbiliya. He was not afraid of anyone.

'If I may speak, Your Majesty?' General Rashad said.

'What?'

'Ibn Nagrilla suggested that the only way to defeat Abbad was to first conquer his allies and leave him weakened and without support.'

Yahya, who had been about to storm out of the room, hesitated and asked, 'What did he mean by that?'

'He said that although the Zirids wouldn't help us to attack Isbiliya, they would be prepared to support us in an attempt to conquer Qarmuña. He thinks that such a move would weaken Abbad considerably.'

'Qarmuña, you say? Well, that is interesting. They are staunch allies of Abbad I; I know he relies on them. Qarmuña, eh? Maybe this Jew is more cunning than I thought.'

'What's that, brother? Which Jew are you talking about?' asked Idris, striding into the room and throwing himself down next to the khalifa.

'As-salama alaykum, dear brother,' he said. He was fond of Idris; they were full brothers and grew up together. 'I thought you were in Sebta? What is the governor doing so far from his charge? Is something wrong?'

'Wa alaykum e-salam, Your Majesty,' Idris said, embracing his brother. 'Don't worry I've left everything under control. Ibn Baqanna is in sole charge; you can imagine how happy that makes him. I just came to see if the rumours were true.'

'What rumours?' asked Yahya. And what did Idris mean about ibn Baqanna? Was the vizier after more power? Allah help him. Was there no-one he could trust?

'About Isbiliya. Are you mounting a campaign against Abbad?'

'So you travelled all this way just to check up on my plans? Or maybe to fight at my side?' Yahya, brushed aside his fears and smiled broadly at his brother. 'Well I'm glad you're here Idris, even though I didn't send for you. The plan has changed. We're not attacking Isbiliya. We will attack their ally, Muhammad ibn Abd Allah, instead.'

'The ruler of Qarmuña?'

'Exactly. This time next week Qarmuña will belong to Malaqah. We will defeat Muhammad's army, occupy the city and our presence there will stop Isbiliya's relentless expansion. There is no need to attack Abbad head on.'

'What about the Zirids? Will they support us?'

'Yes, little brother. Listen carefully while General Rashad explains our strategy.'

After the General had given an account of his talk with ibn Nagrilla and left to begin preparations for the forthcoming campaign, Idris turned to his brother and asked, 'Well Yahya, will you be well enough to go with us to Qarmuña?'

'Of course I will. Whatever gives you the idea that I wouldn't want to lead my army into battle?'

'Forgive me for saying this, dear brother, but I'd also heard that you weren't your usual self. That is the real reason I have left Sebta; I wanted to see for myself. There is a dreadful sickness in the country; they say the ships brought it from the east. Many people are ill and some have even died.'

'Well now that you can see for yourself that I am fit and well, your mind can rest easy; I don't have any sickness. But I thank you for your concern. So, will you join us in Qarmuña?'

'I will indeed, brother,' said Idris, putting his arm around him. 'And how are my little nephews? Not long before Hassan will be riding beside you.'

Yahya smiled. His sons were still very young but already they were learning the art of war. Idris was right; they would soon be accompanying him into battle. How good it felt to have two healthy sons to succeed him.

'It'll be a good few years yet before they are old enough for that. Now go and join General Rashad; you need to make plans for the campaign.' He smiled at his brother again, and said, 'I'm looking forward to seeing Abbad's face when we take Qarmuña. He won't be able to ignore us, Hammudid brothers fighting side by side.'

'Yes, and right at his gate.'

CHAPTER 4

Their new home was everything Makoud had wanted; the shop was not large but there was a spacious room at the back where he could prepare his potions and creams, and adequate accommodation above for the family. Better than all that was its position; it was situated right by the wall to the alcazaba which meant many of his numerous customers came from the royal palace: servants seeking precious aromatics for the khalifa, soldiers looking for salves to cure their wounds or potions to either calm their nerves or increase their libido, doctors needing their prescriptions prepared, the eunuchs from the zenana buying cosmetics and creams for the women of the harem, even cooks looking for special culinary herbs that they couldn't find in the souk, or ointments for the many burns that seemed to happen in the royal kitchens. From the first day they arrived, he had been rushed off his feet. Ibrahim, somewhat reluctantly, had joined him in the shop and worked alongside him.

'Baba, can you come. There's a man in the shop asking for something I've never heard of before. Will you speak to him, please,' said Ibrahim one morning, about a month after they'd arrived.

'I expect it's something quite simple,' said Makoud, wiping his hands and coming into the shop. 'As-salama alaykum, how may I help you?' he asked, bowing to the stranger.

'You're the new apothecary?'

'Yes. May I present myself, I am ibn Qasim. What can I do for you?'

'What happened to the other one? The old man?' the man asked, looking around at the changes that Makoud had made to the shop. By the manner of his speech he appeared to be some kind of foreigner, a slave maybe, who'd been sent on an errand by his master.

'I believe he died. Was there something I could get you?' he asked, beginning to feel impatient with the man. He needed to get back to preparing a new batch of deodorant.

'I told the lad. I need some Artemisia absinthium. Do you have any?' He said the words slowly and clearly as though he'd been taught what to ask for.

'Wormwood? Yes, it's one of the plants that we keep but we don't sell it very often. Why do you want it?'

'I don't see that is any business of yours, but if you must know my wife wants it to make some sweetmeats. I'm very partial to its liquorice flavour.'

'Just a moment.' Makoud went into the back room and found a small piece of wormwood. He wrapped it in a piece of cloth and went back into the shop. 'Here you are. Tell your wife to be careful with it. Wormwood can have a strong effect if you add too much.'

'She knows what she's doing,' the man snapped. He unwrapped the piece. 'It's a bit small.'

'It's all I have at the moment. Do you want me to order some more for you?'

'I think you'd better. This won't last any time at all.' He thrust a coin into Makoud's hand and marched out.

'What a rude man,' said Ibrahim. 'What was that all about?'

'I don't know, but I doubt if he wanted it for his wife. In fact, I doubt if he even has a wife.'

'Baba, you know we have a whole box of wormwood in the back. I saw it when I was unpacking but I didn't know it was called Artemisia absinthium.'

'That's its scientific name. You're right son, we do have more of it, but wormwood is a dangerous substance. It can provoke hallucinations and even lead to seizures and death. I have to be careful whom I sell it to. Some people take it especially for that effect. They say it's like being able to fly. But usually it's women who buy it. They either want it, as he said, to make sweetmeats, or they think it will help them to see into the future.'

'Like the wise women?'

'Exactly. But he didn't look like a wise woman to me, and I don't think his wife will be making cakes with it.'

'What should we do if he comes back? He looks as though he could get angry if we refused to sell it to him,' said Ibrahim.

'As he said, it's not our business what he wants it for. We'll just be careful not to sell him too much in one go. That way he may not kill himself, or anybody else for that matter.' Although he wouldn't be much loss to the world, Makoud thought as he went back to grinding the herbs for the deodorant.

He had not been but a few minutes when he heard Ibrahim calling him again.

'What is it, now?' he asked, rather irritably. Then he stopped, feeling embarrassed at his surly manner. Avi's wife and one of her daughters were standing in the shop, examining some phials of perfume.

'Rebekah. What a pleasure to see you,' he said, his face now wreathed in smiles. 'As-salama alaykum.'

'Wa alaykum e-salam, dear friend.'

'How can I help you? Have you come looking for perfume? I only have a few fragrances at the moment,' he explained, 'but I will be making more. Rose water, lavender and a combination of jasmine and myrtle.'

'We haven't come to buy perfume, Makoud, although it all smells divine. Perhaps another time. We've come to visit Aisha. Is she at home?' Rebekah replied. 'I've brought her some typical Jewish pastries; I think she will like them.'

'She'll be delighted to see you,' he said, wiping his hands on a cloth and removing the overall he always wore over his tunic when he was working. 'Our rooms are above the shop; I'll take you up there.'

He pulled back the curtain hiding the staircase and stood back to let them go up first.

'Ibrahim, mind the shop while I show the ladies where we live,' he said, looking back at his son and wondering at the rather silly smile on his face. 'Is everything all right?'

'Yes, Baba. Everything is just fine.'

By the time Makoud had joined Rebekah and her daughter they were already chatting happily to his two wives and Aisha; he felt superfluous and stayed just long enough to sample one of the pastries before returning to his workshop.

But the deodorant was unlikely to get made that morning. No sooner had he put on his overall again and started to grind the herbs, when he heard the sound of horses' hooves in the street. They stopped outside the shop and then someone called his name.

'See who that is, Ibrahim,' he said. He had no idea who could be visiting him, but he was intrigued when he heard loud laughter and shouting. Who on earth could it be? And on horseback too?

His curiosity was about to get the better of him when Ibrahim ran into the back room crying, 'Baba, come quick. It's great-uncle Rafiq. You'll never guess what he has brought.'

Makoud felt his stomach lurch. He didn't like surprises; they usually meant bad news. Had something happened at home? Had someone died? Why would Rafiq come all this way if it wasn't urgent.

'Uncle Rafiq? What on earth are you doing here?' he asked, staring in astonishment at his grizzled old uncle who sat astride an enormous black stallion, the reins in one hand and holding the bridle of a young bay mare in the other. 'Is everything all right?'

'That's not a very nice way to greet your ammu, my man. As-salama alaykum is the usual form of greeting.'

'Wa alaykum e-salam,' Makoud replied with a slight bow but couldn't prevent a big grin spreading across his face. He'd always liked Rafiq. His uncle had a habit of doing things that were out of the ordinary. What was it this time?

Rafiq swung himself out of the saddle, tied the horses to the hitching post then turned and hugged Makoud against his barrel chest. 'So how is my favourite nephew? I see you've settled in. Prime position. Right by the alcazaba. You must have influential friends.'

'Yes. We opened the shop a few weeks ago and since then we haven't stopped. You got my letter?' asked Makoud.

'Yes. Everyone was glad to learn you were safe. And I was especially pleased to hear that young Umar has enlisted. Actually that's part of the reason I'm here. I've brought him a present.' He turned and stroked the black face of the bay he'd just hitched to the post. It was a magnificent young mare, with the typical broad forehead and small muzzle of the Arabian breed.

'That's for Umar? But it's worth a fortune. He won't be able to pay you for it for years—if ever.'

'I told you; it's a present. If he's going to be a soldier then he must join the jinetes and to do that he needs a horse. You can't have a horseman without a horse. And his life will depend on having the right one, so who better than me to pick out the right steed for my little Umar?'

'Not so little. You should see him in his uniform. I barely recognised him, and his mother went into hysterics; she is convinced he will be killed before the year is out. Come inside and we'll go up and see the family.'

'Later. I must take the horse to Umar first, and deliver this one to the royal stables.' He swung himself back into the saddle and stroked the neck of the stallion. 'Now this one really is worth a fortune. I expect to be able to retire with what the khalifa will pay me for him.'

'How will you get back to Ardales without a horse?'

'Do you still have my camel?'

'Of course.' They had left the animal with Avi for the moment, unwilling to sell it. Both the donkey and mule had already been sold to raise money to buy stock for the shop.

'Good, then that's your question answered. I'll go back by camel.' He laughed. 'It's a long time since I rode a camel. It could be fun.'

'Is that you, uncle Rafiq?' asked Aisha, stepping out into the sunlight. 'How lovely to see you.'

'And you, my child. How do you like your new home?'

'Very well, thank you,' she replied, rather formerly Makoud thought. The poor girl still wasn't happy here. 'Baba, I'm taking the children to Rebekah's house, to play. I won't be long.'

'Very well,' Makoud said, pleased that his daughter was at last taking an interest in doing something other than sitting inside all day.

'Will great-uncle Rafiq be here when I get back?' she asked.

Makoud looked at his uncle, 'You'll stay with us tonight?' he asked.

'Of course, nephew. I'm looking forward to hearing all about your adventures. I'll see you all later, insha'Allah.' He pulled his djellaba around his shoulders and said, 'Ma'a salama, Makoud.'

'Alla ysalmak, ammu.'

Just then a squad of soldiers went past them, heading for the Boveda Gate. They marched in unison to the beats of the young drummer who led the way. Makoud watched them, wondering if Umar was among them, but it was difficult to identify any particular soldier, dressed as they all were in their red cloaks, padded tunics and white turbans. Were the rumours true? Was Yahya planning to attack Isbiliya? Would these young men soon be marching to war?

CHAPTER 5

Al-Azdi had a lot to prepare for the campaign; the khalifa expected everything to be just as it was in the palace. He had spoken to the cooks, to make sure that they would have enough of the delicacies that the khalifa liked. No soldier's fare for him. Even eating in a field tent he expected the best cutlery and dishes, and food fit for a khalifa. Woe betide his servants if anything was below standard. Al-Azdi smiled to himself. Maybe he wouldn't be so demanding on this campaign; it was obvious that his health was failing him. He hadn't visited his harem for weeks; a sure sign that he was unwell.

Thinking about Yahya's harem wiped the smile from his face. His beautiful sister, may Allah keep her safe, had been one of his concubines.

'Azdi, is the khalifa's masseuse with us on the campaign? asked the khalifa's doctor.

'As-salama alaykum, Abu al-Jabir. Yes, he's an excellent man. The khalifa needs his daily massage.'

'Good. I think it is more important than ever when he is on campaign. So many hours on horseback will play havoc with his back.'

'Don't worry doctor; it is all organised.'

They never knew how long the campaign would last so everything had to be taken with them. Sometimes they returned to the alcázar within a few months, sometimes it was years. It was on a campaign, many years ago, that al-Azdi had begun working for the khalifa, or Prince Yahya, as he was at the time. Al-Azdi and his sister had lived in a small village outside Qurtubah. While the army laid siege to the city, a plague of sickness had raged through the camp, killing soldiers and servants alike. Many of the prince's personal staff had died and he had sent out his guards to find replacements. They took twelve people from al-Azdi's village, including himself and his sister, Lubaba. She was supposed to work in the kitchens and he was to be a personal servant to Prince Yahya, but when the prince saw her he was bewitched by her beauty and took her straight into his bed.

'Al-Azdi, the head cook wants to speak to you,' said a young lad, who worked in the kitchens.

'Very well. I'll be right there.'

There was still a lot to be done and they were due to leave the next day.

*

Yahya sat astride his new black stallion, a beautiful horse whose ancestry went back to Arabian stud lines belonging to the Omayyad khalifas. He'd wanted the horse the moment he set eyes on him and paid the price asked without a quibble; he knew good breeding when he saw it. He'd named the stallion Zalaam, Darkness, because that was what he wanted him to bring to their enemies. He smiled. It felt good to be at the head of his army again; the black humours that had been running around his head had cleared and the vertigo was gone.

He signalled for his jinetes to stop. They had crossed the mountains, weaving their way through a narrow pass between outcrops of flat limestone blocks which looked as if they'd been placed where they lay by the hand of some giant being. These bizarre rock formations had been the foundation for many local folk tales involving djinns and giants, and strange creatures who were neither man nor beast and lived in the many caves inside the mountains. Now Yahya and his men stood on a wide limestone plateau overlooking the vast plain that stretched all the way to Qurtubah and Isbiliya. Behind these great cities the Sierra Morena lay like a dark shadow on the horizon and between them lay his target, the independent taifa of Qarmuña. Once it became his, he would drive a wedge between Isbiliya and the rest of al-Andalus. He would pick off Abbad's allies one by one until he stood alone, and then it would be Malaqah that was the most powerful taifa in Muslim Spain.

'General. What do you see?' he asked General Rashad, who had ridden up beside him.

'Your Majesty?'

'Come man, what do you see?'

'There is no sign of an army,' he ventured. 'It's possible that they don't know we're coming.'

'Exactly. Have you had any word from al-Muzaffar?'

'Yes, Your Majesty. His messenger arrived just an hour ago. They will approach via Lucena. He says they will be ready to attack tomorrow at dawn.'

'Good, but attack whom? Where is the enemy? It looks as though we must make our way right up to the city gates.'

'There will be no opportunity to make a surprise attack. We will be seen from many miles away,' the general said. 'Maybe we should cross the plain at night, so we can attack at first light.'

'That's a good plan. We will make camp down there, by that stream,' he ordered. 'It's an ideal place, out of range of the enemy but close enough from which to make any sorties. Pass the command to the other officers and their men. Then tell my brother and the rest of the generals to join me in my tent after evening prayers. We need to plan this attack in more detail before we contact al-Muzaffar.'

*

Prince Idris was the first to arrive. He swaggered into Yahya's tent and threw himself down on the mat beside him.

'Well brother, what's the plan? I hear that Qarmuña is a well-fortified city. This is going to be a bloody one.'

'It looks like it, brother.'

One by one, Yahya's officers entered the tent and bowed to the khalifa before taking their places in the circle. General Rashad positioned himself on the khalifa's left side and once they were all seated, began to speak.

'As you can see there is no sign of any army, neither from Qarmuña nor its neighbours. We must send out some scouts to see what their defences are like.'

'See to it right away. If ibn Abd Allah is unaware of our presence then we need to take advantage of it.'

'Very well, Sayyad.' The general motioned to one of the younger officers, who got up immediately and left the tent.

'The weakest point is in the west wall, by the Gate of Isbiliya. The wall is only forty cubits high on that side,' said one of the quaids, a round, stocky man, wearing the loose tunic of an archer.

'Not that weak, there are catapults on the top of the tower,' snapped another officer.

'And it's on the road to Isbiliya. What happens if it's a trap and ibn Abd Allah has turned to Isbiliya for help. We could find ourselves caught between Abbad I's army and that of Qarmuña. No, I think it's too risky,' said an older man with a long scar across his cheek. He was one of Yahya's most experienced commanders.

'They will expect us to attack at the weakest point,' said Yahya. 'So let's consider the alternatives.'

Yahya knew Qarmuña well. When his father had been Khalifa of Qurtubah, he had visited the city a number of times. The defences were impressive; the city had been built on the side of a steep hill and was completely surrounded by a huge stone wall that was virtually impregnable. It wouldn't be easy to breach.

'There are four other entrances to the city: the Gate of Sedia in the corner of the north wall is heavily defended by a high bastion that dominates the land outside, and there's a deep trench running along the entire length of the wall,' he told them. 'It's difficult to put up ladders, the only way to scale the walls is with grappling irons.'

'But that would mean encircling the city and attacking from the north,' said the quaid with the scar. 'We're approaching from the south.'

'We cannot attack from the south; it's out of the question. The wall is built on a foundation of solid rock; it will be impossible to breach it and we'll never get through the Gate of Yarni.'

'Indeed. But remember, we have the Zirids to help us. Al-Muzzafar will be bringing five thousand men from Garnata. He can approach from the east.'

'Yes, that's probably our best chance, but the approach to the east wall is steep and across difficult terrain and there're many watch towers guarding the Gate of Qurtubah. On the other hand, it would give us the element of surprise because they won't be expecting us to come from the east,' said Idris, speaking for the first time.

'If the enemy don't come out to fight us on the plain then we have no alternative but to attack the city walls,' General Rashad said. 'Which gate we go through is immaterial. Thanks to the support of the Zirids we have enough men to attack on more than one front.'

He was right. They needed to divide the city's defences, not concentrate the attack on a single point. But they needed the advantage of surprise. What Yahya didn't want was to become embroiled in a long and bloody siege. He wanted a quick campaign so that he could return to defend Malaqah. All the time his army was away, the city was only lightly protected and they were not short of enemies: pirates were a constant menace, as was the threat from North Africa, and Isbiliya could easily take advantage of their absence when Abbad saw that they were focusing on Qarmuña.

'Very well. I don't think ibn Abd Allah will want to engage in a long siege. If we show enough force I think he will surrender,' said the khalifa. 'What are your thoughts on this, Prince Idris?'

'I agree. But first we should wait until the scouts return and see what they have to report.'

Yahya looked across at General Rashad. 'Make sure we have news before nightfall. Now, all of you go back to your troops and make sure they're well prepared. We will move out tomorrow night and attack at dawn. I will review the troops in the morning. See that they are ready.'

'And al-Muzaffar?' asked General Rashad.

'Send word to al-Muzaffar that we will attack the day after tomorrow. He is to strike from the east and enter the city through the Gate of Qurtubah. Tell him to have his men ready to meet a robust defence.'

'Very well, Your Majesty.'

'And ensure all the men are well rested.'

'Very well, Your Majesty.'

'If there is nothing else, then I will see you all tomorrow,' he said.

One by one his officers left until only Prince Idris remained. Yahya watched General Rashad mount his horse and ride back to his troops. He noticed that he used the new high saddle—copying the Christian horsemen—and that he rode with a straighter leg now.

'Do you have one of those new saddles?' he asked Idris, nodding towards his general.

'Of course. It gives you greater control over the horse. I don't know why you don't try it.'

Yahya shook his head. 'I'm too old to alter my ways. I prefer the traditional Berber saddle; it's done me well all these years. No need to change what works well.'

'And still no stirrups, brother. You'd think you were a Berber jinete riding through the Rif mountains with your tribal ancestors rather than being khalifa of Malaqah.' Idris sounded very scathing.

'Well that's what I am and you too; so don't forget it. The Berbers are the best horsemen in the world. You should be proud of your heritage.'

There were times when his brother, much as he loved him, could be very irritating.

*

Umar brushed the mare's back, talking to her softly all the time. She was a beautiful Arabian bay and had the softest brown eyes he'd ever seen and she was his. His own horse.

He had named her Basil, because his father said the name meant valiant. That's what he wanted her to be, valiant in battle. She nuzzled Umar gently, encouraging him to continue brushing her.

'Leave that now,' the nazir said. 'The quaid wants to talk to us. Line up with the others and wait for your orders.'

He could hardly believe that he was here, camped on the foothills overlooking the plain where there was to be a battle the next day. His mother had been horrified when he told her he was going with the campaign to Qarmuña. The truth was that Umar had been a bit surprised to be thrust into the front line so early in his new career, but the quaid explained that it was because of his excellent horsemanship. They needed men like him, even if he was still wet behind the ears.

It was his great-uncle Rafiq who had encouraged him to ride when he was very young; Umar had grown up feeling as much at home on the back of a horse as on his own two legs. Rafiq was a retired jinete and he'd explained how a good horse could make the difference between life and death for a soldier, but you had to treat it properly. His ammu only bred the pure Arabian horses that the khalifa needed for his cavalry; it was a breed which made excellent war horses, with great speed, endurance and intelligence. However, although Arabian horses were quick learners and easy to train, he warned him, they didn't respond well to harsh treatment and became nervous and jittery if they were unhappy. Neither of which was a good thing if you were going into battle. Umar couldn't understand why anyone would want to be cruel to one of these beautiful animals; he certainly would never hurt Basil. He rubbed her ears affectionately.

When Rafiq knew that Umar wanted to become a soldier, he told him that his chances of surviving life in the army would be greatly increased by having a good steed under him but he hadn't realised that he intended to give him one from his own stud farm. Umar remembered him talking with great affection about his old war horse, Antarrah and how she'd saved his skin on many an occasion.

'Hurry up Umar, we'll be late,' said another new recruit, his friend Talib. They had enlisted on the same day and so spent a lot of time in each other's company.

The nazir waved them across to join the rest of their squad. Umar and Talib were the youngest, and probably the only ones who'd never been into battle before. The entire battalion were gathered together waiting to hear their khalifa speak to them. At last he rode up on his black stallion and turned to face them. Umar had never seen him before. He was an imposing looking man, with a dark complexion and eyes like a hawk. The last rays of the evening sun glinted on his helmet and shimmered across his chainmail hauberk; he was dressed for war.

'Men, tonight we ride to Qarmuña and as dawn breaks we will attack. Our scouts have told us that there is no sign of an army anywhere; if they are waiting for us then they are inside the fortress itself. But they cannot hide from us. We will find them and we will destroy them.' He paused while the men cheered then continued, 'Tomorrow we take the city of Qarmuña.' More cheers. 'Tomorrow our prize will be the taifa of Qarmuña.' Once again he waited for the cheers to die down and then said, 'We will not be alone. Our allies, the Zirids will be fighting by our side.' Cheers. 'Allah be with us. Let us now pray to Allah to keep and protect us from harm.'

Five thousand men knelt and prayed. Five thousand voices rose in the air, reciting the words they all knew by heart.

When they had finished, the khalifa climbed back on his horse and faced them again. He pulled his sword from its scabbard and lifted it into the air. 'Tomorrow victory will be ours. Go now, make your peace with Allah and prepare for the battle to come. Allah grant us victory.'

'Allah grant us victory,' the men shouted.

After he'd left, their quaid came to inspect the jinetes. 'Right men. Most of you have been here before. You know the drill. Make sure you're ready for the fight; it won't be easy; they're a canny bunch the people of Qarmuña. Ensure your horses are rested and fed, your weapons sharpened, your armour secure. Don't let me down now, men. If we win, the rewards will be high. If we lose we will have less than nothing. I know which I prefer.' He grinned at them and then moved away to speak to his commander.

'What will I do?' Talib asked the nazir. 'I don't have a horse.'

'Don't worry lad. You're staying here and you too, soldier.' He nodded towards Umar before continuing, 'Someone needs to remain in camp and I have a feeling that you two will be more use here than running around the battlefield like a pair of headless chickens. Now, check that all the horses are ready, saddled and bridled and make sure that they have their protective armour. The men will inspect their own weapons. Some will have already seen to their horses, but you just check to be sure.'

Umar's emotions were a mixture of disappointment and relief; he was eager to go to battle—the air around him was charged with excitement and it was impossible not to feel its effects—but he knew he was ill-prepared despite the training that his ammu had given him in Ardales. As he moved from one horse to the next, checking the stirrups, adjusting the multi-coloured rugs on their backs, making sure the new curb bits were fitted correctly, giving a final polish to the saddles, he felt a great pride to be a small part of this magnificent group of jinetes. The cavalry were the elite of the armed forces, charismatic, dashing and brave. Tonight they had dressed for battle, in long hauberks which covered everything except the bottom of their tunics; even their legs were covered in fine chainmail. Each carried a long lance and a studded round shield, and in their belts instead of broad swords they carried slender, curved scimitars, better for harassing the enemy, slashing and cutting their way through them, weakening them, breaking down their defences.

'You're doing a great job, lad,' said one of the jinetes, swinging himself into the saddle. 'We'll see you when we get back.'

'Yes, next time you're coming with us,' said his companion. 'And look after that mare of yours or someone might take a liking to her.'

Umar grinned. Since his ammu had ridden into the Dar al-Jund with the two horses, everyone had treated him differently. Rafiq ibn Ahmad was well known for the quality of his Arabian horses; to give one to a young recruit was something special. They'd all heard of the old man's reputation as a warrior—he'd had years of experience on the battlefield and was still around to tell the tales. He'd fought against Sulayman and though he'd had many commanders over the years he'd always been loyal to the caliphate. So his great-uncle was a legend on two counts. Now that Umar had joined the khalifa's jinetes, he had a lot to live up to.

*

The camp was eerily quiet that night. A full moon lit up the plain below them and he could just make out the army moving towards Qarmuña like a dark cloud drifting across the land.

'What are we supposed to do?' asked Talib. 'I'm really tired.'

'Well why don't we take turns in sleeping. When the men return we'll have plenty to keep us busy. It might be a good idea to get some rest now,' said Umar.

Up to now his duties had been more to do with working alongside the grooms and caring for the animals than learning how to be a soldier, but that would come he was told. There was a lot for him to learn if he was to become part of the khalifa's professional army.

'But the nazir said we were to take care of the camp,' Talib whined. He was really quite young, probably not as old as Umar's youngest brother.

'That's all right. You sleep for a bit and if there are any problems I'll wake you.'

Talib flashed him a grateful smile and lay down in his tent. It wasn't long before Umar could hear the sound of heavy breathing as his friend drifted off into oblivion.

So what should he do? If he lay down he'd fall asleep in a heartbeat. He'd better keep moving if he wanted to stay awake. He wandered over to where the horses had been stabled, and where Basil was still munching away on her evening hay. He was about to call out to her when he heard voices.

'How many do you think there are?' one man asked.

'Not sure. Six thousand, maybe seven. And I heard someone talk about the Zirids. They could be attacking from the east.'

'So what shall we do? We need to warn ibn Abd Allah that it looks as though they plan to attack at dawn.'

'Well you're no use. Your horse is lame; you shouldn't have ridden him so hard.'

'We'll ride yours.'

'What both of us? Do you want to knacker my horse as well? Anyway we'd be too slow. By the time we'd arrive it would all be over. I'll have to go alone.'

'No wait. I'm sure I heard a horse whinnying earlier. Let's have a look around. It came from that direction.'

Umar was frozen with horror. Had these men been sent to check on them? Or was it just bad luck that they had crossed their path? Whichever it was, if they got back to Qarmuña tonight ibn Abd Allah would soon know about the dawn attack. What could he do? He had to think quickly. The cook and his staff were here; they'd be asleep no doubt. Everyone else except Talib and himself had left with the soldiers. Well it would have to be enough. He extinguished his lamp and crept back to his tent. Talib was still snoring happily, his arms thrown back in complete relaxation.

'Wake up, Talib,' Umar said, shaking him roughly. As soon as he saw his eyes open, he clamped his hand over the boy's mouth and whispered, 'Don't make a sound. We have visitors.'

Instantly the young man was awake. 'Who is it?' he asked.

'I don't know but I think they're from Qarmuña, ibn Abd Allah's men. We have to stop them. Go to the cookhouse and get as many men as you can. Tell them to arm themselves with whatever they can find and come to the stable yard.'

'Where will you be?'

'I'm going back. I think they intend to steal Basil.'

Talib scuttled away in the direction of the cookhouse and Umar double-backed to the stables. The men were still there. One had placed a bridle over Basil's head and was pulling her towards the gate. The other was searching for something.

'Hurry up, Fadl. This brute is so stubborn she might as well be a mule.'

'Give her a whack with the flat of your sword. That'll teach her to obey,' replied the other, a squat little man wearing the short tunic favoured by jinetes.

Umar gritted his teeth. He knew which of them was the brute and it wasn't his mare.

'Ah, here it is. Hold her steady now.' Fadl had found what he'd been looking for: Basil's saddle. Umar remembered he'd set it aside to give it a good polish while he was waiting for the soldiers to return. What should he do? If he hesitated they would ride out of here and there would be nothing he could do to catch them. He had to stop them but the odds weren't good; there were two of them and only one of him. Where was Talib? Surely he had roused the cook by now.

The man had tightened the saddle in place and was about to mount Umar's horse. Something had to be done right away. Umar bent down and picked up a small pebble then taking his catapult from his pocket, he fired it at Basil's rump. The mare let out a snort and thrashed out her hind legs, catching one of the men on the chest. He fell backwards, cursing madly.

'What the devil is wrong with this horse? Is she cursed?'

'Maybe that's why she's here and not riding with the others,' said Fadl.

Umar fired another pebble at poor Basil's hindquarters. This time she reared up on her hind legs and pulling away from the man holding the bridle, she galloped over to the gate, just as Umar pushed it open.

'Stop her. She's going to get away,' the man shouted, rubbing his bruised chest.

'Oh, forget her. I'll go on my own. If you can find yourself a horse you can catch me up. We have to get this information to Qarmuña before dawn,' said Fadl.

He walked over to where he'd left his own mount tied to a tree then stopped in astonishment. It was gone.

'What's this? Where's that damned horse of mine? Useless animal,' shouted Fadl.

'Are you sure this is where you left it?'

'Of course I am. They were together, I think you're right; this bloody place is cursed. Come on, they can't be far away. Help me look. They've probably wandered off in search of food. Yours won't have got far with a crook leg.'

'Didn't you tie yours up?' asked his companion.

'Of course I bloody tied her up. What do you take me for?'

The two men were becoming so angry and frustrated that they didn't notice the gang of enraged kitchen workers creeping up on them until it was too late. Before they could do any more about the runaway horses, they were surrounded by irate men and boys of varying ages and sizes, brandishing a selection of cooking utensils: wooden ladles, iron pots, paddles, sticks and vicious looking kitchen knives. The cook, a fearsome man, carried an axe that was normally used to cut up carcasses.

'Grab them and tie them up,' shouted the cook, waving his axe around dangerously. 'Don't kill them, unless you have to.'

Hearing his words, the two soldiers immediately moved into a defensive position, back to back, their swords unsheathed and lifted ready to strike, but they were not used to the unconventional methods of the cook's little army. Before anyone knew what was happening, a lad no older than Talib, lobbed a round gourd at Fadl's head; its hard skin struck him with enough force to knock him off balance and give one of the older men the opportunity to grab his sword. Meanwhile two more kitchen lads threw a pot of boiling water at the other soldier. He let out a furious roar and rushed at them, but partially blinded and enraged by pain, he didn't notice the blow that came from behind. Within minutes they had both men hog-tied and sitting on the ground wondering what had happened.

'Well done, lads,' said the cook, an enormous barrel of a man who probably could have taken on the two men on his own. He patted one of the lads on the head. 'Great shot that, Sandi. He never saw it coming. I think we'll make a soldier of you yet.'

The boy beamed with pleasure.

'What about their horses? We can't let them find their own way back to Qarmuña. They'll know something has happened to them,' said Umar.

'Don't worry. I tied them up. I thought it was the best way of stopping them from leaving,' said Talib, grinning at his own initiative. 'One of them was lame, anyway. It wouldn't have got far.'

'And Basil? Where is she?' Umar felt sick. What if she didn't come back? What if she tried to get back to Ardales? Someone would catch her and he'd never see her again. How would he tell his uncle?

'She's fine. She's with the others. In fact, I didn't even have to catch her, she just went straight over to join their mares,' said Talib.

When Fadl heard that, he spluttered with rage. 'You boy. You'll be sorry for this when you're defeated. And you will be defeated. You don't think Abbad will let you take Qarmuña, do you? You will all be dead once he gets to know what Yahya is planning.' He spat on the ground beside him. 'Damn you and all the Hammudids.'

'You're all talk,' said the cook, kicking Fadl so that he fell on his side. 'But there's not much you can do about it now, except wait until the victors return. They'll know what to do with you both.'

CHAPTER 6

Yahya ducked his head into the bowl of cold water and held it there for a minute to try to clear his mind. The hallucinations had returned during the night ride across the plain; ghostly figures rode out to meet them, swords waving in the air, with shrieks and cries of agony that only he could hear. What on earth was wrong with him?

'Your Majesty, is everything all right?' asked al-Azdi.

'Yes, just a touch of dizziness. Come, help me with my helmet. It's almost dawn.'

The servant pulled the chainmail hood up so that it covered the khalifa's head and placed his helmet on top of it. Yahya took the jewelled scimitar he offered him, and thrust it into his baldric.

'Your lance, Your Majesty,' al-Azdi said.

The lance felt strange in his hand as though it would metamorphose into a snake at any moment. Yahya put it down quickly and said, 'Bring me something to drink. An infusion of juniper berries and lavender mixed with a little lime.'

That should reinvigorate him. He had to have a clear head before the attack. He was the Supreme Commander; he couldn't go into battle scared of his own shadow. He breathed deeply and searched inside himself for a moment of calm. The sun would be up soon. He had to concentrate on the campaign if he wanted to win the prize.

Everyone knew the battle plan now. General Rashad would attack from the west with a contingent of two thousand men, horse archers and infantrymen while Prince Idris attempted to breach the south wall. His archers would shower the city walls with arrows while the engineers moved the trebuchet into place, ready to bombard them with rocks and heavy stones. The Zirids would attack the Gate of Qurtuba and the Gate of Qalsaña simultaneously. His own men, all on horseback, would make numerous short, sharp attacks on the defensive walls, to weaken and dispirit the enemy.

'Your drink, Your Majesty,' said al-Azdi, handing it to him.

Yahya took the silver goblet and stared at the infusion within it. Was it safe to drink? He was so befuddled; he had to clear his mind of these clouds of confusion, the unearthly figures that whispered in his ear, the strange apparitions that taunted him. Whatever it was, he had to fight it. He swirled the liquid around in the goblet. Well, let it kill him or cure him. He lifted it to his lips and drank it all in one draught. The taste was slightly bitter, the juniper berries no doubt—he hoped it was only that.

Now it was time to move out. The others were already in position. He took the horse's bridle from his groom and swung himself onto Zalaam's back. Instantly he was more in control; he always felt better when he was astride a horse. He patted him gently—unable to stroke his coat for the quilted layers of protective armour that covered the animal's sides and chest— then tucked his battle axe into the horse's breast strap. Zalaam fidgeted impatiently, pawing at the ground in his eagerness to get going; he knew the battle was about to begin. As he snorted with excitement, his breath floated in the cold air like plumes of white smoke.

'All right boy, we're going now,' Yahya whispered to his steed.

He took one last look at his troops; they were ready and, like Zalaam, impatient to get started. His army, a mixture of professional soldiers, local militia, free men, mercenaries and slaves had commended themselves to Allah—they fought in His name and for His glory only—each man hoping that He would be by their side that day. Now the hour had come. Yahya could see the banners of each corps fluttering in a wind which blew directly from the south, from the city of Malaqah. That was surely an auspicious sign. His brother's shatrang, with its green and white chequered squares was clearly identifiable in front of him, as were the red and white diagonal stripes of General Rashad's banner as he and his contingent of men prepared to peel off to the west, to the Gate of al-Agamm. Now the Royal Standard Bearer lifted aloft the khalifa's banner of Islamic green with its gold crescent so that all could see it. The drummers began to drum out the signal to advance and Yahya's army moved forward, the infantry in perfect step, the sound of their footfall echoing rhythmically across the plain, files of lightly clad archers behind them, their bows in one hand and long shields in the other and then the jinetes, the most splendid of all, with the first rays of the morning sun catching their helmets as they trotted in the rear, astride their magnificent horses. The attack was about to begin.

*

Prince Idris heard the drums and signalled for his men to attack. With a roar of rage that echoed through the valley like thunder, his corps of light cavalry galloped straight for the south wall, letting loose a flood of arrows at the dozing guards positioned on the ramparts. Then they wheeled away, reloaded and fired again, and again. He could see the consternation among the soldiers of Qarmuña as they rushed to their posts. The last thing they'd been expecting on this beautiful clear morning was an attack; they'd grown too complacent. They had thought that because Isbiliya was their ally that they were safe; that no-one could assail them, certainly not the taifa of Malaqah. They were wrong.

Idris raised his hand and signalled for the trebuchet to be brought forward; this would take a while because it was heavy and cumbersome but once it was within range of the city walls it would be well worth the effort. The sight of it alone would instil fear into the people of Qarmuña. The infantry archers moved into position to give cover to the engineers manoeuvring the trebuchet. By now other infantrymen had raised ladders against the south wall and were climbing up, swords and axes in hand.

The prince could hear the screams of men within the city and the shouts of their commanders as they tried to regain control of the situation. Their archers were now on the ramparts, shooting down on the men trying to scale the walls while others attempted to dislodge the ladders and repel the attackers, but there were too many of them and although some men fell when the ladders were knocked out of place, there were always others to take their place. His infantrymen were now inside the city, fighting hand to hand. Blood was flowing. Soon the Gate of Yarni would be open and he and the jinetes could ride inside and then the slaughter would begin in earnest.

He looked back to where his brother sat, proud and kingly on a low mound which elevated him above the plain so that he could survey the battle. How easy it could be for the khalifa to fall in battle but that was unlikely because the Supreme Commander's role was to oversee and direct everything and to remain well out of harm's way; Yahya was too experienced a soldier to try anything different. But Yahya was growing old; one day he'd make a mistake and then it would be Idris's chance. He would be there, close by, so that when the opportunity came, he would take it.

By now the engineers had the trebuchet in position and were loading it with huge rocks. The first one catapulted easily over the wall and landed with an enormous crash. Then a second and a third. It was chaos inside the city walls but still the gate remained closed. Bodies littered the ground below the walls, soldiers maimed, shot, some screaming with burns from the boiling oil that had been tipped over them, some lucky ones who'd died immediately from a well placed axe blow, or broken their necks as they fell from the wall.

The jinetes galloped past him towards the eastern end of the wall and sent a shower of arrows into the defenders, then whirled away and, reloading their bows, returned to repeat the attack. More cavalry joined them, and again and again they charged, sometimes to the east, sometimes to the west and each time they shot a thousand arrows that harassed and confused the enemy.

*

Yahya could see smoke rising from the area of the al-Agamm Gate; General Rashad must have broken through the west wall despite the war catapults that were supposed to be in place. Of al-Muzzafar and his troops he could tell little from his position, so he sent a squad of men to the east of the city to find out what was happening and another to the west gate. Ahead of him he could see his brother's corps desperately trying to scale the high south wall. With a quick word of command he sent another contingent of horse archers to back them up

The fighting continued, hard and bloody; the bodies were piling up at the foot of the south wall. But what was happening elsewhere? Was it the same or were they gaining ground? At last he saw a horseman galloping towards him.

'Well, what's the situation with the Zirids?' he asked as the breathless jinete leapt down from his mount.

'They have succeeded in breaking down the Qurtuba Gate, Your Majesty, with a battering ram. The Zirids are now engaged in hand-to-hand combat, fighting their way into the city.'

'Right. Tell your quaid to send a contingent of jinetes to back them up, immediately,' Yahya commanded. Then he turned to the second breathless nazir, who had just returned, 'And what news from the west, soldier?'

'Your Majesty, General Rashad has gained access to Qarmuña. The al-Agamm Gate is open and our troops are inside the city walls. He says the governor has surrendered.'

Yahya gazed across at the beleaguered city. It was true; a soldier was walking along the ramparts waving a white flag. They had won. Qarmuña was now his. The fight was over but he could still feel the adrenalin racing through his body. The battle was done but his body wanted to continue. He sheathed his sword and turned to face his quaid.

'Send your men to help with the wounded,' he ordered. 'I will wait here to accept their surrender.'

It had been a great victory but now they would have to count the casualties. He did not expect them to be high. The battle had been ferocious but quick and they owed this speedy victory to the element of surprise. There had been no opportunity for ibn Abd Allah to send word to Isbiliya and ask for help. If he had, it could have turned out very differently. Yahya was not too proud to admit that, even with the help of the Zirids, they would have had a much greater battle on their hands if Abbad I's army had been involved.

CHAPTER 7

Maryam was skipping ahead of them in her eagerness to get to Rebekah's house; she loved playing with the children, but she also enjoyed the company of the women. Today Rebekah had promised to teach her to sew.

'Slow down, Maryam. Remember I have Imran to carry,' Aisha called, but she was happy to see her daughter so enthusiastic. Yesterday she had pestered and pestered her grandmother until she had found just the right piece of white cotton to take with her. Now she carried it carefully folded, in her basket.

It was mid-morning when they arrived at Avi's house. Aisha knocked at the outer door and waited until one of the servants came to let them in.

'As-salama alaykum, Musif. Is the sayeda at home?'

'Wa alaykum e-salam. Yes, she is in the garden with her daughters. You are to go right through.'

Maryam knew exactly where they would be and raced along the path while Aisha followed more slowly, drinking in the fragrance of this beautiful garden tucked away in the middle of the city. A footpath made of blue and white tiles wound its way through bushes of myrtle and rosemary, past orange and lemon trees, still covered in late fruit—how beautiful the garden must smell when their blossom was out —through hedges of roses, their flowers still waiting to bloom, and on up to the main door. She abandoned the path and rounded the corner; there they were, the women of the house sitting on the ground sewing. Maryam of course was already seated beside them and chattering away in her usual happy way.

'As-salama alaykum, Aisha,' said Rebekah, getting up and kissing her on the cheeks.

'Wa alaykum e-salam, dear friend,' Aisha replied. She felt at home in this welcoming household; everyone was so kind to her.

'Well, little one, are you ready to learn how to sew?' Rebekah asked Maryam.

'Yes. Look I have brought some material with me. My seedo wants me to make him a handkerchief with his initial on it.' Aisha's daughter lifted the now slightly crumpled cotton square up for Rebekah to see.

'Very well. In that case we must take care to make it a very special one for your grandfather.'

Maryam nodded enthusiastically.

'Come and sit here by my side and I'll show you how to begin.' She lay down her own piece of sewing on which she was embroidering tiny sprigs of lavender. It reminded Aisha of springtime in Ardales, when the land was covered in a carpet of wild flowers: lavender, daisies, broom, wild orchids, heron's bill, stork's bill, blue pimpernel, goldilocks; she loved their names as much as their colours. When she went to tell her father that it was time for lunch, she used to walk through a mosaic of yellow, blue and pink flowers.

'Your garden is so lovely,' said Aisha, putting her own bag of material on the ground beside her daughter. She hoisted Imran onto her back; his head lolled to one side. He was fast asleep.

'Yes, it's always at its best at this time of year, before the heat of the summer. Why don't you leave Imran here with us and take a walk around. He's no bother, and Maryam's got other things on her mind,' said Sara.

'I think I will,' Aisha said, gently laying her son down on the grass and taking care not to wake him. 'I won't be long.' Much as she loved her children it was good to walk freely for a few minutes, unencumbered either by Imran's increasing weight or Maryam's endless questions.

The garden encircled the house like a sweet-smelling girdle and soon she was out of sight of the women, hidden in bushes of myrtle and winter jasmine. It had rained the previous night and the garden smelled fresh and fragrant. She felt again the ache of homesickness for her old home; those were happy times. She sighed and sat by the fountain, her eyes downcast.

'Aisha. Is everything all right?' a man's voice asked.

She blushed as she recognised him; it was Gideon. She had been hoping to see him today but sometimes he was too busy in the warehouse to come out and greet her and then she was left with an irrational sense of disappointment.

'As-salama alaykum, Gideon.'

'Wa alaykum e-salam, Aisha. What are you doing here alone in the garden? And why so sad?' He looked around, searching for signs of his sisters or his mother. 'And your children?'

'So many questions, Gideon.' She smiled at him. 'I'm not sad, just thinking of my old home. Your lovely garden has reminded me of it. I love the springtime when all the flowers come into bloom. In Ardales I could walk amongst them whenever I wanted. Here in Malaqah gardens are enclosed, private, for the enjoyment only of those who create them. This beautiful garden, for example,' she said waving her arm to encompass the carefully manicured space around her, with its closely clipped box hedges and neatly tiled path. 'Who would know it even existed? It is locked away behind high walls and closed gates.'

'But you can enjoy this garden whenever you want to; you know that. My parents are delighted to have you visit their home. You and your children are always welcome here?' He looked at her quizzically. 'The children?'

'They are with your mother and your sisters. Imran is asleep and your mother is teaching Maryam to sew.'

He sat down beside her on the garden bench. She could smell the light sweat of his body and the perfumed oil he used on his hair. Her heart began to beat more quickly.

'A garden, however lovely and well cared for, is not the same as the flowers of the countryside, wild, free and untamed,' she said.

Gideon looked at her and smiled. 'I think there is something of that in you, Aisha. Wild, free, untamed and beautiful. You are like a lovely, wild flower.'

She felt the blood rush to her head and jumped up in embarrassment. 'I must get back to the children.'

'No, stay a while,' he said. 'I rarely get the chance to speak to you alone. Let's talk some more about gardens and I promise not to embarrass you again.'

'I'm not embarrassed,' she said, trying to sound convincing but she knew the blush rising up her neck was giving her away.

'Malaqah is surrounded by beautiful countryside,' said Gideon, diplomatically returning the subject to the wild flowers. 'You only have to go outside the city walls and you would be knee deep in them. Do you ride? We could ride out for you to see them.'

'Baba would never permit me to leave Malaqah. Not even with you as my escort. He says it is not safe.'

Gideon said nothing at first then he plucked a stalk of lavender and handed it to her 'There is one place I can take you where the wild flowers grow in abundance, and we wouldn't have to leave the city to see them.'

'Really?'

'Yes, come with me now. It's not far from here.'

'But the children? Your mother? She will wonder where I am.'

'Don't worry; Musif will tell them.'

She knew it was not the correct thing to do, to leave the house with Gideon, an unmarried man, but she smiled happily and said, 'Very well but we mustn't be away too long.' She felt carefree, like a young girl again.

He took her hand and led her through the garden to the gate.

'Musif, I'm just taking the sayeda to visit Rabbi Isaac. We won't be long,' he informed the gateman.

'A rabbi? Why are we going to visit a rabbi?' asked Aisha. 'Why would he even want to speak to me, a Muslim woman?'

'No more questions. You wanted to see wild flowers and I'm taking you to see them,' said Gideon with an enormous grin on his face. He seemed to enjoy keeping their destination a secret.

They walked the whole length of the Jewish quarter, heading east all the time. Ahead of her she could see the high stone walls of the Jbel-Faro and sentries patrolling the battlements, and beyond the fortress the mountains rose, tree covered peaks one after the other, that stretched as far as her eyes could see. How wonderful it would be to be up there in those mountains; from there it must be possible to see to the ends of the earth.

'I wonder if my brother is on duty today?' she said, pointing to the crenellated ramparts.

'Who? Umar? He's the soldier, isn't he?'

'Yes.'

She was about to ask if it was much farther when Gideon suddenly stopped and said, 'Well, here we are.'

In front of her was an iron gateway, its gates ajar; even from where she stood she could see a carpet of colourful flowers covered the ground within.

'This is the Jewish cemetery,' he said. 'The gates are always open and at this time of year the wild flowers take over. No-one weeds it or tries to control them. Come inside and enjoy what you said you've been missing.'

It felt strange going into a Jewish cemetery but, she reminded herself, it wasn't the same as going into a synagogue. And she was only there to see the flowers. Nevertheless she still didn't feel comfortable. She bent down and picked a sprig of lavender.

'Is everything all right?' Gideon asked. 'You did ask for wild flowers. Are these not wild enough for you?'

She laughed. 'They're beautiful. And the smell...' Aisha breathed in deeply, enjoying the moment. The Jewish cemetery was a multi-coloured gem set below the walls of the Jbel-Faro, somewhere she would never have found alone and if she had, would never have entered.

Gideon smiled at her in pleasure; he really was such a kind young man. She couldn't help thinking of him as a young man although he was probably a couple of years older than her. Marriage, children and now widowhood had aged her; they had robbed her of her youth.

'Is that you, Gideon?' asked a deep voice.

Reluctantly she pulled her eyes away from the garden and turned to see a rabbi standing behind them.

'Good morning, Rabbi Isaac,' Gideon said, 'I've just brought a friend of our family to see the lovely wild flowers in the cemetery. I hope you don't mind.'

'Now why would I mind? It's not as though you're going to disturb any of the residents, is it?' he replied with a chuckle. He looked at Aisha and said, 'Good morning, child.'

'Good morning, sayyad,' Aisha said, unsure how she should address a rabbi. She had never met one before and couldn't help staring at his long white beard; it was the longest beard she'd ever seen. He made an imposing figure in his flowing dark robes and turban, which was wound neatly around his head. The usual yellow sash was tied loosely about his waist.

'Gideon, I really must get back to the children,' she said. What would the rabbi be thinking of her, a widow alone in the cemetery with a young Jewish man? She imagined she could see the disapproval in his eyes.

'Of course. Goodbye, Rabbi.'

'Peace unto you, my son.'

She and Gideon didn't speak until they were out of the cemetery and heading back down the hill towards Avi's house. 'He'll tell your father,' she said.

'So what if he does? We were only looking at the flowers,' he said, but without conviction.

'Thank you for taking me to see them,' Aisha said, hurrying ahead of him as they grew near the grounds of his house. She nodded at Musif as he opened the front gate and hurried past him to where she'd left her children. It was all she could do to control her racing heart; she prayed no-one had noticed how long she'd been away.

'Ah, there you are, my dear. Come and see how well your lovely daughter is getting on,' said Rebekah as she approached the women. No-one appeared to have moved and Imran was still lying on his back, snoring lightly. She bent down and kissed him gently.

'Yes, Mama, look what I've done.' Maryam held up her sewing for Aisha to see. She'd hemmed two sides of the white square and was about to start on a third.

'That's lovely, sweetheart. What neat little stitches,' Aisha said, taking the cotton square and examining the sewing carefully; she held it in front of her face to hide her confusion.

'Do you have any sewing, Aisha?' asked Sara.

'Yes, I'm making a tunic for the baby,' she said, relinquishing Maryam's cotton square and pulling a length of green material from her bag and spreading it out before her.

'Did you see Gideon while you were in the garden?' Rebekah asked, her eyes firmly fixed on her embroidery.

'Yes, briefly. I think he's very busy today,' Aisha replied, feeling guilty at having to lie to her friends. For the next half hour she would concentrate on making Imran the most perfect tunic possible and pray that her flushed cheeks wouldn't give away her thoughts.

*

As Aisha walked home through the winding streets of the alcaiceria, past the colourful displays of wools and cottons, she felt happier than usual; the black clouds that had tormented her since Daud's death were lifting. She adjusted the sling in which the baby lay, his long black eyelashes delicately framing his dark eyes; what a beautiful child he was and so like his father. She smiled down at him, resisting the urge to pinch his chubby cheeks and see him smile. Gently she moved him onto her other side. He had grown such a lot in the past few months; she would be glad when he was walking.

'Mama, can we go and play with Sara again tomorrow?' asked Maryam, skipping along beside her. Her daughter had blossomed since they'd arrived in Malaqah. When her father died, she hadn't said very much; she asked where he was and what had happened to her grandparents but then she withdrew inside herself and never mentioned them again. Now, thanks to the kindness of Rebekah and her family, they were all beginning to enjoy life once more.

'Yes, if you want to. But only for a short while; we don't want to bother them by going there every day,' she replied.

'It's no bother, Mama; aunty Rebekah said we could go anytime. She says I will be a good seamstress because my stitches are so small.'

'I know, sweetheart, but we can't leave your teta Abal at home all on her own, can we?'

'No, Mama. Because she might go to heaven like my other teta and then I won't see either of them again.' The child's eyes widened as she said this and Aisha realised that she was still missing her grandmother.

'Why don't we ask teta Abal to come with us tomorrow? Would you like that?' She wanted her mother to meet Rebekah and her family, especially Gideon, who had been so nice to her. She took the sprig of lavender from her pocket and lifted it to her nose.

'What's that, Mama?' asked Maryam.

'It's lavender, just like the flowers Rebekah was embroidering. Here you can have it. It smells nice.'

As she thought of Gideon she couldn't prevent the warm feeling that came over her. He was a handsome young man and he made her laugh in a way she hadn't done for a long time. What had he called her? A wild flower.

CHAPTER 8

Yahya rode back to Malaqah at the head of three thousand troops, banners flying high. He was elated. Victory was theirs. He'd appointed Prince Idris governor of Qarmuña and left him with two thousand of his men to defend the city. It wouldn't take him long to swell the numbers with recruits from Qarmuña; when given the choice between death and changing allegiance, soldiers invariably chose to change sides. The remainder of Yahya's army: the wounded, infantrymen, engineers, cooks, grooms, archers, servants—scarcely depleted after the battle—trundled back to Malaqah at their own pace with all the equipment of war, including the trebuchet.

The only cloud on the horizon was the fact that Muhammad ibn Abd Allah, ruler of Qarmuña had escaped and nobody had been able to find him. His family, including his wives and four sons were now imprisoned in the fortress. Yahya had left orders for them not to be harmed. He wanted to lure ibn Abd Allah back to his city so he could be captured and put to death. Free he was a dangerous man. A Berber warlord of the Zenata dynasty, he was a fierce and experienced opponent who was not going to rest until he had both his family and his city back. Yahya would sleep easier when he saw his head on a stake outside the gates of Qarmuña.

Family was important to all Berber tribes, Yahya was well aware of that. He'd been thinking of his sons, still children it was true but they needed to know that their father believed in them. On his death—insha'Allah not for some time yet—Hassan would inherit his throne. In the meantime he intended to keep them close to him here in Malaqah, so no harm could come to them. Besides which he loved their mother, Fatima and she was still young enough to give him more sons.

They entered the city of Malaqah amid cheers and shouts of joy. Ecstatic crowds of people lined the streets all the way to the Boveda Gate of the alcázar, where his palace guard were waiting, resplendent in their green and gold uniforms. For once the clouds that had been disrupting his thoughts had cleared. He had taken the first step towards defeating Abbad, now he would plan the next.

*

'Where is Umar?' Basma cried, when she saw the soldiers returning. 'I can't see Umar. Has something happened to him? He's not there. Where is he?'

They were standing in the street outside the apothecary's shop, along with dozens of other citizens eager to see the victors. Everybody had turned out to greet the soldiers, happy that for once Malaqah was victorious. Men, women and children, young and old, stood shoulder to shoulder along the main street, from the city walls to the Boveda Gate, shouting and cheering, and scattering flowers before the tired soldiers. The air was filled with the scents of jasmine and lilies that lay crushed beneath the horses' hooves.

'Stop panicking, wife. He'll be with the bulk of the army. What did you expect, that he'd ride home beside the khalifa?' Makoud said, pulling at his wife's arm. Nobody was taking any notice of her; they were all too busy shouting and waving at the khalifa. 'He'll be another couple of days at least and then I doubt if he'll be given leave to come and see his mother. If he's survived I'm sure he'll find a way of letting us know. For now, that will have to do you. Stop your bawling and come home.'

Although he was determined not to show it, he too was anxious to know how his son had fared in his first campaign. He'd silently cursed his Uncle Rafiq when he arrived with the horse for Umar. If there had been any doubts in his son's mind, then that present had swept them all away. After all, what young man could resist the allure of becoming a jinete in the khalifa's army? He watched the elite force riding past, splendid in their dashing uniforms with their red capes around their shoulders, astride beautiful horses who held their tails high and their heads higher. Who were the proudest? The jinetes or their steeds? How could Umar resist such a life? Even staid, middle-aged Makoud could feel his heart beating faster as he watched them ride into the alcazaba.

*

Ibrahim stood at the door of his father's shop, trying to get a glimpse of the soldiers; the noise was deafening. People were cheering and shouting 'Long live the khalifa' and 'Praise be to Allah'; there was music playing and the steady sound of the horses' hooves as they clattered up the cobbled streets towards the alcazar. For a moment he thought of locking the shop and running out to get a better view but just as he was about to close the door, a customer arrived. It was the man who had bought the wormwood the week before.

'Hey boy. Not going anywhere are you?' he said, less as a question and more as a threat.

'No. I was just trying to see the victory procession.'

'Victory? Pushover if you ask me. It would have been a different outcome if Isbiliya had been involved. The khalifa's head would be stuck on a pole by now.'

'But it was still a victory,' said Ibrahim, defensively. Who was this man? And why did he behave so aggressively?

'If you say so. Now, are you going to serve me or do I have to stand here all day?'

It may have just been an automatic reaction, but Ibrahim saw his hand move to the hilt of his sword.

'Of course, sayyad. What would you like?' asked Ibrahim. Baba had told him to always be courteous to the customers even if they didn't deserve it. And this man certainly didn't.

'Don't tell me you've forgotten me already? Wormwood. That's what I want and more of it than the last time. That scrappy little bit didn't last any time at all.'

'I'll just see if it's arrived,' said Ibrahim. 'I won't be long.'

What was he going to do? Baba wasn't keen on selling this man much wormwood but Baba wasn't here. He opened the box. There had to be thirty pieces of it in there but he wasn't going to tell him that. He carefully selected three of the smallest pieces he could find and wrapped them in a vine leaf.

The stranger had taken the top off a large Ali-Baba jar and was smelling the contents. He coughed and replaced the lid quickly.

'That's sulphur,' explained Ibrahim. 'We sell a lot to the local alfareros; they use it to make the glazes for their pots.'

'Bloody stinks,' the man growled. 'Well have you got my wormwood?'

'Yes, here it is,' said Ibrahim, putting the packet on the counter.

'I hope there's more than there was last time,' the stranger said, snatching up the packet and unwrapping it. 'Hmmph. Still a bit on the miserly side. Well I suppose that will have to do.' He threw a coin on the counter and strode out.

For some reason, Ibrahim felt he should make a mental note of the man's appearance; he had a bad feeling about this stranger, especially after he had spoken so ill of the khalifa. He silently recalled the man's features: tall, skinny, with a long, thin face and a black beard. He sighed. He couldn't remember any particular distinguishing thing about him; that description could fit anyone. He was dressed simply, more like a servant than a soldier, but he did wear a sword. Of course, his sword hand! How could he have forgotten? On the back of his hand there was a distinctive scar in the shape of two crossed sticks, just like one of the brands that farmers put on their sheep to mark them as their own. People didn't normally brand their slaves, but he had heard of it happening. Did this mean that the man was a freed slave? Or maybe a runaway? Whatever he was, Ibrahim knew instinctively that he was not a man to be trusted. He hoped he wouldn't come back; let him buy his wormwood somewhere else.

The cheering outside continued, louder and stronger than ever; if he hurried he might just be in time to see the end of the procession. He quickly locked the door to the shop and ran down the lane towards the alcazaba. As he mingled with the crowds lining the main street, he caught a glimpse of the man again; he was heading towards the Boveda Gate.

*

Yahya's sons were waiting for him in the alcázar when he arrived. Immediately they ran across to him, taking no heed of protocol, and jumped into his arms.

'Baba. You've been away a long time,' said little ben Yahya.

'And you won,' said Hassan. 'Our army has defeated our enemies.'

'Yes, my boys. We have had a great victory but that doesn't mean we have defeated our enemies. There is still a lot to be done before we can rest in peace. Now tell me what you've both been up to in my absence,' Yahya said, sitting on some cushions and pulling his sons down beside him.

'I have been learning to ride,' said five-year-old ben Yahya. 'I have my first pony.'

'Good. A prince needs to be able to ride.'

'And I've been training a new falcon,' said Hassan. 'And learning how to use a sword.'

'Excellent. All important skills for a khalifa. And you will be khalifa one day, Hassan, when I am dead,' said Yahya, ruffling the boy's black curly hair.

'Are you going to die, Baba?' asked ben Yahya, looking at his father with huge brown eyes filled with tears.

'One day, son. We all die one day.'

'But not soon?' asked Hassan. 'They say you're not well. Does that mean you will die soon?'

'Not well? Who says I'm not well?' Yahya snapped at his son. 'Don't believe all the rumours you hear, my boy. How could I have defeated my enemies if I was unwell? Tell me that.'

'Sorry, Baba.'

'So you're not going to die, Baba?' repeated little ben Yahya.

'No son, not for a long while yet,' he said, hugging him to him. His youngest son was the image of his mother.

'People die when they get old, don't they Baba?' the boy continued. 'Are you old, Baba?'

Yahya didn't know what to answer; he was supposed to be in the prime of life but he didn't feel like it. He clapped his hands to summon his servant al-Azdi. 'Take my sons back to their mother. Tell her I will join her later.' All this talk about death had left him feeling weak. 'I am going to rest now. It was a long ride from Qarmuña. When you have seen to my sons, bring me some refreshment in my room.'

'Yes, Your Majesty.' Al-Azdi bowed and led the two boys back towards the harem and their mother. Yahya knew he should be arranging a big to mark their victory but he didn't feel up to it. The clouds were gathering in his mind again; he just wanted to lie down and sleep. Hassan's words came back to him. So the gossip in court was that he was ill. Well, he'd have a few days to rest and then he'd show them all that he was still a fit man. Next time they'd go straight for Isbiliya.

CHAPTER 9

Basma was waiting for him when he came home for his lunch and before he could sit down she grabbed his arm and said, 'I must speak to you, Makoud. Alone.'

'What is it, wife? What can't wait until I've eaten?'

But she refused to speak until they were alone on the roof terrace then she shut the door behind her and said, 'It's Aisha. She's spending too much time at the Jew's house. It's unseemly.'

'I suppose you mean my friend Avi, the Jew who has been such a good friend to our family? Is that who you mean?' he asked, annoyed that she should speak in such a tone. 'And what pray is so unseemly about visiting my friend's home? I assume his wife is there?'

'Yes, of course she is. But Aisha goes there every day and it's not to see Rebekah. It's to see that son of theirs.'

'They have four sons. Which one are you talking about?' He began to feel a little worried. What was his lovely Aisha getting herself into now?

'The eldest one, Gideon. He's there every time she visits.'

'That's not surprising as it is not only his home but his place of work. But tell me, wife, how do you know all this?'

'Maryam told me that uncle Gideon makes her Mama laugh.'

At this, it was Makoud who laughed. 'What nonsense you talk, wife. What harm is there in laughing? Allah likes us to laugh; it is good for the soul.'

'But not if you are a widow. It is unseemly for a widow to visit a house where there are young men, and even worse to be laughing and joking with them,' she said, scowling at him. His second wife had never really liked Aisha; while his daughter was married and living with her in-laws she had tolerated her but now her dislike was becoming more apparent. 'It's time you found another husband for her,' she continued in a tone that brooked no discussion.

Makoud didn't reply; much as he hated to admit it, Basma was right. It wasn't appropriate for a young widow to wander about the city on her own; people would talk about her. He felt sure that this relationship with Gideon was nothing more than friendship, at least on the part of Aisha; of Gideon he wasn't so sure. His daughter was a very beautiful woman and if anything her sorrow had enhanced her beauty; he was sure she could make any man's heart race. But Gideon could never marry her; he would know that. A Jew was prohibited by law from marrying a Muslim woman.

'I'm going to eat,' he said rather abruptly.

'Will you think about it?' she asked, standing between him and the door.

'Yes, I will think about it. Now let me pass, woman. My stomach thinks my throat's been cut and I can smell the food from here.'

She stepped aside and he made his way down to the room where the whole family were seated around the table, waiting impatiently for him to arrive so that they could begin their meal.

He knew he should think about a new husband for Aisha but he still felt it was a bit soon. She had only just started to return to her old ways, singing as she worked in the kitchen helping her mother with the cooking, spending more time playing with her children, discarding the veil that she'd started wearing when Daud died and, best of all, going outside the house. He'd hated seeing her sitting in her room hour after hour, wasting away like a plant deprived of sunlight, and how happy he'd been when Rebekah had come that day and persuaded her to go out into Malaqah. Now Basma wanted him to upset his lovely daughter by telling her to stay away from Avi's house and, on top of that, to find her a husband. Hadn't Aisha had enough upheaval in her life for a while? Why couldn't she just live with them for a little longer, at least until her broken heart had mended?

'Seedo, why did you go upstairs? We've been waiting for you? We're all hungry and teta Abal is getting cross because the food is going cold,' said Maryam, wagging her finger at her grandfather.

'I'm so sorry to keep you waiting, my little princess. Shall we eat now?'

She smiled at him—the same smile as her mother—and began to eat.

'Everything all right, husband?' asked Abal, as she placed a plate of lentils on the table in front of him.

'Yes, nothing to worry your head about, my dear,' he replied and made a point of not looking at Basma as he said it.

This evening, after he'd closed the shop, he would go and talk to Avi.

*

Makoud waited until he was sure that Avi's family would have finished their evening meal and then set off along the narrow, cobbled alleyways to his friend's home. The lamps that lined the main streets of the city cast yellow pools of light that barely reached these dark alleys, so he carried his own lantern. In his other hand he had a thick staff in case he met any unsavoury characters and a dagger tucked in his belt, precautions that were probably unnecessary but this was Malaqah, a busy port where cutpurses, foreigners and opportunists thrived. He wanted to be well prepared.

Avi's house was in darkness but after he had knocked a few times he heard the bolts being drawn back and the voice of Avi's servant enquiring who was there.

'I am Makoud ibn Ahmad,' he said. 'A friend of your master.'

There was silence for a few moments and then the final bolts were pulled back and the door swung open.

'Makoud, this is a surprise. Come in. Come in,' said Avi.

He had obviously been preparing for bed because he wore a loose grey robe instead of his usual djubba and his hair, normally neatly caught up under his pointed cap, was loose and fell to his shoulders in loose curls.

'As-salama alaykum, dear friend. I'm sorry to call so late, but I wanted to speak to you when you were alone. I thought that this might be a good hour,' said Makoud.

'Any hour is a good hour to see friends. Come in and sit down, please. I will ask my wife to bring us some tea.'

'No, please don't bother. I prefer to speak to you alone,' said Makoud, sitting down on the sofa.

'Very well. I can see that you're worried about something. I hope it is within my power to help you.'

Makoud hesitated. How could he explain to Avi about his concerns without offending his friend? Personally he would be delighted to welcome Gideon to his family but that would be flying in the face of convention and openly defying Muslim law. A sudden doubt prevented him from speaking. Was he being too hasty? After all what evidence did he have? That Aisha was smiling and singing again? That her daughter had seen Gideon make her mother laugh? The spiteful accusations of his wife? Were they enough to jeopardise his friendship with Avi and his family? Without realising it, he let out a tremendous sigh.

'My goodness, Makoud, you must have the weight of the world on your shoulders. Come, tell me what is worrying you,' said Avi, giving him one of his familiar smiles.

'It is nothing.'

'Tell me, has it anything to do with Aisha? And perhaps my son Gideon?' he asked, a twinkle in his eye.

Makoud looked up in surprise. This was Avi; he'd always been able to second-guess him. He smiled sadly and replied, 'I don't know how you do it, but you've always been able to read my thoughts. I think your mother must have been one of the wise women.'

'Don't blame my mother. It's written all over your face. Who else would you be coming here to talk about, in the middle of the night?'

'Very well. You're quite right. My wife has informed me that Aisha has been visiting your house every day and she is worried that my daughter is becoming too fond of your son, Gideon. I have come tonight only to ask for your opinion. Nothing else.'

'My wife and I have spoken of this, too. When Rebekah invited your daughter to come to our house with the children, it was so she could make friends with my daughters and would feel a little less lonely. Neither of us expected Gideon to fall in love with her.'

'Your son is in love with Aisha? In the name of Allah, what can be done?' Makoud cried. It was worse than he thought.

'We both know that their love is doomed,' said Avi. For once his usual jolly face was grave. 'My son knows it too, but love can be very powerful. I fear that he might do something stupid.'

'And what about Aisha? Does she love him?' asked Makoud.

'This I cannot answer. She smiles a lot when she is with him. They talk and laugh but it is he who looks at her with eyes that speak of love. You will have to ask her yourself.'

'What I must do is find her a husband. She has been a widow now for almost a year; it is time she remarried. If I can find anyone,' he added sadly. He knew the usual fate of widows. They either remained with their parents-in-law for the rest of their lives, working as unpaid servants, or they were married off as a second or third wife to some old man. Aisha's parents-in-law were dead and he didn't want the second option for his lovely Aisha, his little princess.

'She is a beautiful woman. Some man will want to marry her,' said Avi, but without a lot of conviction.

Makoud knew that the Jews were as strict as the Muslims when it came to marriage. It would be difficult to find anyone to marry a widow with two small children, no matter how beautiful she was. Well if he couldn't find her a good husband then she would stay with him, no matter what Basma had to say about it. She was his daughter and she wasn't going to be given to anyone who would treat her badly.

'Have you said anything to Gideon?' asked Makoud.

'Not directly. I have told him that he is to go to Garnata and set up a new business for me there. We have a lot of friends in Garnata—you know it is primarily a Jewish city — and I had already planned to arrange a marriage between him and the daughter of a gold merchant who lives there, a man I've known for many years.'

'Does Gideon know about this?' asked Makoud, suddenly worried that such an action might precipitate the couple into running away together. Disgrace would then be inevitable for both families.

'He knows he must go to Garnata. In fact he leaves next week. I have already bought some premises for him to use as a warehouse. But of the marriage I have said nothing. I will travel with him next week to help him settle in and while I am there I will speak to the goldsmith. I will see if we can arrange the marriage to be performed before the end of the year.'

'It will break his heart,' said Rebekah, who'd come into the room to see if they needed anything.

'Maybe. But what else can we do? Do you want him to end up in prison for marrying a Muslim woman? His heart will mend. If he goes to gaol, his spirit might be broken forever,' said Avi.

Makoud could see that he was not happy with his decision but like him, he knew it was the only one to make.

CHAPTER 10

General Rashad almost ran into the royal apartments; his face was flushed and he was breathing heavily. 'I must see the khalifa right away,' he said to a palace guard, standing by the doorway to the khalifa's private rooms. 'It's urgent.'

'The khalifa is resting. He has been unwell since he returned to Malaqah,' the guard replied.

'I'm sorry to hear that but I must speak to him at once,' Rashad insisted. He could feel his pulse racing. What would be the khalifa's reaction? Rashad had suggested they leave more men to defend the city; he'd told him that Prince Idris would need more reinforcements in case ibn Abd Allah returned but Yahya had paid no attention. Two thousand men were all he could spare, he'd said. Malaqah was more important; he didn't want to risk losing it, he said. And now, after a successful and short campaign with very few men lost, he'd thrown his victory away because he'd refused to leave enough men to defend the conquered city. The unthinkable had happened.

'Wait here.'

The guard pulled the heavy wooden door open and spoke to someone inside.

'His doctor says you must keep it short. His Majesty is not well enough to be bothered by trivia, however urgent you think it is,' said the guard, with a smug look. He was enjoying giving orders to the khalifa's second-in-command, and would have liked it even more if he could have denied him access. But orders were orders and rather reluctantly he had to stand aside to allow General Rashad to enter.

It was true; the khalifa was ill. He looked ghastly lying there on his black silk pillows, the colour of which only emphasised more than ever his yellowy-grey skin and the enormous shadows beneath his eyes which made him look like some ghoul or creature from the after-life. As the general approached the bed, Yahya opened his eyes and stared at him as though he were a phantom come to haunt him. He was terrified. But of what? The general had seen many men die in battle, but none had looked as frightened as the khalifa did at that moment.

Yahya lifted his hand and signalled weakly for the general to approach. 'What is it, Rashad?' He whispered, his voice trembling as he spoke.

'Your Majesty, please forgive the intrusion. I thought you'd like to hear this right away. A messenger has just arrived from Qarmuña. I'm sorry to inform you that the city has fallen. Abbad I has taken Qarmuña and reinstated Muhammad ibn Abd Allah as its ruler. It was all for nothing, Sayyad. Our victory has turned to defeat.'

The general knew he was babbling but there was nothing he could do to stop himself. Did the khalifa understand what he was saying? He had expected him to fly into a rage at the news but there was no reaction from him. None at all. This was strange. He'd never seen the khalifa like this before.

'Qarmuña? But...' Yahya's voice faltered and he lay back on the silk pillows and closed his eyes.

'What are your orders, Your Majesty? Do you want us to launch a counter attack? I can have the army ready to leave within the week.'

He didn't add that he'd also received word from their ally al-Muzzafar who'd also heard that Qarmuña had fallen into Abbad I's hands. Al Muzzafar's message to the general had been short and sharp, but as clear as crystal: 'Do not expect help from the Zirids if you intend to retake Qarmuña.'

'Your Majesty?' He leant closer to the ailing khalifa, who was drifting off to sleep.

'Prince Idris? Where is he?' Yahya asked suddenly, pushing himself into a sitting position. The man looked as though he was at death's door.

'Prince Idris is on his way to Malaqah, Your Majesty. He will be here tomorrow.'

'My army?'

'They are lost, Your Majesty.'

'But he is alive?'

'Yes, Your Majesty. You will see him soon.'

'Two thousand men lost,' the khalifa whispered, as though to himself.

'The army, Your Majesty. Would you like me to start the preparations for war?'

General Rashad knew it was a hopeless task but he felt it was his duty to ask. They'd had too few men before; now they had even less and no support from Garnata. The campaign had been a folly from the start, a whim on the part of the khalifa and then, just as impulsively, when the battle was over, he'd turned for home and left his feckless brother with a handful of men to guard it.

'Leave me now, dear friend. I must rest. I will speak with you tomorrow. You and Labib. And Idris. And Hassan. We will talk then.' The khalifa lay back on the cushions and closed his eyes.

'Very well, Your Majesty,' General Rashad said, backing away from the prostrate figure on the bed in front of him and wondering if he would survive until the morning.

As he left the room, the doctor called after him. 'A moment General, if you would.'

'Yes, Abu al-Jabir, what can I do for you?'

'I just wanted to ask you about the khalifa. Did you notice anything unusual in his behaviour while you were away on the campaign?'

General Rashad hesitated. It didn't seem right talking about Yahya I in this way; he was Khalifa, and Supreme Commander of the army. It was true that Rashad had noticed him acting strangely at first but then, once the campaign was under way, he seemed to be back to his old self. What was the point in mentioning it?

'No, I can't say I did.'

'Nothing strange? He didn't see people who weren't there? Or cry out for no good reason?'

'People who weren't there? Of course not. He's not mad, you know. I expect he's just exhausted. Don't *you* know what's wrong with him?'

The physician shook his head. 'Between you and me, Rashad, it looks very much like a case of poisoning, but I daren't say that openly in case people assume that someone is trying to murder him.'

'Well if he's being poisoned, doesn't that make it a case of attempted murder?' asked the general.

'Not necessarily. It could have been something he ate without realising it. I don't want to start a witch hunt.'

'Speak to his servants. Tell them to check everything he is given and where it comes from.'

'I will. I just hope I'm not too late. Al-Azdi tells me he's been having terrible nightmares for some months now.'

'I don't know anything about that. But I do know that you mustn't believe all that the servants tell you. Well, if there's nothing else, I must leave you. I have a lot to see to today,' the general said, and marched away from the inquisitive eyes of the physician.

Was the doctor right? Was someone trying to murder the khalifa? If so, who could it be? General Rashad ran through all the people who would like to see Yahya out of the way and all he could come up with were members of the khalifa's family; they were the only ones to gain if he died. But that didn't make any sense; his sons were too young and that only left his brother, Idris and he was devoted to him, or so he always said.

*

Prince Idris was in a foul mood. He'd managed to escape from Qarmuña by the skin of his teeth, vowing that he'd return immediately and retake the city from that meddling despot, Abbad I. What right had he to interfere? The ruler of Isbiliya hadn't even wanted the city for himself; he just wanted to demonstrate to Malaqah that he was the stronger of the two. Now General Rashad had said that it was impossible to mount another campaign. What an old woman he was; he'd been the khalifa's second-in-command for too long. It was time for a change; he'd speak to his brother about it at the first opportunity.

'Your Majesty,' Idris said, leaping to his feet and bowing as Yahya came into the throne room, leaning heavily on the arms of two servants. 'Dear brother, you look exhausted. What has happened to you?' He turned to the grand vizier and shouted, 'Where is the doctor? Where is the khalifa's physician? Is no-one caring for my brother? Why are we meeting today when my brother is so ill?'

'Calm yourself, Prince. The doctor is caring for him. And as for the meeting, it is expressly at the request of the khalifa,' replied the grand vizier.

They waited until the khalifa was seated and then all sat down beside him. Yahya was breathing heavily from the exertion and had to lean back on the cushions for a few moments to recover; it took a while before he could speak.

'I have some news for you all. Labib, you will have to record this officially,' he said, struggling to keep his eyes open. Clearly even the effort of speaking was tiring him.

The grand vizier signalled for his secretary to approach. The scribe, a tiny, wizened man whose eyes were constantly screwed up, sat by his side and took out his pen and ink, then unrolled a piece of clean parchment. He dipped his quill pen into the ink and looked at Labib expectantly.

'We are ready, Your Majesty,' said the grand vizier, with a nod to the scribe.

'Very well. I, Yahya I, ibn Ali ibn Hammud al Mutali, Khalifa of Malaqah have decided to divide my kingdom into two separate taifas: the taifa of Malaqah and the taifa of al-Jazira.'

Idris couldn't contain a gasp of astonishment. He hadn't been expecting this. Why was Yahya doing this? What did it mean? He'd been so sure that Yahya would leave everything to him; he'd hinted as much on many occasions. So why split his kingdom into two?

The khalifa laid his head back on the cushions for a moment before continuing. 'Some dreadful ague has taken hold of my body and I fear that Allah may be calling me. Before I go to join Him in Paradise, I must ensure that my succession is secure, which is why I want you all here to-day to witness what I have to say.' He waited a moment to regain his breath and then said, 'As you know, Allah has blessed me with two wonderful sons but that blessing came late in my marriage; my sons are still very young. But they are my heirs and as such I leave the taifa of Malaqah to my son Hasan ibn Yahya ibn Ali, together with the title of khal-ifa, and to my younger son Idris ibn Yahya ibn Ali, I leave the governorship of the taifa of al-Jazira.'

He looked across at Idris and paused again, wiping a tear from his eye, then continued, 'If I do die before they come of age then I look to you, dear brother, to care for my sons and help them in their new roles.'

'Of course, brother. I will care for them as if they were my own. But what of the people?' asked Idris, desperately trying to keep his anger hidden inside him. How could his brother do this? They were surrounded by enemies and he was making a ten-year-old and a five-year-old rulers of his kingdom. There was definitely something wrong with him; he would never have made such a decision if he were in his right mind. He would realise that Abbad would see such a move as an open invitation to attack Malaqah.

'What about them?' Yahya managed to croak. He was growing weaker by the minute; Idris could see that he wouldn't last much longer.

'They will be angry that you have favoured your sons instead of choosing someone with more experience. You are leaving the door open for our enemies to attack us.'

'Rubbish. My ministers will have to deal with it. This is my decision and it is final.' With that he collapsed back on the cushions and closed his eyes.

'Your Majesty,' ventured General Rashad. 'What shall we do about Qarmuña?'

'Qarmuña? Oh, nothing. You have said yourself that we do not have enough men. When I am dead you can discuss it with my son. Now, please leave me. I am tired and would rest.'

General Rashad, Prince Idris and the grand vizier backed out of the room, leaving the ailing khalifa with his physician.

'Well, what are we going to do now?' asked Idris, barely containing his rage. 'We can't let Hassan become khalifa, not yet. When he's older maybe, but not now.'

'The khalifa is not dead yet. He may recover and then there will be no problem. Let's just wait and see how he fares,' said the grand vizier.

'Yes, I agree. We can't go against his wishes. That would be treason,' said General Rashad.

'Very well. But I think we should be ready with some plan; he doesn't look as though he will live much longer,' said Idris. 'When he dies, we must move quickly before anyone makes a bid to take over the throne.'

'So, you're not returning to Sebta?' asked the grand vizier.

'Of course not. I need to be here, by my brother's side. He is obviously unwell. There is no way I can leave him.'

'So, who is governing Sebta, while you are here?' asked General Rashad.

'Our friend Ibn Baqanna is there. He is more than capable of looking after our interests.'

'You are mistaken, Prince. I saw him only this morning; he is in Malaqah,' said the general.

'What? I didn't send for him. Why has he come here?'

'I asked him the same question and he replied that he thought he'd be more useful here than in Sebta. He seems to be under the impression that the khalifa is about to die and that you will need him by your side.'

'Does he indeed?'

What was ibn Baqanna playing at? He obviously hadn't heard that Yahya had left everything to his sons. He was expecting Idris to become khalifa. Well he'd soon find out he'd had a wasted journey. He smiled to himself. He liked ibn Baqanna—they'd been friends for many years—but he didn't always trust him. What did he want? Why was he really here?

CHAPTER 11

Umar loved being a soldier; this would be his life from now on, fighting for his home, his city and his khalifa. What greater work could a man have?

'Hey, soldier. Stop fussing with that horse and get on with your training,' shouted the naqib in charge of his contingent.

'Sayaad,' Umar replied, bowing quickly and then hurrying across to the parade ground.

He was dressed in white loose-fitting trousers and tunic for the training, which began each morning with a wrestling match. The rest of his squad were already there; they'd been divided into two teams and the result would be determined when all the members of one team had been defeated.

'Come on Umar; we're depending on you. We're one down already,' said one of his team mates.

Today Umar was pitted against a huge jinete, a man so big that he was the constant butt of jokes about his horse collapsing under him. But strength wasn't everything as Umar had been quick to learn. Speed and cunning could overcome the largest of men.

'As-salama alaykum, my little friend,' said his opponent, with a broad grin. Umar could see from his expression that he expected to get the match over very quickly. Well, he would see about that.

The nazir drew a fresh circle in the sand with a stick and, once the two men were standing inside the circle, he gave the signal for them to start. Within seconds Umar was flat on his back but he leapt up instantly and resumed the attack. Only two falls were required to win a bout and already he'd had one—touching the sand with any part of the body, except the feet, represented a fall. He couldn't afford to make any more mistakes.

The rules were simple; there were only three moves: grasping, blocking and deflecting. His opponent had the advantage in the first two because of his superior height and strength so Umar had to concentrate on deflecting his moves and using his opponent's own strength to unbalance him. Punching, hitting and trying to strangle your opponent were forbidden, no matter how much you thought they deserved it.

His opponent grasped his tunic and tugged hard, trying to pull him to the ground but Umar was too quick for him; he tucked his right foot behind his opponent's and pushed him off balance so that he fell on his elbow. One fall each. The next fall would be the decider.

The huge jinete was angry now and tried to use his strength to block any of Umar's moves; they wrestled back and forward for ages, neither one giving way until at last Umar managed to get a handhold on the back of his opponent's tunic, and neatly slipping his foot behind him, pulled him to the ground. The jinete was up again immediately, but not before his hand had brushed the sand. It was over. Umar had won his first match, against all the odds. The two men bowed to each other and sat down to watch the next pair. The score was now two all.

His friend, Talib was next to wrestle, but he was too slow and his opponent soon had him on his back, not once but twice and his match was over; now the score was three-two. Talib still had a lot to learn about wrestling.

'I don't know how you did it,' said Talib, sitting down beside him. 'He's much bigger than you. How did you manage to win against such a brute?'

'I've told you before; you have to try to outwit them. That's why it's part of our training. It's not just about physical exercise but learning how to use all your body to fight and how to read your opponent's moves.'

'So, if I look closely at my opponent I can guess what he's going to do next?'

'Yes, something like that.'

'But I don't have the time to look at him. I'm usually on my back before then,' he said with a laugh.

'Hey you, don't sit there gossiping like an old woman, archery practice now,' said the nazir. He'd been particularly nice to them both since he'd heard how they had stopped the soldiers getting back to Qarmuña.

'Yes, sayaad,' said Talib. 'Shall I get my horse?'

'Only if you're planning on shooting it through the eye with an arrow. No. I think you need to learn to shoot straight before you try it on horseback, don't you?'

'As you wish, sayaad.'

'Well I *do* wish, so get a move on or you'll end up scrubbing out the stables.'

Umar turned his attention back to the wrestling match. The score was now three-two against his team. They needed to win this one or morale would slip.

The latest vanquished competitor slumped down beside him.

'Did you see that? That clown punched me and the nazir said nothing. It was a foul. He should have been disqualified,' he protested.

'Well it looked all right to me,' said Umar. He didn't really want to get into an argument with this soldier; he was someone who was always looking for trouble. 'Anyway, it's only a training exercise; it's not a real competition.'

'Not real? Well I'll tell you what is real.' He leaned closer and whispered, 'The khalifa is dying.'

The man's breath smelt of rotten eggs.

'What?' Umar looked around to make sure nobody had heard him. It was treasonous to speak like that.

'It's true. I heard it from one of the palace guards. He's gone mad, raving and shouting all the time. Thinks someone is trying to kill him. I tell you, it's all they can do to contain him.'

Umar thought of the tall, proud man he'd seen outside Qarmuña. Could this be true?

'Well, even if you're telling the truth, I think you should be careful whom you talk to about it. Everyone has enemies, even the khalifa.'

'Especially the khalifa.'

'So all the more important not to spread it around. Keep it to yourself.'

'I think it was losing Qarmuña that sent him over the edge,' said the soldier, disregarding Umar's advice. 'All that effort for nothing. The only people who gained from that campaign were the bloody Zirids. They cleaned up before they left. Plenty of booty for them but nothing for us. All we got was our marching orders. Back to Malaqah as fast as you can ride.'

His rather strident way of speaking had alerted their commanding officer, who now walked across to them. 'Complaining again, soldier? Well I think it's time you got on with your training unless you'd sooner spend your time cleaning out the latrines? You're out of the wrestling match so there's no need for you to hang around here. Off with you. Sword play,' instructed the nazir then he pointed at Umar. 'And you, you're wrestling again. Get ready.'

*

Umar's team lost the wrestling match by a slight margin. Unlike Talib, who never got past the first round, Umar had an even score of wins and losses over the time he'd been there. He didn't mind about getting beaten occasionally; the most important thing for him was that he was learning his new craft. His sword play had improved to such an extent that he now did all his practising on horseback, charging at and slicing up sacks of straw that hung from gibbets. He learnt how to defend himself by disabling his attackers: a slash at the inside of the elbow, or across the wrist or knee. He learnt the position of the most important organs in the body—the heart, the liver, the kidneys, the stomach—and, if he was on foot, how to position his dagger below the rib cage and drive it upwards. His range of weapons was wide; besides the scimitar and dagger that he carried at all times, he had a lance, a bow and an axe which he took into battle. His archery had improved to the extent that he could now hit a moving target at a hundred paces, but still couldn't quite manage it from the back of his horse. They trained hard every day and when they weren't training they were exercising and grooming their horses, or else they sat around, chatting and cleaning their weapons. There was never much time for anything else.

Today, however, he had a half-day pass and he was going home to visit his parents. He hadn't been to their new home since they'd moved in six months before, so he was looking forward to seeing them all and proving to his mother that life as a soldier did not necessarily mean instant death.

While some of the troops were stationed inside the alcazaba, the majority of the khalifa's army—including Umar —were located at the top of the hill, in a garrison beside the lighthouse, the Jbel-Faro, the rock of light. This immense fortress was surrounded by high, thick walls and its magnificent situation presented the soldiers on guard with a panoramic view along the coast; any enemy ships would be spotted long before they got to shore.

He stopped to stare at the sea below him; it was rough that afternoon and he could hear the wind lashing it against the walls of the fortress. Part of Malaqah's navy was moored at the far end of the harbour, close to the ship building area; these light and rapid longships had probably been in for their winter repair.

It was almost spring and from now on there would be a lot more activity in the harbour: merchant round-ships and trading vessels that toured the Middle Sea buying and selling their goods, flat-bottomed qaribs that could sail easily up the rivers and bring back the wood that was required for ship building, fishing boats and galleys. He'd even seen naval ships which were used to land horses, galleys fuelled by oarsmen that could back onto a beach and unload up to forty horses through the stern. He wondered how brave his Basil would be on such a ship.

His stomach started to grumble; if he hurried he might arrive home in time to eat with the family. The Jbel-Faro was connected to the alcazaba by a defensive corridor, so that the army could support any attack on the khalifa's palace. It was an ingenious design and meant the troops could move into action quickly. It was along this defensive corridor that Umar strode that afternoon, with his mind firmly focused on a plate of his mother's vegetable stew.

*

It didn't take him long to find his father's new apothecary's shop; it was far closer than he'd realised. Before he could enter, Ibrahim came rushing out of the shop, a big grin over his face.

'Umar. What a surprise. Mama will be so happy to see you; she hasn't stopped wailing about her little boy going off to be a soldier.'

Umar hugged him and said, 'It's good to see you, brother. How are you?'

'Not having as much fun as you, I expect. I like working with Baba, but sometimes I long for a bit more adventure.'

'Don't get any ideas about enlisting; that really would upset Mama.'

'Who're you talking to, Ibrahim?' Makoud called from inside the shop. 'Who is it now?'

'Come and see for yourself, Baba,' Umar said.

'Is that you, Umar? At last. I thought you'd forgotten us,' said Makoud, with that familiar look on his face which said he was delighted to see you but not willing to show it. How did he ever think he could fool them?

'They don't give me much leave. But here I am now.'

'Yes indeed.' His father enveloped him in a long embrace; if his face wasn't going to reveal how much he'd missed him, then his actions did. 'Come inside. I must call your mother, at once.'

Umar followed his father into the shop, his eyes—now keener from his training—taking in all the details: the long counter with rows of glass bottles, phials and narrow-necked jars where medicines and creams were stored, the larger amphoras sitting on the tiled floor, baskets of dried herbs and fresh ones hanging from the ceiling on lengths of coloured flax, the low sofa where the customers could sit and talk in confidence to the apothecary, and the open door which led to his father's workroom. The shop smelled of thyme and rosemary, of the pungent smell of garlic and fennel, the aromatic scents of camphor and anise, of sandalwood. This was much larger than the previous shop in Ardales, where his father had only one small room to do everything, prepare skin and hair treatments, toothpaste, depilatory creams, make-up, tonics, perfumes, in short, almost everything that his skill could produce and that the physicians prescribed.

Despite the fact that he'd never been there before, this new apothecary's shop felt like home and Umar was transported back to his childhood; he'd liked spending time with his father, watching him grind the herbs and mix the ingredients. To him it was a kind of magic, but when he once mentioned that to Baba, his father had been angry and said that it wasn't magic; it was science. Magic was forbidden by the Quran; only witches performed magic. Forbidden or not, Umar knew there was magic in the world; he saw it when a new born foal took its first steps; he saw it in the sunrise when the world changed from grey to gold and he saw it in Basil's eyes when he spoke to her and stroked her muzzle.

'Here he is, wife. Your son returned from battle, safe and sound. Didn't I tell you that nothing would happen to him? Allah was looking after him, just like I told you he would,' said Makoud.

Basma stared at Umar as if he were a ghost, then she burst into tears.

'Well Mama, that's not much of a welcome. I thought you'd be pleased to see me,' said Umar, hugging his mother.

'I am. I am. I have prayed night and day for Allah to keep you safe and my prayers have been answered. Let me look at you? Are you well? Have you been injured? Let me see.'

She held him away from her and inspected him in the same way she used to when he was a boy and had hurt himself playing. He half expected her to pull up his tunic to see if he had any bruises.

'I'm perfectly fine, Mama. No injuries. Nothing.'

'Is that a bruise on your cheek?'

'Probably, Mama. I'm in the army; it's not all soft beds and feather pillows. We're soldiers.'

'Leave him alone, wife. You have what you want; he is home and he is well. Now come inside, son. You've arrived in time to eat with us. Come. Your little brother and your sister will be so happy to see you.'

*

It was strange how different he felt; his months in the army had changed him. Now he was much more aware of the undercurrents in his family; he could sense that although the men of the house were quite content with their new life, there was a sadness about the women. Were they missing Ardales?

'Where's Dirar?' he asked, accepting a huge plate of lentils and vegetables from Basma.

'Your brother is a fisherman now,' said Makoud. 'He'll be home soon.'

'So, plenty of fresh fish, then,' said Umar, spooning the lentils into his mouth. This was one thing he did miss, home cooking.

Abal put a plate of fresh figs on the table and a basket of bread.

'Dirar likes his work,' she said. 'He's happy here.'

'I thought he was going to finish school first?'

'He didn't want to. What was the point in making him stay at school if he wanted to work?' said Makoud, chewing the warm bread.

'And what about you, Aisha? Are you well?' She looked better than when he had last seen her but Umar still felt uncomfortable talking to his sister; she had been so unhappy when Daud died. What could he say to her? They had been very close once; he, Aisha and Daud had spent a lot of time together when they were children. Now he felt tongue-tied. Daud's death had built a wall between them and he couldn't work out how to scale it.

Aisha smiled her sweet smile and said, 'I'm well thank you brother.'

'So how's life in the army?' asked Makoud. He was eager to hear all about it.

Umar began by telling them about his normal routine, the wrestling, the training, Basil.

'But what about when you went to Qarmuña?' asked Ibrahim. 'Was it exciting? Did you kill anyone?'

'Ibrahim,' his mother exclaimed.

'It's all right Mama. No, I didn't kill anyone because I was left behind in the camp.'

'So you weren't involved in the fighting?' asked Makoud. He could see that both his father and Ibrahim were disappointed to hear this.

'No, but I did play an important role in our victory.' He told them how he and Talib had managed to stop the two soldiers from getting back to the enemy. As he recounted his tale he saw their looks of admiration and was happy that he had given them something to be proud of.

'You did well, son. Kept a clear head. Very important that, not to panic,' said Makoud and there was envy in his eyes.

For the first time in his life, Umar wondered about his father's life. He knew they had fled from Qurtubah when he was a similar age to himself, but none of the details. What had life been like for them living in a besieged city? How had they escaped? He vowed that he would talk to him about it next time he came home.

'What happened? How did we lose Qarmuña so quickly?' Ibrahim asked. 'Do you know?'

'Not really. They say that there weren't enough men to defend the city and Abbad I saw his chance and attacked. That's all we've been told.'

'But why didn't the khalifa send more men?' asked his brother.

'That's a question everyone has been asking. It could be that he was frightened of leaving Malaqah poorly defended. Or maybe he just made a mistake.'

'Made a mistake? How can the Supreme Commander make a mistake?' asked Ibrahim, his eyes wide in surprise.

'Well, there are rumours—and you mustn't repeat them —that the khalifa is not himself. He has been behaving rather oddly lately and the gossip is that he's been poisoned.'

'How could that happen? I thought that the khalifa's food was always tested by one of his servants before he ate it? Who would have the opportunity to poison him?' asked Ibrahim.

Makoud put out his hand and touched Ibrahim's arm. 'I think we should leave this for now. We don't want to upset your mother.'

His father looked directly at him; there was something he wanted to tell him but not in front of the others. What could it be? Did he know what was happening to the khalifa? Was he somehow involved? Surely not.

CHAPTER 12

Musif was waiting for them by the front gate, holding the mules by their halters. They would not arrive in Garnata until nightfall, which was why they were leaving so early.

'Come Gideon. Do you have all you need?' asked Avi, looking at the small bag that his son was tying onto the back of the mule.

'Yes, Baba. Just a few clothes. We're not staying more than a couple of days, are we?'

'A couple of days? And then what? Do you think you can run the business from here, in Malaqah? No matter. I will have your things sent on to you later.'

His son looked crestfallen. 'I know you said you wanted me to run the new business in Garnata, but I didn't realise you meant straight away. I thought you were talking about sometime in the future, Baba.'

'There comes a point, my son, when the future has to become the present. What's the problem? I thought you were excited about being your own master and taking this on?'

'I am, Baba. It's just that…' His son hesitated and a pink flush tinged his smooth, beardless face.

'If you're worried about Aisha, your mother will tell her that you've moved to Garnata.'

At that Gideon's face grew scarlet. 'Why do you say that, Baba?' he stammered.

'Relax Gideon, you are not the first Jew to fall in love with a Muslim girl. When I was your age, I too had feelings for a beautiful woman whom I knew I could never marry. We can't control whom we fall in love with but we can control whom we marry. I knew there was no future for us together and so I married your mother instead. I have never regretted my decision for one moment. I knew that the only way I could be with a Muslim woman was if I turned my back on my family, my religion and all that I held dear. It was a sacrifice I was not prepared to make and it's one that I won't allow you to make either.'

'But I love her, Baba.'

Avi's heart ached for his son. Young love was so painful. There was no point telling Gideon that the pain would pass, that in time he would come to realise that his father was right. He was not ready to hear those words; right now it was his heart which led him.

'I understand, my son. But what of her? Does she love you?'

'I don't know. We have never spoken of it.'

'She is a lonely, vulnerable young woman, Gideon. All she has is her family and her children. You can't take her away from her family; it would be cruel.'

'I just want to see her one more time, Baba. Please. Let me say goodbye and then I will go with you to Garnata, I promise. And I will never speak of her again.'

Avi looked at his heart-broken son and knew he had to close this in his own way. If he dragged him away from her like this, Gideon would never forgive him and the love he had for Aisha would smoulder in his heart forever.

'Very well. Your mother tells me that she comes every morning. We will leave tomorrow.' He turned to the patient Musif and said, 'Take the mules back to the stables. We are leaving tomorrow morning at dawn.'

'Thank you Baba.'

*

'Mama. Mama. Sara is getting married. Look, we are making her wedding clothes,' Maryam cried, excitedly holding up a square of embroidery.

'Is this true?' Aisha asked, sitting down with her friends and picking up a piece of the sewing. Each of the women was embroidering a large square of thick cotton in various shades and patterns; it would be a rainbow of colour by the time it was finished. 'Are you really getting married, Sara? You never spoke about it before.'

'Oh, it's not for months yet,' said Sara, stretching across and picking up Imran. She tickled his tummy and when he started to laugh a broad smile spread across her face. 'I hope I have beautiful children like yours,' she said, burying her head in his soft body.

'Yes, it is not until the end of the summer, which is fortunate,' said her mother, 'because we have only just finished the dress; this cloak will take at least a couple of months to complete.'

'I will help you,' said Aisha. 'You will have to tell me what you want me to do, but I am skilled with a needle and thread.' She put her own sewing to one side.

'Oh that's wonderful, an extra pair of hands. Here you can take this over from me; just continue joining together the finished squares as I have been doing. Then I can get back to embroidering new ones,' said Avi's mother.

She was an old woman whose eyesight was failing and she held her sewing very close to her eyes but despite that Aisha could see that her stitches were still minute and even; she seemed to be doing it by instinct.

Aisha picked up a needle, threaded it with some white cotton and began to sew. She liked needlework; it was relaxing and she could chat to her new friends at the same time.

'So, Sara, you must tell me all. Who is your husband-to-be? What is he like? When did you meet him?' she asked, feeling as excited for her friend as if it were her own wedding.

'His name is Aaron, Aaron ibn Jaheem and he is a merchant in Garnata. He came here with his father once, to do some business with Baba. I didn't realise it at the time but part of that business was a marriage deal; I was quite young at the time,' said Sara.

'And now that you're older, you're still happy with the arrangement?' asked Aisha.

'Why wouldn't she be?' said Rebekah, rather snappishly. 'He's a kind man, from a good family. They will look after my daughter well. What is there not to be happy about?'

Aisha lowered her head and stared at her sewing. Baba had arranged her own marriage and it had been successful, so why was she querying the wisdom of Sara's betrothal? Was it because she and Daud had been so much in love? Did she hope for something similar for Sara? She certainly did for her own daughter.

'Won't you be lonely living in Garnata?' she asked, quietly. 'Away from your family?' In the short time she'd known Avi's family she could see that they were all devoted to each other. Why would they send one of their daughters to Garnata? Surely there were suitable husbands here in Malaqah?

'Oh, I won't be alone,' Sara said with another of her beaming smiles. 'Gideon will be there. I'll be able to see him whenever I want to.'

Aisha felt a shiver run through her body despite the warm sun that, a moment ago, had been so pleasant. 'Gideon? Your brother, Gideon?' she asked, as calmly as she could.

'Yes. Have you not heard?' interrupted Rebekah. 'Gideon is to open a new branch of my husband's business in Garnata; it is a wonderful opportunity for him. He will be in sole charge and if he makes a success of it, then Avi will give it to him. Only twenty-five and owning his own business, that's a great start in life for any young man.' She didn't look at Aisha as she spoke, which was strange as Rebekah was usually a very open and direct person.

'So he will live in Garnata?' Aisha asked.

'Yes, my dear, that's what I'm telling you. He leaves tomorrow. The premises are already bought; all he has to do is buy the stock and get started,' said Rebekah.

'What about your other sons? Don't they want to go to Garnata?' she asked.

'His brothers? I don't know. All I know is that Avi needs them here.'

Aisha finished sewing her square and handed it back to the grandmother. 'I'm sorry. We must go now. I'll come again soon and help you with the sewing,' she said.

'Oh, Mama. Why do we have to go? We've only just got here. I haven't had time to play yet. Just a bit longer, please,' wailed Maryam.

'I'm sorry, sweetheart, but we must go now. I promised Seedo we wouldn't be long.' She turned to Sara and taking Imran from her arms, added, 'Good luck with your wedding preparations. Please let me know if I can do anything to help. Ma'a salama, my friends.'

'Alla ysalmak, Aisha. Come again soon.'

It was all Aisha could do to stop herself from running out of there; but she couldn't risk them knowing how upset she was at the news. It was silly of her to react in this way but Gideon had never mentioned anything about leaving Malaqah. Not a word. She brushed away a tear. Maybe she'd been mistaken. Perhaps what she'd taken for love was nothing more than pity. How stupid she'd been. This was what happened when you became too wrapped up in your own grief; you stopped seeing the world as it really was.

The sun was already high in the sky; she would have to hurry if she wanted to be gone before Gideon appeared for his morning break.

'Mama, you're hurting me. Why do we have to run like this? What's happened? Is Seedo sick?' cried Maryam.

Aisha stopped and bent down to her little daughter. 'No, sweetheart, Seedo isn't sick. It's Mama's fault. I forgot you have such little legs. Come we'll walk nice and slowly now.'

'One day my legs will be as long as yours, Mama.'

'Yes, darling. They will. One day, when you're a big girl. Come, take my hand.'

Together they walked down the path to the gates, but before Musif could finish unlocking them for her, she heard someone shout her name.

'Aisha, wait. Aisha.' Gideon was running down the path towards them. 'Are you going without speaking to me, today?' he asked with his usual big grin. 'I thought we'd have a glass of tea together.'

'I'm in a hurry this morning,' she whispered, trying to hold back her tears.

'Mama is upset,' said Maryam. 'She wants to go home.'

'Really? What's upset you? Has one of my sisters said anything?' asked Gideon, his smile gone.

'Maryam, just go and play in the garden for a moment, please,' Aisha said. She waited until her daughter was out of earshot and then continued 'I hear you're going to live in Garnata.'

'They told you?'

'Your mother thinks it's a great opportunity for you,' she said, unable to stop her eyes filling with tears.

'I wish they could learn to keep their mouths shut, just once in a while,' he said.

'So you were going to leave without telling me?' Aisha said, brushing away her tears in anger.

'Of course not. You're my friend; why would I do that? No, I wanted to tell you myself.'

His friend? Well, why would she expect anything more? He was a good friend; she should be happy with that. She smiled at him and took his hand. 'I hope we can remain friends when you're living in Garnata.'

'You don't understand. I want you to come with me. To be my wife. I love you Aisha.'

His wife? She looked at him in disbelief and suddenly she realised the dangerous game she'd been playing. Lonely and desperate for affection and companionship, she'd allowed this kind young man to fall in love with her. How

stupid of her. She knew there was no future for them together. She was a Muslim and a widow. He was Jewish and
unmarried. Neither his faith nor hers would allow them to
marry. She felt ashamed. Her heart was telling her that she
could be happy with him; he would be a good, kind father
to her children and a husband to her. But her heart was also
telling her that she still loved Daud and so how could she
marry someone else when she knew that was true.

'Aisha. Did you hear me? I love you, Aisha. I know it
will be difficult at first, but we will find a way.'

She took his hand and whispered, 'I'm sorry, Gideon. It
won't work. I'm so sorry. Please forgive me.' Then she
pulled away from him and called to her daughter, 'Maryam.
Come here. It's time to leave.'

'Aisha, please don't leave. Let's at least discuss this. I'll
tell Baba that I don't want to go to Garnata. I'll stay here in
Malaqah. I'll do anything to be with you, Aisha.'

'Come, Maryam, we're going home,' Aisha said, as her
daughter came running down the path towards her. She
took her hand and walked through the open gates without
looking back.

Imran began to cry; he could sense that his mother was
upset. She patted his back and whispered comfortingly to
him.

'Aisha, wait. Aisha, I love you,' called Gideon, regard-
less of the fact that Musif was standing by the gate.

She brushed away the tears from her cheek before
Maryam could see them and hurried home. How could she
have been so thoughtless?

CHAPTER 13

Makoud left Ibrahim to close up the shop and hurried down the narrow alleys that led to the Jewish quarter. He'd hardly had time to see his friend Avi since he'd spoken to him about Gideon; he'd been so busy with the new shop and building up his stock. It would be good to just sit and chat with him over a glass of mint tea.

As he expected Avi was in his warehouse, examining some bales of cloth.

'As-salama alaykum, my friend. I hope I'm not disturbing you,' Makoud said, entering the darkened room.

'Makoud. Welcome. Welcome. What a pleasure to see you. Just one moment while I finish this and I'll be with you.' He folded the cloth carefully and stacked it with the other bales, then pulled back a curtain and shouted, 'Rebekah, bring some tea for our friend. Tea. Mint tea.'

Makoud smiled to himself; Avi had never lost the habit of repeating himself when he was excited.

'Come, dear friend. Come with me. You have time to share a glass or two of tea with me, yes? Of course you do. Why else would you be visiting me at this hour? Come, we will sit on the terrace where it is cool.'

He led Makoud through his spacious house and up onto the roof, to a wide terrace that looked out over the city towards the sea and the mountains across the bay.

'Sit down. Please sit down. Tell me how everything is going? Are you happy with the shop? What about the customers? Are there many of them? There are a number of apothecaries in Malaqah, you know. I hope there is enough business for you. I hope you aren't disappointed.'

Makoud sat down on a low sofa and looked at the view. It was very peaceful up there, above the bustle and noise of the city. And Avi was right; it was fresh and cool. There was a roof terrace above his own shop, but it was only used for storing odds and ends. He must speak to Abal about cleaning it up so that they could all sit there in the evenings, like they used to do in Ardales. Two gulls flew overhead cawing loudly and landed on the roof next door where they sat eyeing him, no doubt wondering if there was going to be any food for them.

'I am very happy with the shop, Avi. You chose wisely. And there are plenty of customers, including quite a few from the alcazaba. It hadn't occurred to me that there would be so many people working there that would have need of my services,' he replied.

'Good. Good. I am pleased for you.'

'I've brought you a gift,' Makoud said. 'Well, it's for your wife as well, actually.' He handed him a small packet.

Avi took the package and grinned like a little child. 'A present? How lovely? Rebekah loves presents. Ah, here she is. Rebekah look, Makoud has brought us a present.'

His wife laid the tray with the glasses and jug of tea on the table and took the packet from him. She bowed and murmured, 'Thank you.'

'Well open it, my dear one. Open it,' said Avi, who couldn't hide his impatience to know what the package held.

'How lovely,' she said, unwrapping a small jar and removing the top. 'Thank you, Makoud. It smells wonderful.'

'What is it?' asked her impatient husband. 'What has he given us?'

'It's a perfumed oil,' she replied and looked at Makoud for further explanation.

'It's a massage oil, made from frankincense, geranium flowers and sandalwood. It's very good for relieving tension or curing insomnia,' he said.

'Excellent. Excellent. Rebekah you can try it out on me tonight. You know I haven't been sleeping well lately,' said Avi with a wide smile.

'I'm sorry to hear that you're having sleepless nights,' said Makoud, when Rebekah had left them.

'It's this problem with the pirates. The khalifa doesn't do enough to protect the merchant ships from piracy. Each month at least one of the ships is attacked on its way across the Middle Sea, sometimes more. It's costing the merchants a lot of money. Last month I lost forty bales of good quality silk. That's a great deal of dinars. But what can we do about it?'

'Can't you put armed men on the cargo ships to protect them?'

'We do. But they're not much use. The problem is that our ships are too slow. We can't outrun the pirates; their boats are both lighter and faster than ours.'

Makoud didn't know very much about ships and sailing; he'd always lived inland. Although he could remember seeing longships set out on the Guadalquivir from Qurtuba; as a boy he and Avi had stood on the Roman Bridge many times and watched the oarsmen propelling the ships towards the estuary.

'Like the warships we used to see on the Guadalquivir, you mean?'

'Exactly. But these pirate ships also have sails.'

Since Dirar had become a fisherman Makoud had become more interested in the ships that sailed into the harbour. He often stood outside his shop and looked out to sea, hoping to catch a glimpse of his son's fishing boat.

'Oars and sails?' he asked.

'Yes, so not only are they fast but they can travel further. They're impossible to catch.'

Avi explained that the ships that he and the merchants used to bring goods from the other side of the Middle Sea were altogether different. They were wide, heavy round boats that could carry enough provisions for a long journey and weather any storm, and because speed was not an issue they had no need of oarsmen and that gave them more space for their cargo.

'The problem is, our ships, which although they have triangular lateen sails that can catch the slightest breeze and rarely have to ship anchor, are not built for speed,' Avi explained.

'But you could ram the pirates' boat,' said Makoud. 'They're heavy enough for that.' He'd seen the merchant ships moored by the quay, heavy-duty wooden boats built to carry as much cargo as possible.

Avi laughed. 'Yes we could if we were quick enough, but usually they are upon us before we know it, assaulted our men and taken our goods. Sometimes they throw the crew overboard and take the whole ship, cargo as well. Remember cargo ships are crewed by seamen and merchants; they're not fighting men and no match for heavily armed pirates.'

'Can't you chase them to their base?'

'These pirates are too well organised; they're like a collection of private armies. They have hiding places in coves and bays all along the north African coast. Some operate from the Balearic Islands, some as far afield as the Fortunate Isles. It's impossible to stop them.'

'But who are they? Where are they from?' Makoud asked.

'Most are Arabs. Some are disgraced seamen, or soldiers; some are men who escaped prison; some are deserters; a few are infidels—Vikings who attack coastal towns or travel up the rivers and kidnap people to sell as slaves—and all are desperate men. They'd cut your throat as soon as look at you.'

'I've brought you some almendrados to go with your tea,' said Rebekah, coming out onto the terrace with a large plate of almond sweetmeats in her hands. 'Avi told me how you were always stealing almonds from your neighbour's tree when you were a boy because you loved them so much.'

'Did he say that? I'm not sure it's wholly true. If I remember it was you who wanted to climb into his garden,' said Makoud, looking at Avi with a smile.

'But it was you who got caught,' laughed Avi and popped a sweetmeat into his mouth.

'And Gideon?' Makoud asked when Rebekah had left. 'Where is he?'

'He's in Garnata. I told him I needed him to work there from now on. He wasn't happy about it but he understands that he must do as I say. I feel sorry for him. I know what it is to love someone you can never have.' He looked at the stairs to make sure his wife had not returned. 'You remember Musa?'

'Yes I do. She was a beautiful girl but in the end you did the right thing,' said Makoud.

'I had no choice. If I'd run away with her it would have destroyed my family; they would never have spoken to me again. I would have been disinherited.'

'Such decisions are hard to make,' Makoud said, thinking of Aisha and what he should do about her. 'You will all miss Gideon.'

'That's true. My children are not happy about it but they would understand if they knew the real reason. And Aisha?'

'I don't know. She's stopped visiting your house and spends most of her days helping my wives with the housework.'

'Yes, my wife told me that Aisha doesn't call in to see her anymore. She is worried that this business with Gideon will mean the end of their friendship. She suggested to me that she go and visit her instead, but I said it's best to wait a while.'

'I think you're right. Whatever went on between them, it will take time to heal,' said Makoud, wondering just how much Aisha was missing Gideon.

'Well, I have arranged a marriage for him now. That should help him to forget.'

'To the goldsmith's daughter?'

'Yes. The wedding will be at the end of the year.'

'What has Gideon said about that?' asked Makoud.

'He wasn't really surprised. He knew I had a girl in mind for him for some time; you can't keep anything secret in my house.'

'But he understands, doesn't he, that he and Aisha could never be together?' His heart went out to the young man; he could understand him falling in love with his daughter.

'I believe he has accepted it. He's never spoken to me about her after that day when I told him he was going to live in Garnata.'

'You think she said something to him?'

Avi shrugged. 'All I hope is that whatever it was is now over. Gideon knows it couldn't work. Come drink some tea and tell me what your sons have been up to.'

*

Aisha went up on to the roof terrace to be alone. She moved aside some of the sacks of rice that were stored there and sat down. The letter she'd received that morning was burning a hole in her pocket but she couldn't bring herself to read it. Why had Gideon written to her? The look on his face when she'd told him that she wouldn't go with him to Garnata kept coming back to haunt her. She had hurt him and for that she was very sad. What more was there to be said?

She pulled the parchment out of her pocket and opened it carefully. It read:

Sitting here in the moonlight, dearest Aisha,
I can see your face before me.
Day and night I dream of you.
I feel your presence in the soft rays of the sun
It lingers in the cool breeze floating across the sea
How I long to touch your soft skin
And taste those sweet lips.
You are in the very air that I breathe
But our love can never be.
My head and my heart are in conflict

but in the end reason must prevail
And I must awake from this dream.
Maybe, if God is merciful, we will be together
in another time, another life
Until then always remember, my dearest
You are my love now and will be forever more.

It was unsigned but she knew it was from Gideon.

'Aisha? Are you up there?' It was her father.

Hurriedly she folded the parchment and put it back in her pocket. 'Yes, Baba. I'm coming down now.'

'No, stay where you are; I'm coming up.'

Within a few minutes her father's unruly mop of grey hair looked around the door. 'What are you doing up here, child?' he asked.

'Just enjoying the cool breeze,' she said, trying not to blush. Lying had never come easy to her.

'Yes, it's cooler up here; you're right. I've been thinking of getting your mother to clean it up so we can use it as a proper terrace instead of an extra storeroom. What do you think about that?' She saw him look at her then continue, 'I've just been round to have a glass of tea with Avi and we sat on his roof terrace. It was very pleasant and got me thinking about ours. I think our view is even better than his, you know.'

Her father prattled on and on but she barely listened to him, until she heard him speak Gideon's name. 'Sorry Baba, what did you say?'

'There's to be another wedding in Avi's house. Young Gideon is to get married now.'

'Really? When?' She kept her voice steady and calm but inside her heart was beating wildly. So that was the reason for the letter. He had accepted the inevitable, that they would never be together. This is what her father had been wanting to tell her.

'Before the end of the year. The wedding will take place in Garnata. I expect all the family will go.'

'So soon,' she murmured. 'Barely six months away.'

'Yes, and it's Sara's wedding next month. Avi has invited us all to go to the celebrations. You'd like that, wouldn't you, to see your friend get married?'

'Of course, Baba. I must ask Mama to help me make a suitable dress for the wedding.'

'And for little Maryam.'

'Yes, of course. I ought to go downstairs now and see what she's up to. She can be very naughty these days.'

'Is everything all right, my dear? You seem very sad, lately,' he said, taking her hand in his and stroking it gently.

'Everything is fine, Baba. It's just sometimes I feel so lonely.'

'I know child. It's time I found a new husband for you. You're too young to be on your own.'

'That's how Allah has willed it, Baba and I must accept His will,' she said and went down to see to her daughter, leaving her father sitting looking at the stars.

CHAPTER 14

The khalifa was dead. Umar felt strangely sad for this man whom he hardly knew and had only seen on a couple of occasions. He remembered how impressed he'd been the first time he'd seen him, such a proud, noble man; everything about him said he'd been born to rule. Umar had felt privileged to serve him. He was a man who deserved a warrior's death, not to die in such a horrible way. Rumours had spread through the alcazaba like wildfire. They said that on his death bed he cried out in terror at phantoms only he could see, and writhed in pain as the sickness worked its way through his emaciated body. It was said the physicians still had no idea what had caused his death; they'd been able to do nothing to help him. Now it was too late. According to the gossip they stood around his bedside and had no explanation for such a rapid decline in a man still in his prime. The grand vizier had put out an announcement that Khalifa Yahya I had died from an injury sustained in the battle of Qarmuña, but the rumour that Yahya had been poisoned persisted.

Weeks ago, when his father had told Umar about the customer who had repeatedly bought wormwood from him, he hadn't given it much thought, but now that the khalifa was dead he couldn't get this information out of his mind.

So were the rumours true? Had the khalifa been assassinated? Had that man who'd gone to Baba's shop poisoned him? Was he the murderer? And if so, what should Umar do? Should he speak to his commander about it? But if he did that, then he'd have to tell him that it was his father who'd sold the wormwood to the man, and then his commander might think that Makoud was complicit in the murder. It was too risky. No, first he needed to find out more about this man and try to track him down. But how? The obvious place to start was at home; both his father and his brother had seen him. Maybe they knew more about him than they'd told him. What had made them suspicious in the first place? Was it something he'd said? More importantly, had they seen him again? Maybe he lived close by. Yes, it made sense to start by talking to his father again.

*

It wasn't until almost a week later that Umar managed to find the opportunity to leave the barracks and visit his father. It had been raining all night; the air was cool and moist, and the cobbles of the coracha were glittering in the early morning sunshine. He held Basil on a loose rein as he trotted meekly down to the alcázar, through the gates and into the town. After he'd spoken to his father, he would take Basil for his usual exercise. His friend Talib followed behind on a grey mare, and ahead of them rode the rest of their squad.

'Talib, this is my father's shop. I must stop and speak to him for a moment. You carry on and I'll catch you up.'

'He's an apothecary?' asked Talib, rather surprised at this news.

'Yes. Look, I won't be long. Just follow the others and take the route we went on the other day, along by the river and down onto the beach. We can really stretch their legs there. And Talib, don't mention to the others that I've stopped here.'

'All right.'

Reluctantly Talib spurred his horse forward and left Umar outside the apothecary's shop.

'Umar. This is a nice surprise,' said his father, opening the door and coming out to greet him.

'As-salama alaykum, Baba. Are you busy? I need to speak to you for a moment.'

'Come in. Your mother will be so pleased to see you. Have some tea with us.'

'No, I can't. Don't call Mama. I really shouldn't be here; I'm supposed to be training. Is Ibrahim about?'

'He's inside. You've time to come into the shop?' his father asked, beginning to look concerned. 'Is something wrong?'

'Not really. Well not with me, anyway. You've heard that the khalifa is dead?'

'Yes, of course. Everyone is talking about it. Poor man. They say he died a horrible death and in his bed too. No way for a khalifa to die.'

'That's what I want to talk to you about,' said Umar, following his father into the shop.

'You're thinking about the wormwood? I thought about it as soon as I heard. Is it possible? It certainly sounds as though it could have been the cause. But that doesn't mean it came from my shop. All apothecaries sell wormwood. It could have come from anywhere.'

'But it's a bit of a coincidence don't you think?' said Umar.

His father nodded. 'So what are you going to do?'

'I wondered if you could tell me anything about the man? What did he look like? Was he from around here?'

'Are you talking about that strange man who bought the poison?' asked Ibrahim, joining them now that his last customer had left. 'I don't know about him being from around here but I saw him go into the alcázar. The guards didn't even question him; they just stood aside and let him pass.'

'So he's a soldier?' said Makoud.

'Not necessarily. Did he look like a soldier?' asked Umar. 'He could work in a dozen other jobs.'

'Like the kitchens?' asked Ibrahim. 'The guards obviously recognised him or they would have stopped him and questioned him.'

'Exactly. And in the kitchens he'd have access to the khalifa's food,' said Makoud.

'No. He'd have to be able to get closer to Yahya than that. All the khalifa's food is tasted before it's taken to him. If the poison was put in the food, then it had to be after it left the kitchen,' said Umar.

'So it's someone he trusts?'

'I don't think he was a soldier,' said Ibrahim. 'He was too scruffy and he didn't walk like a soldier. But he did have a sword.'

'What can you tell me about him?' asked Umar.

'Well, he was thin and had a black beard.'

'That tells me nothing. Ninety-nine percent of all men in this city have black beards and at least half of them are thin. How old was he?'

'Difficult to say. Not really old and not really young,' said Ibrahim, wrinkling his forehead in an attempt to recall the man's features.

'There must have been something to distinguish him. Did he say anything?' Umar was feeling frustrated now.

'Apart from making rude comments about the khalifa and his victory at Qarmuña? No. Wait a minute, I remember thinking he might have been a slave. Now why was that?'

Umar was getting impatient now. He wished his brother would get to the point so he could rejoin his squad before he was missed.

'So? Why *was* that?'

'I remember now. He had a brand on his hand. Two crossed sticks. On his sword hand. It made me wonder if he was an escaped slave.'

'Why would a slave want to kill the khalifa? What motive could he have?' asked Makoud.

'No, Baba, wait. That's interesting. If the man's a slave then someone else sent him to buy the wormwood. And if he's a freed slave then he's probably someone's servant now and his master sent him. Either way, somebody else is behind this and that person must have something to gain from the khalifa's death.'

'But who would benefit?' asked Ibrahim.

'His brother,' said Makoud.

'But surely his brother wouldn't have him killed. Everyone says how fond they are of each other,' said Umar.

'What about his two sons. They would benefit, in time,' suggested Ibrahim.

'But they're just children. No, it has to be someone else.' said Makoud. 'Your first task is to find the man with the crossed sticks and then you'll discover who his master is.'

'You're right, Baba.' said Umar. 'Thanks, brother. You've been a great help. Now I'd better go, before my nazir finds I'm missing.'

'Take care, son. Don't do anything stupid. Even if you find out who killed the khalifa, there's nothing you can do to bring him back once he's dead.'

'Don't worry, Baba. Ma'a salama.'

'Alla ysalmak, son. Be careful.'

Umar untied Basil from the iron ring in the wall and leapt easily onto her back. She whinnied in greeting and started off down the hill into the city. Together they picked their way carefully through the crowds of people heading towards the early morning souk. The air was ripe with the odour of freshly caught fish, and the pungent smell of spices from newly opened sacks, so full they looked in danger of spilling their exotic contents out onto the ground.

'Hey. Watch where you're going, soldier,' said a young man, balancing two baskets of fish across his shoulders.

'Dirar? Is that you, you cheeky pup?' Umar reined his horse to a stop and looked down at his young brother.

'Umar, what are you doing here? Why aren't you with the rest of your squad? I saw them ride through at least a quarter of an hour ago.'

'Never you mind.' He bent down to look at the fish. 'A good catch, I see. I hope some of them end up in the army kitchens. I like a nice fresh bream.'

'I'll put your name on it, brother,' said Dirar with a grin. 'Take care.'

That was the second time that morning that someone had warned him to take care. Umar gave his mare a gentle nudge with his toe to move her forward and rode towards the city gate. It couldn't possibly be Prince Idris that gave the order to kill the khalifa. Brothers were supposed to protect each other; they were united by blood. There wasn't any stronger tie than that.

CHAPTER 15

Makoud had found a suitable matchmaker in the city; she'd been recommended by one of his customers. He was on his way to visit her when he met Aisha coming back from the market. She carried a wicker basket filled with vegetables and walked with her head down, oblivious to all around her.

'Aisha, my dear,' he said.

'Oh, Baba. I didn't see you there. Where are you off to?'

'Just some business. I'll be home in time for lunch.'

'Good. Mama is making your favourite dish: rice and vegetables. Look what I found in the market, asparagus. The season has just begun.'

She smiled at him sadly.

'Yes, of course. You used to go into the fields and collect it when we lived in Ardales,' he said and instantly regretted mentioning their old home because a tear ran down her cheek. Poor child she was so unhappy. Well he'd do all he could to find her a husband she could love, someone to bring a smile back to her face.

'I must hurry,' she said. 'I have to get some fish. Dirar didn't bring any home with him this morning.'

'Ma'a salama, my child.'

He watched her head in the direction of the fishmonger. How comely she was. It shouldn't be too hard to find someone who would love his daughter.

*

The matchmaker lived in a narrow street beyond the main mosque. Makoud knocked on the door of a small white house and waited. After a few moments the door opened to reveal a tiny, dark skinned woman in flowing robes of green and white—the colours of Islam.

'As-salama alaykum. I'm looking for Afra, the matchmaker,' said Makoud rather nervously, because although this woman was very small she stared at him with eyes which penetrated to his very soul.

'Ahlan. You have found her. I am Afra, matchmaker for all the best families in Malaqah. Come in and take a seat,' she said, leading him into an interior gaily decorated with bead curtains and multicoloured cushions. There was a strong scent of incense. For a moment he wondered if he'd stumbled into the home of one of the wise women, the soothsayers who claimed they could tell the future.

He sat down on a low divan and looked about him. Flickering oil lamps burned in each corner and another sat on a table beside them, casting a garland of golden flowers across the table. Cool air wafted into the room through open patio doors, beyond which was a fountain that bubbled and sparkled in the sunlight that fell from above.

'How can I help you?' Afra asked. She poured two glasses of water and handed one to him.

'I need a husband for my daughter.'

'How old is she?' the woman asked, straight down to business.

'She's twenty.'

'That's a bit old to be looking for a husband. What's the problem with her?' she asked, looking straight at him with those piercing eyes of hers.

'Nothing's wrong with her. She's a beautiful girl, with a sweet nature; she can cook and sew and would make someone an excellent wife.'

'So? Why wait until now?'

'She's a widow,' he reluctantly admitted. 'Her husband died of the plague when we lived in Ardales. My daughter and her children survived and now they live with me in Malaqah.'

'And your wives want rid of her?' she said with great prescience.

'Yes. My second wife has never really liked her; now she insists that I find a husband for my daughter. She won't accept that it is not a simple task.'

'You're right; it won't be easy. Let me see. I have two or three who might be ready to take her on. Beautiful, you say? What's her temper like? If she's a bit of a shrew it doesn't matter how beautiful she is, they won't take her.'

Makoud bit his tongue. She was talking about his beloved Aisha as if she were a camel in the auction. He was feeling more and more uncomfortable. Nobody in his family had ever used a matchmaker before. It hadn't been necessary in Ardales; everyone knew each other. Matches were made when the children were young; you knew the parents and the grandparents and what sort of people they were. It was easy to find a husband or a wife for your child. That's what he'd done with Aisha. She and Daud had been friends; his mother was a friend of Abal. There was no danger she would be married to someone who would not care for her. Now it was different. Who were these men whom the matchmaker thought might be suitable for his princess?

The woman got up and rifled through a bundle of old parchments. Makoud watched her, thinking of his own marriages. He hadn't really wanted to take a second wife; he had been happy with Abal. He loved her. He still did. But when Abal gave birth to Aisha something had happened to her insides and the doctor told him that she would never have any more children. That meant that unless he took another wife he would never have any sons. Abal had been very unhappy when he told her he was going to marry Basma—she knew her family and didn't like them—but she knew he wanted sons and so she had no choice but to agree.

'Ah here we are. Now this one might be suitable. He's a bit old, but he's wealthy. She would have a comfortable home and servants.'

'How old exactly?' asked Makoud.

'He tells me he's forty-six but I calculate that he has to be in his fifties. He has ten children and the eldest is at least thirty.'

'Ten children?'

'Yes, but don't worry; she wouldn't have to look after them all. He has three other wives. I think she would have an easy life in their home.'

'Three wives? Is he royalty? If he has three wives why on earth does he want another one?' Makoud asked, getting more agitated by the minute. He mustn't do anything hasty. A marriage contract signed was binding for life—at least as far as the woman was concerned. A husband could divorce his wife for the slightest thing.

'I think he wants more children. He said something about his wives getting old.'

'No. Definitely not. He's not at all suitable for my daughter.'

The woman stared at him. 'You do realise that it won't be easy to find a husband for your daughter as she's a widow and she's not young.' She paused and added, 'And of course she has children. How many does she have?'

'Two. A girl of three and a boy of just over a year,' he said. His heart sank. This was not going to be easy.

She shook her head, making the strings of beads around her neck jangle like sheep bells. 'Not good. Well at least she has one son. But no-one wants to take more girls into their home. This is not going to be easy,' she said, echoing his own thoughts. 'Let me see. There's this one. He might consider her.'

She pulled a second sheet of parchment out and read it carefully. 'Single, says he's forty and has no children.'

'What is his occupation?' asked Makoud.

'He's a farmer. He lives in the mountains to the north of the city. He needs someone to help him with the farm.'

'Why doesn't he hire someone?' asked Makoud, although he could guess at the answer. He didn't want to pay anyone; it was cheaper to take a wife and get her to do the work for nothing. Besides which she would cook and clean for him as well.

'So you're not interested in him, either,' she said.

'No. I was hoping you'd have someone in the city.'

'I'm sorry I can't help you; that's about all I have at the moment. I will ask around and see what I can come up with,' the matchmaker said, with a sigh.

'Very well. Thank you for looking,' he said and placed a small dirham on the table. 'Ma'a salama.'

'Alla ysalmak my friend and may Allah help you in your search,' she said, taking the coin and slipping it into her pocket.

Makoud felt very dispirited as he trudged back to his shop. Basma was going to be in a bad mood for days now.

Well it couldn't be helped. He done as she requested and visited a matchmaker. It wasn't his fault if there were no suitable men about at the moment. He wasn't going to rush into this; his decision when it was finally made would affect Aisha for the rest of her life.

CHAPTER 16

During the next week Umar kept his eyes and ears open, hoping to pick up some information that might reveal the identity of his father's customer, but he saw no-one even remotely of that description. One pair of eyes wasn't enough. He needed some help.

'Talib, did your father have any slaves?' he asked his friend as they sat, polishing their horses' saddles.

'Yes, he had quite a lot. We lived on a huge estate and he used his slaves to dig new irrigation channels, to cut down trees, all the heavy work. Then there were two wo-men who worked in the house. Why do you ask? Didn't your family have any slaves?'

'No. We had no need of slaves. I just wondered if you branded them?'

'Branded them? The slaves? What like sheep or horses?' Talib asked, his eyes opening wide in surprise.

'Yes, that sort of thing?'

'No, we never did that. That would have been inhumane. My father would never do anything like that. He looked after his slaves well. A few of the older ones are freemen now. And another couple converted to Islam; they moved into the city to work.'

'So you never saw any slaves with marks on their hands, like a brand?'

'What kind of marks?'

'Crossed sticks?'

'No.' He hesitated and then added, 'Do you mean crossed swords? Only I've seen some soldiers with crossed swords tattooed on their arms. They were Christians.'

'Really.'

So maybe the man in the shop was a soldier and the crossed sticks his brother saw were actually swords. That would make sense. But if he was here inside the alcazaba, where in the name of Allah, was he?

'Why are you so interested in tattoos all of a sudden?' asked Talib. 'Are you going to have one done? You know it's against our religion.'

'No, I'm not thinking of having a tattoo; it's a barbaric custom.'

'So what's all this about?'

Talib was much more confident and outspoken than when he'd first arrived; it was good to see. He was becoming a competent horseman and fought well in the training sessions. He was also discreet, an unusual thing for a soldier.

'Very well, I'll tell you. I'm looking for a man with two crossed sticks, or maybe swords on the back of his sword hand. I don't know if it's a tattoo or a branding, but I believe it's permanent. But the thing is, I don't want him to know I'm looking for him.'

Talib's usual smiling face grew serious. 'Has he done something bad?'

'The truth is that I don't know, yet, but I think he may have had something to do with the khalifa's death.'

At this, Talib's eyes almost popped out of his head. 'What are you saying? That the khalifa was murdered?'

'I told you it was only a suspicion. I need to find this man and discover what he knows about it. You have to admit that the khalifa died in strange circumstances and even his doctors were not sure what caused his death.'

'Well I never believed that story that he died from his wounds. I never saw any wounds,' said Talib.

'Neither did I, but then we were in the rearguard; we didn't see the khalifa after the battle was over.'

'It's possible but you know how the gossip flies around the barracks. If he was wounded we would have heard something.'

'So how did he die?'

'Well, poison would explain his strange behaviour.'

'But if he'd been poisoned the doctors would have been able to tell.'

'Maybe they just didn't want to admit it.'

'You mean in case it was someone close to the khalifa who'd poisoned him?'

'Yes, they could be frightened for their own lives.'

'You have a lively imagination, my friend, but who knows, there may be some truth in what you say,' said Umar.

'Have you told the nazir?' asked Talib.

'No. You're the only one I've told and I want it to stay that way.' He glowered at his friend to emphasise the point. 'But I would like you to look out for anyone with that description.'

'You can rely on me, Umar. I won't say anything. And as I usually get knocked out of all the training bouts in the first round, I'll have plenty of time to sit and look at the other soldiers. I'll soon pick him out.'

'Remember we don't know for certain that he's a soldier, but if what you've told me is true about the crossed swords then it seems likely that he's been in the army at some time in his life. But which army?'

'Probably chose to serve whoever paid the most.'

'Or was captured during a campaign against the Christians and changed sides.'

'He could be one of the palace guards,' said Talib. 'Most of them are foreigners and non-Muslim. He'd have better access to the khalifa than one of us; I only ever saw Yahya once, when we were in Qarmuña. The palace guards must get to see him all the time.'

'You're right. That makes sense. All we have to do now, is make an inspection of all the palace guards and examine their sword hands.' He laughed at the ridiculousness of the idea. But Talib's reasoning did mean that he would be better off looking for the man inside the alcázar rather than in the barracks where they were stationed.

*

Prince Idris was in mourning. He stood beside his two nephews while they lay their father, his only brother, Khalifa Yahya I, ibn Ali ibn Hammud in his shallow grave. He was buried according to their custom in the grounds of the mosque, with his head pointing towards Mecca. Stripped of all his finery and wrapped in a plain white shroud he was no longer the proud, powerful ruler he had been. Illness and death had stripped that all away from him. For a moment Idris felt a wave of sadness; he would miss his brother.

'With the Name of Allah and according to the Sunnah of the Messenger of Allah,' chanted the imam.

The grave diggers began to cover the body with soil.

'O Allah, forgive him. O Allah, strengthen him,' continued the imam.

Yahya's sons began to weep as they watched their father disappear beneath the layers of earth.

'Hush, boys,' Idris said. 'We leave the tears for the women. You must be brave. Your father has gone to Paradise. There he will be with Allah.'

'But will we see him again?' asked little ben Yahya.

'When we go to Paradise, we will,' said his brother. 'When we die.'

'But, I don't want to die,' said ben Yahya.

'Hush children, the imam is speaking,' said Prince Idris.

The grave was covered; the gravediggers had tamped down the soil and now laid a wreath of flowers on it. Later there would be a simple headstone to commemorate the man and ruler. The imam now turned his attention to the mourners.

'Surely, Allah takes what is His, and what He gives is His, and to all things He has appointed a time ... so have patience and be rewarded.'

The mourners would stay for hours, until the next call to prayers, but Idris had things to do; he wanted to talk to ibn Baqanna to find out why the vizier had come to Malaqah when he was supposed to be governing Sebta.

*

Ibn Baqanna was standing outside the throne room talking to Naja al-Siqlabi, the young princes' tutor.

'What the hell is going on? Why are you here, ibn Baqanna? I told you to remain in Sebta until I returned,' Idris barked.

'Sayyad, I heard about your brother's death and thought you would need me here. So I came straight away. My apologies if I was wrong to do that,' the vizier said, bowing to the prince. 'You need have no concerns about Sebta; I have left everything under control.'

Idris felt slightly mollified by the vizier's obsequious tone and replied, 'Very well. You are here now. Has the grand vizier arrived?'

'Yes, Sayyad. He and General Rashad are waiting in the throne room.'

'Well, let's see what those two old women have to say.'

He strode towards the heavy oak doors which two palace guards hurriedly opened to let them enter.

'As-salama alaykum, gentlemen,' he said. 'What is so urgent that I have had to leave the funeral of my dear brother?'

'Wa alaykum e-salam, Prince.' The grand vizier rose to his feet. 'Prince Idris, gentlemen, I am sorry to have to call this meeting in such haste. I know that our friend and ruler, Yahya I—may Allah have mercy on his soul—is not yet cold in his grave, but we owe it to him to keep his kingdom safe and that means appointing a ruler as soon as possible. His Majesty's mind was somewhat troubled at the end and I believe that when he appointed his son Hassan as his successor he didn't realise that the moment for him to succeed him would be quite so soon. Hassan will make a fine khalifa one day, but at the moment he is only ten years old. If we comply with the wishes of our esteemed Yahya I we will be putting the taifas of Malaqah and al-Jazira in danger,' he continued.

'I agree with you, Grand Vizier. Something must be done, and quickly,' said ibn Baqanna. 'May I make a suggestion?'

'Of course. We must come to an agreement with all possible haste.'

'Well, as I see it, I believe that if Yahya I had been in his right mind he would have appointed a regent for his sons, and the man he would have most likely selected is his brother, Prince Idris ibn Ali.'

There was a great deal of nodding heads and murmuring at this suggestion. Idris was pleased to see that it had obviously been in all their minds.

'So, what I suggest,' ibn Baqanna continued, 'is that Prince Idris takes over the throne of Malaqah, and his eldest son, Muhammad rules al-Jazira. In that way we still comply with Yahya's wish to divide the taifa into two parts.'

'But what of his sons? We can't ignore the fact that Hassan is the rightful heir,' interrupted the grand vizier.

'Yes, what you're proposing is not the same as appointing a regent. You're discounting Yahya's heirs entirely,' said General Rashad, raising his voice above the babble of conversation that this suggestion had set off.

'Please allow me to finish. When Hassan comes of age, then he can claim his right to the throne and Prince Idris will abdicate,' said ibn Baqanna.

'And if I don't want to?' asked Prince Idris. This didn't sound a workable solution, at all. What was ibn Baqanna planning? And what did he hope to achieve for himself?

'Then we will look for someone else to stand as regent,' said Labib, brusquely.

Idris glowered at him; how he disliked the man. He'd never understood why his brother had kept him as grand vizier so long.

'What happens with Yahya's sons in the meantime?' asked Naja.

'They go to Sebta. We will make Hassan the governor of Sebta and you will go with him. You will be his right hand man. It will be good training for him before he takes up his inheritance.'

Idris stared at the vizier; he'd given this a great deal of thought and he'd obviously discussed it with Naja, but not with him, the rightful successor. Were they plotting something together? He was beginning to wonder whom he could trust.

'Thank you ibn Baqanna. That has been most helpful. Take a few minutes to discuss this proposal amongst yourselves and then we will reconvene,' said the grand vizier.

This wasn't what Idris had in mind. He'd assumed that they would instantly turn to him as his brother's heir. Instead ibn Baqanna had come up with this alternative. Well, it looked as though he had no option; if he refused they would find a regent to rule until Hassan was of age and Idris would have to remain governor of Sebta. No, he would agree to ibn Baqanna's suggestion and worry what to do about Hassan when he was old enough to be a threat to him. He might not live that long anyway; there were plenty of tropical diseases in North Africa, and he'd always looked a rather sickly child. And then there were the various Berber tribes bordering Sebta; they had coveted the thriving port for years. Yes, anything could happen to Hassan before he came of age. Maybe that was also in ibn Baqanna's mind.

*

It wasn't long before everyone had drifted back into the throne room, ready to continue with the meeting.

'Well, gentlemen. Do we have any other proposals?' asked the grand vizier. There was a general shaking of heads, so he continued, 'In that case I assume we will agree to ibn Baqanna's plan?'

'Yes, I think it's a good idea,' said General Rashad.

'Idris?'

'Yes, I agree with his proposal.'

'In that case there is no time to waste. We will crown Prince Idris ibn Ali our new Khalifa of Malaqah.'

He faced Idris and bowed low, 'Your Majesty.'

Idris could feel the adrenalin rush through his body. He was Khalifa and Supreme Commander at last. It felt good. He beamed at them all and said, 'Very well. Thank you gentlemen, but as our esteemed grand vizier has said, there is no time to waste. Send for my son, Muhammad and I will tell him the news.'

He looked at the grand vizier. What was going through his mind? Labib was a secretive man and Idris had never felt he could truly trust him. Besides which he was far too conservative in his ways for Idris. Well now was time for a change.

'Naja, arrange for you and my nephews to go to Sebta by the first available ship. I will speak to Hassan myself to explain what is happening and to reassure him that he will become khalifa when he comes of age. Labib, I would like you to accompany my nephews; there is no-one better than you to prepare Hassan for his future role.' He saw the look of shock on the grand vizier's face but turned to Ibn Baqanna before he could interrupt him, and continued, 'Ibn Baqanna, I want you to stay here. Your experience will be invaluable to me. Now gentlemen, is there anything else?'

'Your coronation, Your Majesty? It should be as soon as possible,' said Labib, somewhat subdued by the turn of events.

'Of course. Ibn Baqanna will take care of that. He will take over your role as grand vizier while you are in Sebta.'

It was vital to keep ibn Baqanna close where he could keep an eye on him. His friend was ambitious and ruthless and Idris was sure there was something he wanted. Was it the throne?

'Very well, Your Majesty.' Labib bowed and withdrew from the room, leaving Prince Idris alone with his new grand vizier.

It was done. He was Khalifa of Malaqah and his son Muhammad ibn Idris ibn Ali was the ruler of al-Jazira. He could already feel the power surging through him. With a new grand vizier and a fresh council of ministers he was going to make Malaqah as great a city as Qurtuba had been under the Omayyads.

CHAPTER 17

Three weeks after his futile visit to the matchmaker, Makoud was working in his dispensary when he heard voices in the shop. A conversation between Ibrahim and a man seemed to go on forever and his curiosity was about to get the better of him when his son pulled back the curtain and said, 'Baba. Come and look at this man. He's cut himself rather badly and I don't know what to do for him.'

'Send him to a doctor.'

'But he won't go; he says he just needs something to stop the bleeding. Please come and talk to him.'

'Very well.' Makoud washed his hands and removed his soiled overall.

A tall, well-built man was standing in the shop holding a blood stained cloth against his leg.

'What can I do for you, sayyad?' he asked, approaching the man and signalling for him to sit on the low divan that ran along one of the walls.

The man lowered himself down carefully, stretching his injured leg out in front of him.

'I cut myself at work,' he said. 'Stupid accident. It's not much but it won't stop bleeding. I thought you could give me something.'

Carefully Makoud removed the bloody cloth and examined the leg. Immediately the wound began to bleed again, the blood running down the man's calf and onto the ground. He replaced the cloth at once and said, 'You need to see a physician. The wound isn't fatal but it needs stitching; that's the only way it will heal.'

'I can't wait to see a physician. I have to get back to work. Can't you stitch it for me? I will pay you well.'

'It's not a question of money; I am not skilled enough to do it.'

'What about Aisha?' Ibrahim said. 'She stitched up Dirar's head when he fell off the mule that time.'

'Who is this Aisha?' asked the man.

'She's my daughter, but she's not qualified to tend to wounds. She's neither a doctor nor an apothecary.'

'But you are. You could supervise her. Please. I really must get back to work. If you won't do that then sell me some ointment and some bandages and I'll just bind it up until the bleeding stops.'

He tried to stand up but the movement only increased the bleeding and he collapsed back on the divan.

'Very well. Ibrahim run upstairs and get Aisha while I prepare the necessary implements,' Makoud replied. He couldn't be sure that the wound would not get infected. If the man was going to be so mulish then he had no option but to help him.

'So what work is it that you do that's so urgent?' he asked, taking down some calendula from the shelf. He measured out a small quantity and placed it in a glass dish and added a little water. Then he took down the jar of yarrow; this would stop the bleeding. He placed a fine silver needle on the tray and laid a length of cat gut alongside it. He had silk thread but if this man was about to go straight back to work he needed something stronger than that, and anyway he doubted if he'd be bothered if he was left with a scar when it healed. He didn't look like the sort of man who would be overly worried about his appearance.

'I'm a ship builder,' the man replied. 'The khalifa has put in an order for two new warships. We have to complete them by the end of the month. I can't afford to be away from the yard, not even for a day.'

'Baba, what is it?' asked Aisha hurrying into the shop. Her face was flushed and she looked more radiant than ever. 'Ibrahim said there was someone bleeding to death in the shop.'

Makoud laughed. 'Not exactly, my child, but I would like you to help me sew this man's wound. It is quite deep but I don't think he's bleeding to death. Not yet anyway.'

The man was staring at Aisha as if he were bewitched. Whatever he'd been expecting, Makoud could see it wasn't this angel of mercy.

'First of all I'd like you to wash his leg; make sure there're no splinters of wood in the wound,' he told Aisha.

'My name is Bakr,' the man said.

'Very well, Bakr, let me roll up your robes so that we can get a clear look at the wound,' Makoud said. He removed the cloth and saw his daughter wince at the sight of the ugly cut across the man's shin. Whatever tool he'd been using, it had slipped and sliced right through to the bone. He examined it carefully. Bakr had been lucky; it was a clean cut and no tendons or major arteries had been touched. It was a simple matter of cleaning him up and stitching the wound.

Aisha knelt down beside the man and gently bathed his leg, wiping away the congealed blood and dirt, and every so often stopping to extract a splinter of wood with the tweezers.

'I think it's all right now, Baba,' she said.

'Good.' Makoud knelt down and bathed the cut with the disinfectant solution he'd made up and then said, 'Now you can stitch it. Keep the stitches as close together as you can. And small.'

'Yes, Baba. I know how to sew,' replied Aisha, threading the needle with catgut and kneeling once more beside the man.

The man didn't flinch as she began to sew up his wound; he just continued to stare at her with a look of bewilderment on his face.

'You are a fortunate man to have such an accomplished daughter,' he said at last.

'My little angel of mercy? I am indeed,' said Makoud. 'And you, do you have any daughters?'

'I do. I have a son and a daughter, but they are both very small. My daughter is but a year old.'

'Then you too are fortunate,' said Makoud, measuring out some of the yarrow. He felt disappointed; for a moment he'd thought this man might make a good suitor for Aisha, but if he had two small children he probably wasn't looking for a second wife just yet. He realised that he was coming to terms with the idea that Aisha would have to be someone's second, or even third wife. Although it pained him to admit it, he knew that no bachelor would consider a widow for a bride.

Just as he expected, Basma had been furious with him when he returned from the matchmaker empty handed. He'd tried to reason with her but she flew into a rage and then began to sulk. She was still not talking to him, but he didn't really care; while she was sulking she wasn't nagging him.

'That's it. All done,' Aisha said, looking up at Bakr for the first time and giving him one of her beautiful smiles.

The man was tongued tied but managed to smile shyly in return.

'Just a moment before we bandage it up, we need to slow down the bleeding,' said Makoud, sprinkling the wound liberally with the yarrow.

'Thank you,' said Bakr, at last. 'I am very grateful to you and your daughter.'

Makoud tied off the bandage and said, 'Remember you have to come back in two weeks' time so I can remove the stitches for you.'

The man nodded. 'Thank you. Ma'a salama and may Allah look after you and your family,' he said.

'Alla ysalmak friend.'

*

Bakr hurried back to the ship yard; it was not far from the apothecary's shop, located in the perfect position right by the harbour and close to the river Guadalmedina. His leg was throbbing but at least it had stopped bleeding. It had been an interesting morning. He couldn't get that girl's face out of his mind; she reminded him of his beloved Juml although her features were quite different. Her face was oval and her eyes were like deep brown pools; he felt he could lose himself in them forever. Her nose had an aristocratic arch to it and her mouth—he felt his loins stir as he thought of her mouth—was wide and full. Juml, whom he'd loved at first sight and whom he still loved although she'd been dead for over a year now, had a much softer and sweeter face, yet there was something about the apothecary's daughter that reminded him of her. They both exuded a radiance that made those who saw them feel good about themselves. They both were easy to love.

'Sayyad, is everything all right?' asked his foreman as he arrived back at the atarazanas. The man stared at his master's blood soaked robes.

'A small accident, nothing more. Now how are the galleys coming along?'

'We have ten men working on them, sayyad. Another week and the first one should be finished.'

He nodded at the carpenter and walked through a rounded arch and into the vaulted building where his men were hard at work. The tide was in and the water in the shallow basin where they anchored their ships—some half-finished, some in for repairs and others ready to sail—was higher than usual and rocked the vessels gently from side to side. At that moment there were only five garibs and a refurbished round ship floating in the shipyard, although the basin could hold up to twenty vessels. The familiar cacophony of sawing and hammering that reverberated through the air cleared his mind of this morning's interlude and brought him back to earth. The two galleys for the khalifa were set up on wooden trestles and while one was receiving its finishing coat of pine tar, the other was still only half-way through construction.

He walked over to inspect the work. As usual the yard smelled of a mixture of sawdust, the acrid stench of pine tar, and fumes from the blacksmith's forge. Bakr wound his scarf protectively across his face, copying the carpenters who were busy caulking the bottom of the ship with hemp soaked in tar.

'Nearly done?' he asked the foreman.

'Yes, sayyad. Another coat in a couple of days and it'll be ready by the end of the week.'

'What about the other one?'

Without waiting for an answer Bakr walked across to where a dozen of his men were sawing, planing and fitting wooden planks to the hull of the second galley.

'We'll have it ready by the next full moon,' the foreman said.

Bakr examined the joins between the planks. They had been immaculately cut so that each plank fitted neatly over the one next to it and was then secured in place with iron rivets. Not a chink of light was visible between them.

He nodded appreciatively at his foreman. 'And the oars?' he asked, raising his voice above the clamour.

'All finished,' the foreman replied, pointing to where over a hundred oars, made of the finest oak were stacked under the high vaulted nave.

'Good. I'm expecting to receive an order for a warship capable of carrying up to forty horses and a hundred and fifty men.'

'That's a big job,' said the foreman with a beaming smile. It meant enough work for the shipyard for months if they were lucky enough to get the order.

'Yes, but we have a competitor,' said Bakr. 'There's a shipyard in Álmeria who have built one already and they're also after the work So it's imperative that we don't delay this order for the galleys. It's mid-spring already and the fleet will be setting sail soon. I want to keep the khalifa happy. Understood?'

'Of course, sayyad. We will have both ships completed on time. Don't worry about that.'

The new khalifa was increasing the size of the navy. It was understandable; Malaqah was vulnerable to both pirate attacks and raids from North Africa. A strong navy was the best deterrent.

Bakr had inherited the shipyard from his father; in his time it had been far smaller but Bakr had increased the storage facilities, building another domed workshop alongside the existing one and amplifying the anchorage. He'd also built two large gates which secured the premises and prevented raiding pirates from helping themselves to either materials or ships. From the beginning he'd felt the weight of his inheritance. He was his father's only son; there was no-one with whom he could share the responsibility. He had three sisters, but they had no interest in shipbuilding and neither did his only brother-in-law. One day his son would inherit his business; but that would be a long time in the future. Until then he must do the best he could.

'What about the timber we ordered?' he asked his foreman. 'Has it arrived yet?'

'It's on its way. It should arrive tomorrow or the next day at the latest.'

'Excellent. Let me know when it's here.'

The timber they used for their ships was home grown, cut from the forests high in the mountains behind Malaqah and floated down the river Guadalmedina right to their door. It was the finest oak and it made the strongest ships. His father had been wise enough to purchase a piece of the woodland when he was a young man so, unlike many other ship builders, Bakr didn't have to pay exorbitant prices for the wood he used.

He made his way to his own corner of the shipyard, the only place where he could escape from the clamour and the stench, and think in peace. He had a new ship to design; it was going to be bigger than anything he'd built before. But as he sat down at the table to work, it wasn't the sleek outline of a ship that floated before his eyes but the delicate face of Aisha.

CHAPTER 18

Ibn Baqanna plucked a fruit from the vine that trailed along the wall of his new garden and popped it in his mouth. The previous grand vizier had lived in splendid rooms within the alcázar and now they were his. He smiled contentedly; he was feeling very pleased with himself. True, Idris had been annoyed that ibn Baqanna had come to Malaqah without his permission, but he'd soon accepted the situation, just as he knew he would. The new khalifa was not a man who went looking for trouble; he liked a quiet life and time to enjoy the pleasures and luxuries of his new status. Of course there'd been rumblings of discontent when people realised that Yahya's children had been sent to Sebta; some saw it as an insult to the previous khalifa, others as a blatant grab for power on the part of Idris, but in the end people got used to the idea and it had amounted to nothing.

Now that ibn Baqanna was grand vizier, he would be in a good position to influence his actions; he never had any chance of promotion while Yahya was khalifa. Now he would become the power behind the throne. He smiled to himself; he liked the sound of that.

'Sayyad, there is a man who wishes to speak with you,' said ibn Baqanna's servant, bowing so low his nose almost touched the silk carpet on which he stood.

'Who is he?'

'He wouldn't give me his name, Sayyad, but he said he is an old friend from Sebta. He said it was of great importance. Something to do with a death. Shall I send him away?'

'No. Show him in. I want to see what he wants.'

A minute later the servant returned, followed by a thin-faced man in a blue turban. A Christian. What did a Christian want with the grand vizier? And what was so important that he thought he could just walk in and ask for an audience with him?

'Who are you? And what do you want?'

'I must speak to you, sayyad,' the man said with a slight bow of his head. 'Alone.' He looked at the servant who seemed reluctant to leave his master with this disreputable looking man. 'It is a most secret matter, involving the late khalifa.'

'Very well. You may have a moment of my time, but that is all.' He waved away his servant and beckoned for the man to approach more closely. His face looked vaguely familiar.

At least a dozen guards were either inside the room or guarding the entrance, tall Slavs wearing the royal green cloaks of the palace guards and all armed with swords and lances. He was in no danger with 'The Silent Ones'—so called because none of them spoke any Arabic— around him, but nevertheless his hand felt instinctively for his dagger.

'Speak,' he commanded the man.

'Sayyad, don't you recognise me? I am Wada. Once we were good friends, in Sebta. Do you not remember?'

'Why should I know a common wretch such as you?' replied ibn Baqanna, although he now remembered him only too well. 'What is it that you want?'

'I believe I have done you a great service,' he said and waved his arm about to indicate the richness of the grand vizier's rooms. 'And I think one great service deserves an other, don't you?'

'Speak plainly man or go about your business.'

'I'm sure that is the last thing you would want me to do. What would become of your new-found power if people discovered what had really happened to the khalifa?' he said, leering at ibn Baqanna in an over-confident manner. 'And what would the khalifa think if he knew how his brother really died?'

'I have no idea what you are talking about, wretch, but I can see what you are insinuating. Do not come here again or I shall have you arrested,' ibn Baqanna said. He was furious that this abject creature had the courage to come and threaten him, and even demand money from him. He knew perfectly well who he was, but how had *he* become involved? Did he really have some information about the khalifa's death? It was possible. Why else would a man such as him risk ibn Baqanna's anger unless he felt he had some power over him?

The man didn't move. Instead he said, 'I was paid well, sayyad, but the silver will not last long. Soon I will be poor again.'

'That is your problem. Do not expect me to give you any money, whatever it is you say you know,' snapped ibn Baqanna. 'Now, begone with you before I alert the palace guards.'

'Oh, I wouldn't do that, sayyad. Yahya I is not yet cold in his grave and yet here you are, his brother's advisor, wearing fine clothes and living in the palace. I hear that Idris I loved his brother and so did the people of Malaqah. They wouldn't be happy if they knew all the details of his death, now would they?'

The bastard was trying to blackmail him. With what? What was he insinuating? He had to tread carefully.

'So, if you don't want money, what do you want?' he asked.

'I have spent most of my life hiding in the shadows, doing other people's dirty work, moving from city to city, never able to settle down and take myself a wife. I'm tired of that. I want to join the Palace Guards, then I will have an income and a place to live. And when I'm old, I want to have a pension, so I can live out my remaining years in peace and comfort. Now that's not much to ask in return for all that I have given you. Is it?'

Wada's eyes narrowed as he looked at the grand vizier. He was not a man to be trusted; ibn Baqanna remembered him of old. But how had he come to be here in Malaqah? He daren't confront him directly without it looking as if he were somehow involved in Yahya's death. He knew the khalifa; any suspicion that ibn Baqanna was involved in his brother's death would mean the end of the grand vizier's new career. And if the people of Malaqah heard of the man's accusations then it could get out of hand; they were very receptive to rumours and gossip. Before long everyone would be convinced that ibn Baqanna and maybe even Idris I too, had been behind the old khalifa's death. He couldn't have that. What was he going to do? He couldn't be sure that the wretch hadn't already been talking to people; he was always loose-tongued when he'd had a few drinks. He would have to buy some time so that he could find out exactly what it was that Wada thought he knew.

'Very well, report to the commander of the Palace Guards tomorrow at the break of dawn. He will find you a post inside the alcázar. That is all I will give you and then I never want to hear from you again. No word of this is to pass your lips or I will have your tongue cut out. Is that understood?'

'Of course, sayyad.'

This time the man bowed, but not before ibn Baqanna saw the satisfied smile on his pock-marked face.

Once he'd left, the grand vizier clapped his hands and summoned his servant. 'Tell the commander of the guard that I have sent him a new recruit. And be quick about it.'

He felt the rage mounting inside him. Something had to be done about Wada. He couldn't allow any loose tongues to spread gossip about him, not now when he had so much to lose. This wretch was either very clever or very foolish if he thought he could blackmail the new grand vizier. Well he would soon find out. In the meantime he was safe enough in the Palace Guards, where he could keep an eye on him.

*

Fatima sat in the prow of the boat, weeping; she was still dressed in her widow's robes and clutched her two sons close to her. By rights she should still be in Malaqah in her dead husband's harem until iddah had ended, but Idris had instructed her to leave and take her sons to Sebta within days of Yahya's death. Her brother-in-law had robbed her children of their inheritance. Instead of being the new khalifa, her little Hassan was to be governor of Sebta, a Hammudid enclave in a foreign land. What future was that? She wiped her tears on her scarf, smearing the kohl around her eyes.

'Is everything all right, Sayyida?' asked Naja. 'Would you like me to take the children for a while?'

She shook her head. 'No, I want them here with me, where I can keep them safe.'

'They will be safe in Sebta, Sayyida. I will be by their side all the time. I promise you.'

Naja al-Siqlabi was an ex-slave who had been with her husband since before her sons were born. A saqaliba from the eastern part of Europe, he was tall, fair-skinned, with blue eyes and grey hair. He was an educated man and it hadn't taken her husband long to realise that he would make a good tutor for his sons. Since then both boys had come to rely on him. She smiled at him gratefully; he was the only one she could trust. Fatima knew that as long as her sons were alive they would be a potential threat to her brother-in-law, Idris I. She had seen enough family feuds to know she should be worried; her sons would never be safe until one of them was on the throne. Maybe here in Sebta they would be far enough away for him to forget about them.

'Have you been to North Africa before, Sayyida?' Naja asked.

'No. As a girl I lived in my father's court in Qurtuba and then when I married Yahya I moved to Malaqah. I have never been to the land of my ancestors. Is it as beautiful as al-Andalus?'

'It is beautiful but in a different way; it is a drier land and the coast is bordered with high mountains. But no, nowhere is as beautiful as al-Andalus; that is paradise on earth.'

'And now my children have been expelled from that paradise. It is unfair.'

'They are young Sayyida; when they are grown they will return and reclaim their birthright. Al-Andalus will once again be their home.'

Fatima looked at him sadly; his words had the ring of a promise already made. It was always that way in the world of men; they would fight for what was theirs despite the consequences. She hugged her boys more tightly; she would not be able to keep them safe for long. They would come of age and demand to have what was rightly theirs; there was no other path for them to take. She prayed that Allah would keep them safe.

'We're almost there,' said Naja. 'Look there are the ancient Pillars of Hercules at the entrance to the Narrow Straits, with the mountain Jebel Musa above the port of Sebta and on the opposite bank is the other pillar, Jebel al-Tariq.'

She knew the Greek myths of Hercules and how he smote the mountain barring his path with his mace and in so doing created Jebel Musa and Jebel al-Tariq, and formed a channel to link the Middle Sea to the Sea of Darkness. That name had always terrified her and yet here she was, at the gateway that led to this feared sea. She shivered.

'Are you cold, Sayyida?' asked Naja.

'No.' If only she had someone with whom she could confide her fears. She had brought her personal maids with her and there were soldiers to accompany her on the voyage but no member of her family, only her sons and they were too young to understand her fears. Staring ahead at the waves breaking against the fortified harbour walls, she felt very lonely.

'Are we there now?' asked ben Yahya.

'Yes, little one. We'll soon be in our new home. See, there it is rising up above the walls, your palace.'

'It's very big,' said ben Yahya.

'It's a fortress,' said Hassan, scowling. 'To keep out our enemies.'

The crenellated grey stone walls of the alcazaba glowed a warm pink in the sunshine, looking more inviting than forbidding. Perhaps it would be a good place to bring up her sons, after all. The closer they came to Sebta the more attractive it seemed.

Their ship sailed into a wide harbour and directly up to the port. She stood open-mouthed at the bustling cacophony of colour and noise; there were people from all around the Middle Sea: tradesmen from Rome, Syrian potters, Turkish sailors, slavers leading their captives: tired and desperate men, crying women and their stupefied children all manacled together; there were prosperous Jewish merchants with barrowloads of Persian carpets and men whose skin was the colour of ebony carrying baskets of ivory and bone trinkets; there were Greeks, and Ethiopians with silver bangles on their arms, camel drivers and horse dealers, tradesmen of every description. Every nationality, every religion, every trade and every type of commerce was represented in this busy port. How strange it all was; people talking in different languages, some she recognised but most she didn't. There was no mistaking that here she was in a foreign land; once again a feeling of alienation swept over her. She and her sons had been exiled from their home. But one day they would return and her sons would reclaim their birthright, one day. For now, what she needed was patience. Patience and hope.

*

Umar left Talib within the walls of the alcazaba and set off immediately towards the royal kitchens; he knew one of the under-chefs—a man not adverse to exchanging gossip for a few silver dirhams.

'So what's new?' he asked the under-cook when he brought him a plate of cold mutton stew. He placed a small pile of dirhams on the table next to him.

'You know the khalifa died?'

'Yes,' he replied impatiently. 'How, is what people really want to know.'

The man looked furtively over his shoulder and then sat down next to Umar. 'Nobody knows for sure but the rumours have it that he was poisoned. One of those herbs that turn your head funny before it eventually kills you.'

'So who's responsible?'

'Again, this is just rumour. I don't want you coming back here and causing me problems if you've killed the wrong man.'

'I'm not planning on killing anyone. Just get on with it. Or it will be you with the problems,' Umar said, laying his dagger onto the wooden table.

'All right, don't get excited. I'll tell you what I know. About three weeks ago, there was this wastrel hanging about the taverns, close to the alcazaba. A Christian I think, because he had a cross tattooed on his hand. One night he drank too much wine and started boasting that soon we'd be looking up to him, that his life was going to change. Well you often hear that, especially from the foreigners, and especially when they're drunk—that's why wine is forbidden to us Muslims; you lose control of your tongue—so nobody took much notice, but then he said something that

made me sit up. He said he was going to become a palace
guard. Well. I know he went about saying that he used to be
a soldier until he'd fallen on hard times—nobody believed
a word of that either—but to become one of the elite palace
guards. Nobody believed him.'

'That's interesting but get to the point.'

'It's just a rumour, but the next thing I heard, his words
had come true. Someone said that the grand vizier had
made him a member of the palace guards.'

'And you're telling me this because?'

'Because it's strange, don't you agree?'

'What's this man's name?' asked Umar. He agreed. It
was indeed strange. For a start how had the man even been
able to speak to the grand vizier? You couldn't just walk in
and ask to see him. Or could you?

'He said his name was Wada.'

'And where is he now?'

The under-cook shrugged his soldiers.

Umar passed one of the coins across the table to him.
'Let me know if you find him,' he said. He broke off another piece of unleavened bread and used it to mop up the mutton juices. So the man was called Wada. It sounded as
though it was the same man who'd bought the wormwood
from his father. But was he the one who'd murdered
Yahya? It didn't seem possible. For a start, how would he
get access to the khalifa's food? No. Wasn't it more likely
that someone in the palace kitchens had doctored his food?

He took a long draught of water and considered who had
the opportunity to poison the khalifa. The list of suspects
couldn't be that long; it had to be someone the khalifa
trusted, his doctor maybe. But why would his doctor poison
him? It always came back to the same questions; who

would want him dead and what did they stand to gain from it? There was one obvious answer but could he prove it? Was it wise to even try?

'Here take this.' He passed him another dirham. 'Now, one last thing. Where can I find the royal physician?'

The under-cook scooped up the money and slipped it into his pocket. 'His house is close by, but I don't think he'll speak to you at this time of night. The rumour has it that he's scared for his life. When the khalifa died he shut himself in his house and hasn't been seen since.'

'Where is it?'

The under-cook drew him to the doorway and said, 'You see that street lamp, the furthest one? Well just before it is a narrow alleyway. It leads to his house and nowhere else. But you won't get to see him. Nobody can get him to answer. I tell you, he's a frightened man.'

'Ma'a salama, my friend. Remember, if you hear anything else you can find me at the Dar al-Jund.'

CHAPTER 19

Exactly two weeks after his visit to the apothecary, Bakr got up earlier than usual. He washed, trimmed his beard and dressed in his best djubbah then joined his sisters for the morning prayers.

'You're looking very smart,' his youngest sister, Rayya, said after they had finished. She rolled up the prayer mats and placed them carefully in the corner of the room.

'Yes. Not going to work today?' asked Rusa, his inquisitive oldest sister.

They stared at him, desperate to know where he was going and who he was going to see. They never left him in peace, even Rudaba who had a husband of her own to fuss over. His beloved Juml was not cold in her grave before they started nagging him to find another wife. Think of your children, they said repeatedly. They need a mother. You need a wife. As if he didn't realise that. But they didn't understand; for him it was too soon. Marrying someone else would seem like a betrayal of his love for Juml. One day, perhaps. But not yet.

He looked at them and tapped his nose. Wouldn't they love to be able to read his mind.

'Will you be back for lunch, brother?' asked Rusa.

'Of course, sister. Why would I not?' Rusa was due to be married within the month and would go to live with her husband's family, he hoped. Nothing had been decided yet.

His sisters knew better than to ask him outright, but waited eagerly for any crumb of information he might drop them.

'I'm going to have these stitches removed from my leg and then I will go to work. Satisfied? Now will you let me go about my business in peace?'

'Alla ysalmak, brother. Allah go with you.'

Bakr lived in his father's old house, not far from the spice market. It was a rambling old building and he shared it with his mother, his grandmother, his three sisters, his brother-in-law, two servants and five small children, including his own two. Did he really need another wife? Wasn't this family enough for his children? Why couldn't they let him alone with his grief?

He set out for the apothecary's shop, walking first along the street which led to the sea—the one he used every day to go to work—and then turned left onto the main street which led up to the alcazaba—the Street of the High and Mighty it was called by the townsfolk.

The apothecary was just opening his shop when Bakr arrived.

'As-salama alaykum, my friend. How is your leg? You seem to be walking well,' said the apothecary.

'Wa alaykum e-salam. I am well, thank you. I have returned as you said, to have the stitches removed,' Bakr said. He could have pulled them out himself. Indeed he'd sat down with that very intention but then stopped. Was it the hope that he'd see the lovely Aisha again that prevented him from continuing?

'Let me see,' said the apothecary. 'Good. It has healed perfectly. Just a moment and I'll have them all out.'

He took a pair of scissors and quickly snipped each stitch and pulled it free. Then he swabbed the scar with some more calendula, patted it dry and said, 'That's it. As good as new.'

Bakr felt slightly let down that the apothecary had removed the stitches and not called on Aisha to help him. 'How is your daughter today?' he asked.

'Aisha? She is well. Probably seeing to the children, I expect.'

'Oh, she is married then?' he asked, biting back the disappointment.

'Widow. And so young. It's a shame. That's why we came here to Malaqah, to help her get over it,' the apothecary explained and then went on to tell Bakr about Ardales and the sickness that had changed their lives.

'It's hard when you lose someone you love,' said Bakr, his thoughts returning to those long, desperate days after his wife died.

'Yes. They were such a devoted couple. I'm trying to find a suitable husband for her, but it's not easy. I don't want her to end up as a skivvy to an old man; she's too young and beautiful for that.'

'So what will you do if you don't find anyone to marry her?'

'She'll have to stay at home with us. What else can I do?'

'It's not easy to be a father, is it?' Bakr said, with a smile. 'Well, thank you again. I must go to work now. Perhaps we could meet for a glass of tea one evening?'

'Yes, I would like that. I usually go to the bar on the corner next to the souk; they do a delicious concoction of myrtle and pomegranate.'

*

It wasn't until the two galleys were completed and delivered to the admiral of the navy that Bakr had time to take an evening off and seek out the apothecary. The bar he'd mentioned was small and poorly lit, but it had a homely feeling to it; unlike many of the taverns in this cosmopolitan port it didn't serve alcohol and appeared to be only frequented by Muslims. The apothecary was sitting in the corner of the bar playing chess with an older man.

'Good evening, friend. I thought I'd join you for a glass of that myrtle and pomegranate tea,' Bakr said, sitting down beside him.

'Bakr. How nice to see you. Let me introduce my friend, Yazid. He is a phenomenal chess player.' He indicated how few pieces he had left on the board and grimaced.

Yazid smiled at Bakr and gave him a brief nod; his concentration was wholly on the game. He picked up the queen and placing it down with a flourish said, 'Checkmate.'

The apothecary sat back and laughed. 'Not again, Yazid. Can't you let me win just once in a while?'

'Sorry, Makoud. You make it too easy for me. Now I must leave you. See you tomorrow evening?'

'Of course. I must get my revenge on you one time at least.'

He stood up and embraced the old man, who bowed to Bakr and left.

'Do you play chess?' Makoud asked Bakr, replacing the pieces on the board.

He shook his head. 'No, I've never got time; the ship-yard takes up most of my day. Then when I'm at home I like to spend a few hours with my children. They are still missing their mother,' he said sadly.

Makoud called the waiter across and ordered two glass-es of tea. 'You'll like this,' he said. 'It's the best tea in the whole of Malaqah.'

Bakr listened while Makoud told him about his friend Yazid and how he met him there at least twice a week. It seemed he was a retired schoolteacher and when he found that Makoud liked to play chess he began to turn up regularly to seek him out. Now they had a fixed arrangement that neither liked to break.

The myrtle tea was indeed delicious and when it was finished they ordered another pot.

'If you don't mind me asking, how did your wife die?' asked Makoud, nibbling at one of the almond and sesame biscuits that the waiter had brought them.

'She died giving birth to my daughter and the saddest thing was that she never even saw her. Now the women of my house look after the baby and her brother.'

'So your daughter never knew her mother.'

'No, but she is happy in her ignorance. Her brother on the other hand still asks for his mother and wants to know when she will come home. It breaks my heart to hear him. I ask myself which is better, to have memories that pain you or no memories at all?'

'I can't answer that, my friend,' Makoud said, sadly shaking his head. He sipped his tea slowly and asked, 'For-give me for asking but have you never considered taking another wife, someone your children could call mother?'

'One day I will have to do that, but at the moment I can't bear the thought of replacing my dear Juml.'

'Well, if you change your mind, we will talk again,' said Makoud. 'Now let me teach you to play this marvellous game.'

The apothecary was an affable companion; it would be nice to prolong the evening a little longer and relax over a game of chess. 'I suppose you're in need of someone to beat, is that it?' he said, with a smile. 'Well, if it'll make you feel better, then I agree.'

So Makoud wanted a husband for the lovely Aisha. Bakr felt very tempted but he wasn't sure he'd be the best husband for her. After all that she'd suffered she deserved a man who could give her his love. He wasn't sure that he could do that. Not at the moment.

CHAPTER 20

Umar made his way towards the physician's house. The wind had strengthened and it caused the flames in the street lamps to flicker eerily, casting strange shadows along the alleyway. So far everything he'd heard about the khalifa's death were rumours. He needed to establish that their ruler had been poisoned before he did anything else and the only person who could tell him that was the khalifa's physician. It was imperative that he saw him.

From the outside the house seemed to be a modest stone building with a single wooden door as its entrance; there were no windows and the door was reinforced with iron bars and rows of thick iron studs along its panelling. There was no access to the back of the building, nor to the sides; the building cut off the alleyway, allowing him to go no further. He banged on the door and waited but there was no reply. It looked as though the under-cook had been right; there was no way he could get in to see the physician. Well he would have to wait and see what happened. He hunkered down in the corner and pulled his cloak around him. If this was the only way into the house then someone would eventually come here, a servant, a friend, a relative. All he had to do was wait.

After what seemed an interminable length of time, Umar heard the sound of footsteps approaching the house. He shrunk back further into the shadows and waited. A slight figure swathed in a dark robe and djellaba approached the door and knocked gently. Umar tensed, ready to spring up. This was his opportunity. The figure waited and then knocked again. This time a small window in the door opened and a voice asked, 'Noor, is that you?'

'Yes, Baba. I've brought you some food.'

It was the physician's daughter. Umar waited until the door opened slightly and then he leapt up and thrust his foot into the gap. The young woman screamed and flew at him in a rage, her basket of food flying out of her hand, but she wasn't strong enough to prevent Umar pushing his way into the house and shutting the door behind him, leaving her beating the door with her fists and screaming at him.

'Who are you? What do you want? Have you come to kill me?' asked an elderly man, cowering in the corner of the room. His servant waved a sword rather ineffectually at Umar who by now had his own sword at the old man's throat.

'Were you Khalifa Yahya I's doctor?' he asked. 'Speak.'

'Yes. My name is Abu al-Jabir. What do you want with me? Who are you?'

'My name is Umar. I'm a soldier in the service of the khalifa. I haven't come to harm you. You have nothing to fear from me; I just want some information. Were you with him when he died?'

'Is that what this is about? I didn't kill him, if that's what you think. He was a sick man, you know. People always blame the physician when someone dies but we're only human you know; we can only do so much.'

'How sick was he?' Umar let the tip of his sword press a little harder against the man's wrinkled neck. He had no intention of hurting him but he wanted to frighten him into speaking. He had to know something about the khalifa's death.

The physician let out a groan. 'Who has sent you? Is it Idris? Is this how he repays me for caring for his brother?'

'No, Idris didn't send me. Nobody sent me. Why would you think so?'

'I did nothing, I swear. I have been with the royal family all my life. I have served the khalifa faithfully. I would do nothing to harm him.'

'And yet he is dead.'

'That was not me.'

'Tell me how he died and I will leave you in peace and then you can enjoy your evening meal with your lovely daughter.' The pounding on the door had stopped.

'My life will be in danger if I tell you.'

Umar pressed a little harder with the sword so that a bead of blood appeared on the man's skin. 'You have little choice, old man.'

'Very well. Drop your sword and I'll tell you what I know.'

Slowly Umar withdrew his sword from the man's neck, but he didn't sheathe it. 'Speak,' he instructed.

'He was poisoned. I had suspected it for some time but I couldn't see how it could be true. There was no way that any poison could have been put in his food; everything was tasted by his food taster before he ate it.'

'Maybe it was administered in a different way. Maybe it wasn't in his food,' said Umar.

'I can't see how.'

'Do you know what poison was used?'

'I can't be certain, but it was probably something like Artemisia absinthium and given to him over a long period of time. He had been gradually growing unwell for some months.'

'Is that sometimes called wormwood?' Umar asked. Maybe he was getting somewhere.

'Yes. How did you know?'

Umar ignored his question and said, 'And you didn't tell anyone of your suspicions?'

The physician laughed bitterly. 'How could I? What do you think would happen to me if I said that someone was trying to poison the khalifa? I would have been locked up or killed. How could I say anything? And to whom? They would have accused me of treason. Remember I didn't know who was to blame; I wasn't even completely sure that it was poison. But, to be honest, I can't think what else it could have been.'

'So you told no-one?' asked Umar.

'No. I feared for my life at the time and I still fear for it,' he said, collapsing onto a low sofa with a groan of despair.

'And there was no antidote?' asked Umar.

The old man shook his head sadly. 'I liked the khalifa,' he said. 'He was a noble man. He didn't deserve to die like that.'

'You were by his side the whole time? And at the end?' asked Umar.

'I was. He needed constant care. His mind had gone and I was worried he'd hurt himself while under one of his delusions. So either myself or one of his personal slaves was always at his side.'

'Was there a man called Wada who visited him? A foreigner with a tattoo on his right hand?'

'No. No-one was allowed in the bedchamber other than myself, his personal slaves and his brother. Not even his wives and concubines were allowed to see him.'

'One more question, did the khalifa suffer any wounds at the battle of Qarmuña?'

'No, He wasn't wounded. I would have known. That was just something the grand vizier put out to quash the rumours about his death.'

'So there were no wounds at all?'

'No, I told you. He returned from Qarmuña unscathed.'

The knocking on the door resumed with greater fervour.

'That will be Noor. She will be worried. Please let her come in,' the physician said.

'I must go. Enjoy your supper. Thank you for speaking to me,' said Umar, opening the door and slipping out into the night as quickly as he'd entered.

It was late. There was little more he could do now but at least he'd learnt something from the physician. Tomorrow he would rise early and see if he could locate this Wada. Maybe this mysterious man would be able to tell him more.

He stopped, his hand going automatically to his sword. There was someone hiding in the shadows; he was sure of it.

'Who's there?' he called. 'If you have good intentions step out into the light. If not, begone before you feel the thrust of my sword.'

He unsheathed his sword and held it before him. There was no sound. Suddenly a cat screeched and rushed out from the alley, brushing against his legs as it passed.

'Bloody cats,' he swore and put his sword back in its sheath.

*

It was just after morning prayers when a young boy came to the barracks looking for him.

'I have a message for you from my master,' the boy said, eyeing the half-eaten pomegranate on Umar's plate, hungrily.

'Well give it to me and be off with you.'

'I have to tell you in person. My master wouldn't write it down in case it fell into the wrong hands.'

'And who is your master?' asked Umar, his curiosity aroused by the boy's furtive manner. He was a skinny lad in a ragged djubba and his feet were bare but he seemed bright enough and his face shone from a recent scrubbing.

The boy moved closer and whispered, 'He is one of the under-chefs at the alcázar; you spoke to him last night.'

'So what do you have to tell me, boy?'

'My master says that the body of the man you were looking for has been found on the beach. He's dead. Drowned.'

'The physician? How so?' The man had been alive and well when he left him. Was it a coincidence that a few hours later his body was washed up on the beach. 'Are you sure about this? Repeat to me the exact words your master said.'

The boy fidgeted impatiently and said, 'Tell him that the man he is looking for has been drowned. He was found on the beach this morning at sunrise.'

'Did he say the man's name?'

'I've told you what he said. He's dead. Drowned.'

'Very well. Here, take this.' He handed the boy a small coin but instead of grabbing it and running off, he hesitated, looking longingly at the pomegranate. 'Very well, take that too,' said Umar.

The boy grabbed the pomegranate and asked, 'Do you have any message for my master?'

'Give him my thanks and say may Allah protect him.'

Before he could add anymore the boy had rushed away and disappeared down one of the side alleys.

Who was the under-cook referring to, Wada or the physician? If it was the physician then it couldn't be a coincidence. The under-cook had said that the man never left the house. Had someone followed Umar and seen him go into the physician's home? And if so, who was it? He would have to be more careful. But first he needed to speak to Talib to see if he had found out anything in the alcázar.

*

Talib was already at the training ground, sparring with one of their squad; he had a bloody nose but looked as though he was winning. Umar sat down by the ring and waited until the bout finished.

'It looks as though you won that fight,' he said.

'Yes, for once. I'm tired of being knocked on my back by these great big brutes. So I have changed my tactics,' said Talib with a grin that revealed that he'd lost one of his front teeth. It made him look even younger than ever.

'How so?'

'They have to catch me first. I just keep out of the way until I can land a punch of my own.'

'Doesn't look as though you were very successful,' said Umar, pointing at the gap in his teeth.

'Oh that. That's nothing.'

'Have you got time to talk?' asked Umar. The nazir was nowhere in sight and Talib's opponent had gone off to challenge someone else.

'Yes. What about you? Did you find the khalifa's doctor?'

'I did. He was hiding in his own house; hadn't left since the khalifa died. We were right; he was poisoned and Abu al-Jabir is pretty sure the assassin used wormwood. So it's all fitting together. What about you?'

'I went into the alcázar and talked to some of the guards. It wasn't easy—most of them don't speak Arabic—but I found one who said he knew of this man. He'd joined the guards very recently but he was never on duty inside the palace; he was assigned to duty at the gate to the coracha.'

'So, did you speak to him?'

'No, but I found out when he was next on guard. Today at midday. I'll go along then if I can get away without the nazir noticing.'

'I'll come with you.'

'Did you ask the physician about Wada?'

'Yes. He said he'd never seen him. He said nobody got near the khalifa, except his brother and his personal servants.'

'So it has to be one of them.'

'Yes. But I'll tell you one thing; the doctor is a frightened man. He thinks his life is in danger.'

'So, whoever killed the khalifa might kill the doctor. But why?'

'He knows how he died. As far as everyone else is concerned it's only speculation.' Umar hesitated and looked around to make sure nobody was watching them then said, 'They've found a dead body on the beach. I think it might be Abu al-Jabir. He may have been right; someone wanted him out of the way. I'm going down to the darrabun in the town now, to make some enquiries. If the nazir wants to know where I am, make up some excuse, will you.'

'But I thought you said you spoke to Abu al-Jabir last night?'

'I did.'

'Now you think he might be dead?'

'I hope not, but I fear it is so. We need to be careful; it looks as though we're dealing with some dangerous people. People who have a lot to lose.'

Talib lifted his fists and grinned. 'Well I'm ready for them,' he said, flashing his gappy smile.

'Seriously, Talib. You must be careful whom you speak to. Somebody doesn't want anyone to know how the khalifa died.'

*

The darrabun had finished his nightly rounds through the city and was returning to his home by the Boveda Gate when Umar caught up with him.

'As-salama alaykum,' he said, with a polite bow.

'Wa alaykum e-salam, young man. What can I do for you?' he asked, as he extinguished the torch he'd been carrying.

'I heard you found the body of a man, washed up on the beach. I'm worried that it might be my brother; he's a fisherman.'

'Your brother? How old is your brother?' asked al-darrabun, rubbing his eyes. He looked tired.

'He's fifteen.'

'Well in that case, the answer is no; it was the body of a much older man,' he said, turning away from Umar.

'That's a relief. So whose body was it?'

The watchman, who was already unlocking the door, said, 'I can't see why you want to know, but I can see that if I don't tell you, I'm not going to get to my bed any time soon. It's the royal physician. Off you go and let me get some rest.'

'One last thing, how did he die?'

The night watchman looked at him and said, 'His throat was cut. Satisfied?'

'Was it suicide?'

'Suicide? Well I suppose it could have been, but why would an eminent physician commit suicide? More likely some cut-throat after his money. Now be off with you before I report you to your commander.'

'Ma'a salama and thank you,' said Umar, hurrying back towards the training ground.

His head was spinning with questions. Who had seen him at the physician's house? Had the daughter told anyone of his visit? He remembered the figure he thought he'd seen in the shadows. Had he been followed? Or, more likely, had she been followed? But how had the murderer gained access to the house? Had the physician gone out to talk to anyone or had someone forced his way in, like Umar had done? Maybe the murderer been waiting there all the time Umar was in the house. He shivered at the thought. If the assassin had seen him and thought he knew anything, he could have been murdered as well. But that didn't happen, so it probably meant the man was on his own and he didn't want to face an armed opponent. Not a soldier then. A servant? There were so many questions his head hurt. There was one however, to which he already knew the answer, the reason the physician had been killed. He knew too much. Umar felt panic welling up in his chest. They had to speak to Wada before anything happened to him as well. If he died then they would never be able to discover who was behind the deaths.

He began to hurry back to the barracks, then it struck him. It had to be someone Abu al-Jabir knew; he wouldn't have let anyone else in his house. He thought the man was a friend.

CHAPTER 21

Bakr felt exhausted. The plans he'd drawn up for the new warship were still under debate. The khalifa wanted more capacity inside the ship; he wanted to carry at least two hundred fighting men on it, together with fifty horses and then there were the oarsmen. Both the admiral and Bakr had tried to explain that although such an enormous ship could be built, it would be slow and cumbersome, not what was required of a warship. The khalifa was very stubborn but in the end he agreed to reduce the capacity slightly and Bakr had promised to add three lateen sails to the ship, to increase the speed. He didn't have much choice; the khalifa made it quite clear that the shipyard in Álmeria had raised no such objections. Bakr had wanted to say that that was because they were such incompetent fools who would promise anything to ensure they secured the order. He didn't work like that; if he agreed to something he felt honour-bound to complete it. But he bit his lip and prayed that it would work out all right.

He opened the door to his home and went straight through to the patio to sit by the fountain; it was the most peaceful spot in the house. As he sat by the edge of the pool, watching the water bubbling up through the natural spring that fed their well, he was soothed by its gentle murmuring. He closed his eyes and tried to let his mind empty of all the day's problems.

'Baba. Are you all right?' asked a little voice.

'Sandi, my son. Why are you not in bed?' He stretched out his arms and pulled the little boy towards him. He hugged his soft, warm body close to him, burying his face in his silky hair.

'I was waiting for you, Baba. You said you'd tell me a story about the djinn and the princess. Don't you remember?'

'Of course I remember. I'm sorry son; I had to work very late tonight. I'll tell you it tomorrow instead.'

'Mama used to tell me stories every night,' he said, pulling away from his father and looking at him resentfully. 'When is she coming back? She has to look after the baby.'

'Mama is in heaven now, with Allah. You will have to make do with me telling you stories instead.' No matter how many times he tried to tell Sandi that his mother was dead, the little boy still thought she'd come back to him.

'You don't do the voices,' he said, angrily. 'Mama always did the voices.'

'Well you can help me. You can tell me what the djinn sounds like and what the princess sounds like,' said Bakr, trying to appease his son.

'And the old man?'

'Yes.'

'And the angry soldier?'

'Yes. We'll do all of them. Now run along to bed. Baba is tired and he'll be going to bed soon as well.' He kissed the boy on the cheek and watched as he skipped back into the house. It was no good; he would have to find a wife. He couldn't leave his children in the care of his sisters forever;

they needed their own mother. It was time he put his self-ishness behind him and thought more about Sandi and Naila. Juml would always be in his heart but from now on he must think of them.

*

He knew Makoud would be in the bar next to the souk; it was his evening for meeting his chess friend and he wouldn't miss that even though it was a wet and windy night. The streets were unusually quiet and Bakr pulled his djellabah tightly around him, leaning into the wind as he headed towards the tavern. He had come to a decision at last; he only hoped he hadn't left it too late. It had been weeks since he'd last seen Makoud, plenty of time for him to have found a husband for Aisha. He found his steps growing quicker as though these last few minutes were going to make any difference.

The bar was warm and welcoming after the dank night outside and he took off his wet djellabah and shook it before hanging it over the rail.

'Bakr. Welcome, my friend. Have you come to try your skill against the maestro?' Makoud asked, setting the pieces out on the board. He'd obviously lost yet again to Yazid.

'I hear you've taken up this noble game,' said Yazid, leaning back and looking up at Bakr with a quizzical expression on his face.

'Makoud is trying to teach me, but I don't think I have much aptitude for it,' Bakr replied. He turned to Makoud and said, 'I've come to talk to you about your daughter.' There was no point hesitating. His mind was made up.

'In that case, I will leave you two alone. See you next week, Makoud,' said Yazid, getting up and collecting his djellabah. 'Still raining I see.' He pointed to the puddle of water that had collected under Bakr's cloak.

'Yes, next week. You won't be so lucky next time,' said Makoud, grinning at his friend. 'I'm working on some new moves that will astonish you.'

His friend raised his eyebrows as if to say, 'Is that right?' and lifted his hand in farewell.

They waited until Yazid had departed and then the apothecary said, 'Well this is a surprise. You say you want to talk to me about Aisha; I can only assume that you are considering her as a wife? Is that correct?'

'Yes. It is a possibility. But it will depend on whether she will accept me as her husband.' He sat down beside the apothecary. 'As you know I have two young children and they need a mother.'

'Ah, that is the problem,' said Makoud. 'Aisha says she is resigned to living alone but I think she is too young for that. At the moment she is letting her grief cloud her judgement. Her children need a father. Personally I think it is an excellent idea. From the little I know of you, I think you would make a good husband for my daughter.'

'So how shall we proceed?' Bakr could feel his heart racing. Would she consider him? Or would she think he was too old?

'I will need to speak to her. She is a very independent young woman. Of course she still has the bride price paid by her husband's family and the dowry we gave her, but that won't last forever and she has two growing children to consider.'

'I would of course pay a bride price for her,' interrupted Bakr.

Makoud nodded. 'That is very generous of you.'

It wasn't normal to pay the bride price for a widow; usually the family had to offer a substantial dowry to encourage someone to marry her.

'So you will speak to her about it?' Bakr asked.

'Yes, of course and I will send word to you at the shipyard. Now why not have a quick game of chess with me?' the apothecary said, already laying out the chess pieces.

'I'm sorry, Makoud. I haven't time this evening; I must go straight home; I've promised to read my son a story. I look forward to hearing from you. Ma'a salama.'

'Very well. Another time then. Alla ysalmak.'

There was no real reason that Bakr had to hurry home; Sandi would be asleep by now. He'd read him the story tomorrow. For now, his mind was in such turmoil that he couldn't stay there any longer and he certainly couldn't settle it enough to play a game of chess.

The rain was horizontal now and lashed down on him, stinging his face and half blinding him. The waves were crashing on the beach, their white foam breaking into a million tiny parts that gleamed like fallen stars each time the clouds parted to reveal the moon. He thought of the ships anchored in the yard; the water would have risen considerably but they should be safe enough. Not so those at sea; it was a bad night for the fishermen.

*

Makoud could hear the rain thundering on the roof of the tavern and decided to wait a little longer before setting off for home.

'Another glass of tea, please,' he called across to the waiter. 'And a piece of churros.' He felt like celebrating. If he could persuade Aisha to marry Bakr, it would be a good match. The ship builder seemed a genuinely nice man and he had his own business, so he could afford to keep a wife in comfort. Of course Aisha wouldn't see it like that; he knew his daughter too well. It wouldn't be the same for her as when she first got married but then nothing ever would.

As he sipped his tea, he thought back to the day Aisha had married Daud. How lovely she'd looked in her simple white dress, adorned with the jewellery she'd been given as her dowry and her glossy black hair plaited and crowned with fresh flowers. That morning she'd come skipping in to show him her henna painted hands and feet, as excited as a schoolgirl. She raised her hands in the air so that her gold bangles jingled as they slid down her arms and she twirled and twirled like a crazy Dervish, her skirts billowing out, the bells on her anklets tinkling and the rings on her toes flashing in the lamplight. She'd been like a mad woman with happiness. But that was then and this was now. She had to realise that life had to move on. Daud was gone. He'd been a nice lad; in fact Makoud had been very fond of him. He was like one of the family even before they got married, always in their house, playing with the boys— even though they were younger than him—and inseparable from Aisha. They all missed him. Now this was the best news he'd had in a while.

'That was a hell of a downpour,' said a rather corpulent man, coming into the tavern and dripping water all over the earthen floor. 'But it's stopping now, thank goodness. A glass of something to warm me up, waiter.'

'I must be going home,' Makoud said to nobody in particular. He picked up his djellabah and stepped out into the night.

What would Abal say when he told her the news? True Bakr had more years than Aisha and his beard was turning grey but he wasn't an old man; he was still tall and straight. He and Aisha might even have more children in time. That was a point in his favour, he hadn't said he wanted a young wife to give him more sons. He'd never even asked if she was capable of having more children. No, he was more interested in whether she'd be a good mother to the children he already had. He was a caring man. Now the big question was whether Aisha would accept him. And if so, on what terms?

CHAPTER 22

The next morning Umar was roughly awoken by one of his squad. He opened his eyes to see the battle scarred face of his friend Fahad.

'Get up. The quaid wants to speak to you,' he said.

'What? What's it about? What's happened?' asked Umar, still struggling to clear the sleep from his brain.

'No idea, mate. But I think you're in a shitload of trouble.'

Talib sat up, rubbing his eyes. 'What's all the noise about? Umar? What's happening?'

'No idea. Go back to sleep Talib.' This had to be something to do with the enquiries they'd been making. He couldn't think what else it could be.

Umar stumbled out of bed and pulled on his tunic and boots. He reached to buckle on his sword but the soldier stopped him, saying, 'No weapons. Just come as you are. And get a move on. The quaid's in a bad enough mood as it is, without us making him wait.'

Fahad had been right in his assessment; the quaid was pacing back and forth across the room and his face was like thunder.

'Right soldier, what's all this about?' he barked at Umar. 'I have a woman who is accusing you of murdering her father.'

Umar felt his knees go weak.

'I haven't murdered anyone, sayyad,' he said.

'Speak up, man.'

'I haven't killed anyone, sayyad. I don't know what you're referring to.'

'Do you deny you went to visit the physician Abu al-Jabir?'

'No sayyad. I did go to see him but I didn't kill him.'

'His daughter says you threatened him and you drew your sword.'

'I drew my sword but I didn't threaten him. I told him I meant him no harm. I swear on all that's holy, sayyad, I never hurt him. May Allah be my judge.'

Umar's stomach had turned to water. He knew that the punishment for such an offence would be swift and brutal. It was one thing to die on the battlefield but he didn't want to die here, in the prison, a dishonoured soldier. His family would never get over the shame.

'Can you explain why you went to the house of the physician?' asked the quaid.

'I wanted to ask him some questions.' He stopped. What would the quaid think of his speculations? Would he believe them or dismiss them as fanciful rubbish?

'What sort of questions?'

Umar took a deep breath and began to explain to his commanding officer about his suspicions about Yahya's death and how what Abu al-Jabir had told him had confirmed them.

'You see, I had no reason to kill him and every reason to keep him alive. He is the only witness who can say that the khalifa had been poisoned. Please believe me, sayyad; I did not kill him. Surely his daughter is not saying that she saw me murder him?'

'No, soldier, she's not saying that, but she believes that you were the only one who visited him that night. She says no-one else entered the house.'

'She doesn't know that unless she was there all night,' said Umar, gaining a bit of confidence from the quaid's questions. 'Was she there all night?'

'No. She says she took her father some supper, which is when you burst in on them. After you left she stayed about an hour and then went home. The next morning she was told her father was dead. She is adamant that you were the only one to see him before his death. And the servant backs her up on that. He says you were the only one to see the physician that night.'

'Maybe he went out to meet someone?' he suggested.

'I don't think that's likely, soldier. His daughter says he was a very frightened man.'

'Did she say why?' asked Umar.

'No. She didn't know the reason but she said that he thought someone was trying to kill him. The question is, was it you?'

The quaid sat down behind his desk and pulled his dagger from his belt; he began to carefully polish the blade between his fingers. This was a habit Umar had witnessed before when his commanding officer was puzzled about something. After what seemed to Umar to be hours of waiting, the quaid said, 'As I see it, soldier, we have your word against that of the physician's daughter. I have no alternative but to put you in jail until we have sorted this out.' He looked at the two guards standing behind Umar and said, 'Take him away.'

The soldiers grabbed his arms and marched him towards the door.

'But I didn't kill him,' cried Umar, his voice quavering with fear. 'Please believe me, sayyad. I didn't kill him.'

'If we find that is the case, then you will be released, but until then I can't allow you to go free.'

Umar knew there was no point saying anything else; the quaid had made his decision and he was not a man to change his mind easily. But how on earth was he going to prove his innocence if he was locked up? Once he was inside that dungeon he could do nothing; he was at the mercy of his gaolers.

The guards escorted him out of the quaid's office and across the busy parade ground towards the dungeons. When the other members of his squad saw him they stopped what they were doing and looked on in disbelief.

'Umar. What's happening?' called Talib, running across to them. 'Why have you arrested him? Where are you taking him?'

'Out of the way, lad. This is none of your business,' said one of the guards. 'Unless you want to join him?'

Umar saw his friend hesitate and drop back, a look of bewilderment on his face.

'Talib, they think I murdered Abu al-Jabir. You have to let my father know what's happened. And the nazir,' shouted Umar. 'Let them know where I am.'

'Don't worry about that; they'll know soon enough,' said one of the guards.

'Yes, when they see your head stuck on the end of a pole,' laughed the other.

*

Talib walked back to the training area, his head swirling with thoughts of what he should do. From an immediate point of view, it was more important to find out who had killed the physician, but something niggling at the back of his mind suggested that their plans hadn't really changed. He had to find Wada; he was the key to it all. If he found the man who bought the poison then he could trace his way back to who had ordered it. That was the man they really wanted. That would be the man responsible for the physician's death.

But first he must speak to their nazir. And then he had to find Wada. He smiled to himself; yes, after all there were only two thousand soldiers stationed in the alcazaba and a further five thousand in the Jbel-Faro. How difficult could it be to find one man who didn't want to be found?

*

The nazir was amazed when Talib told him what had happened to Umar and what they'd been doing.

'Why didn't you come to me with this information before?' he asked.

'Because you probably wouldn't have believed us, sayyad,' Talib replied. 'We wanted to get some proof before we told anyone.'

'You're right. I think you've both let your imaginations get the better of you.'

'But two men are dead in suspicious circumstances, sayyad,' said Talib. 'And now Umar has been accused of being a murderer. That's not imagination.'

The nazir glared at him; Talib knew his tone was bordering on insubordination.

'Mmn. We have no proof that the khalifa was murdered and the physician could have been killed by any cut-throat —Allah knows we have enough of them wandering around the city,' said the nazir.

'But the two things are linked, sayyad. Abu al-Jabir told Umar that he thought the khalifa was poisoned by doses of wormwood administered over a long period of time.'

'Wormwood? What is this wormwood?'

'It's a poison that creates hallucinations and paranoia, and eventually kills the victim.'

'So did Abu al-Jabir say who had administered this poison?' asked the nazir, showing a little more interest now in what Talib had to tell him.

'No. He didn't know. He said no-one was allowed near the khalifa, only him, the servants and Prince Idris.'

'Prince Idris, you say? The new khalifa?'

'Yes, sayyad.'

'But you have no proof?'

'Not now that Abu al-Jabir is dead.'

'Well unless you can find some proof, your friend Umar is likely to stay in prison and if they decide he is guilty then he will be executed.'

Talib felt his heart sink to the pit of his stomach.

'Can't you do anything to help him, sayyad?' he asked.

'Bring me proof that someone else killed the physician and then I will see what I can do. In the meantime, I'm giving you a week's leave of absence. Get to it, soldier. Your comrade needs your help.'

Talib bowed and left the little man still frowning over this unusual state of affairs.

*

Umar's father was sitting in a small cafe outside the apothecary's shop, drinking tea.

'As-salama alaykum, ibn Ahmad,' said Talib, giving a slight bow and sitting down beside him.

'Wa alaykum e-salam, young man. You're a friend of my son's, I believe,' said Makoud, waving the waiter across to him. 'Where is Umar?'

'I have some disquieting news for you, sayyad.' He saw the smile fade from Makoud's face. 'Your son has been arrested.'

'Arrested? I don't believe you. Why would they arrest Umar? What do they say he's done?'

'They say he murdered a man.'

Makoud let out a long groan and doubled over, holding his head in his hands. 'Allah, save and protect him.' He stayed like that for a minute or two, rocking back and forth, then when he had recovered his composure he sat up and asked, 'What can we do?'

'We have to find the guilty person.' Then Talib told him all that he knew about their discoveries and Umar's meeting with the physician.

'Have you found out any more about that strange man who came into my shop?' Umar's father asked.

'Yes and no. We know more about him now but I haven't actually found him yet. In fact that's my next task, to track him down and question him.'

He began to tell Makoud all that he'd found out. 'He was murdered,' interrupted Umar's father. 'The physician. But not by Umar; I'm certain of that. We heard all about it. I knew the man well. He often came into our shop with his daughter, a nice, modest young woman. I thought she'd make a good daughter-in-law.'

Talib went on to explain how that nice young woman had accused Umar of murdering the good doctor.

He watched Makoud's face turn pale. Somebody would surely pay for murdering the royal physician and in the absence of the true culprit it could well be his son. Umar's father knew this; he knew how the system worked.

'So what are you going to do?' asked Makoud.

Talib ordered a glass of pomegranate juice and then said, 'I have a week's leave, so I will look for this man, Wada. At least I have a bit more to go on now.'

'Ibrahim and I can help you with that. The palace guards often come into the town to spend their pay. We will ask if anyone has seen him.'

'I thought I'd make some enquiries now.' Talib swallowed back his pomegranate juice and stood up. 'All right if I meet up with you later?'

'Of course, come round to the shop.'

'I'll call in this evening and let you know what I've found out.'

Umar's father nodded and drank some more of his tea; he looked very worried. Talib knew he would be upset by the news but if he was going to help Umar, he needed all the assistance he could get.

*

It was on the second day of combing the back street taverns of the city that Umar's brother, Ibrahim, found out something useful. The soldier Wada had taken to frequenting one of the taverns that sold wine; it was in a narrow alley leading up from the harbour and was the haunt of foreign merchants, itinerant workmen and mercenaries. Few Muslims ever went there. Talib and Ibrahim waited outside until they saw someone whom Ibrahim recognised as the man from the shop.

'I'm pretty sure that's him,' he said. 'But we'd have to get closer to be sure.'

'Come on then. I'll buy you a drink,' said Talib.

Ibrahim looked horrified. 'But it's wine. We're not allowed to drink wine.'

'I know but we may have to if it's the only way we can get him to talk,' said Talib. He was sure that would have been Umar's response. Anyway he wasn't going to let the fact that this tavern only sold wine stop him from entering and questioning the man. Who would know? Only Allah and he was sure Allah would understand he was doing it to help a friend.

The tavern was dark and crowded. Smoke from oil lamps that needed trimming added to the gloom. It stank of sweat and stale wine with a background odour of fish hanging in the air.

'There he is, over there in the corner, sitting on his own,' said Ibrahim.

They went across and sat down, giving him no more than a cursory nod. Talib motioned to the waiter to bring them a jarrah of wine.

'Your health,' said Ibrahim raising the pottery mug a bit tentatively to his lips.

'And yours, brother.' Talib turned to Wada and said, 'Not drinking, soldier? Here let me fill up your beaker.' He poured a generous measure into Wada's cup. 'In the Guards I see. Nice cushy life there, I bet. Me, I prefer the excitement of the battle ground.'

The guard took a long draught of the wine and then seemed to see Ibrahim for the first time. 'Hey, I recognise you. You're that kid from the apothecary's. I bet your father doesn't know you're in the tavern, drinking wine.' He laughed, exposing a mouth full of rotten teeth.

'Well I hope you won't mention it next time you go in there,' Ibrahim replied, looking genuinely embarrassed at being caught with a mug of wine in his hand.

'No. You have nothing to fear on that account. I was your age once. Anyway I'm not likely to be going into your father's shop again.'

'Why's that? Your wife refused to make you any more cakes?' Ibrahim asked, with a giggle.

Talib could see that the first sips of wine had gone straight to his head. He stifled a smile.

'No. Don't have any wife. Whatever gave you the idea I did? Me, I'm free and footloose. Always been a wanderer, me. Fighting for whoever would give me the biggest bag of silver. Mind you, I almost took a wife. Once, a long time ago. I was much younger then and soft in the head.' A tear rolled down the man's cheek and he hurriedly brushed it away. 'Lucky escape. I mean, what would I want with a wife who nagged me all day and a bunch of screaming kids? No. Not for me. Free as a bird I am.'

'What happened to her?' asked Ibrahim. 'The one that got away.'

Wada stared at him for a moment, then said, mournfully, 'She's dead. No more to be said.'

This wasn't getting them anywhere so Talib decided to goad him into giving himself away. 'But you're just a palace guard,' said Talib, pointing at his uniform. 'Not a lot of adventure there. Just a well paid nursemaid. What do you do all day? Stand guard over a few old men and their families? That's not a soldier's life.' The tattoo was clearly visible on the back of Wada's hand and he was doing nothing to hide it. This was definitely the man they were after.

Talib took a draught of the wine; it was the first he'd ever tasted and it left a sour taste at the back of his throat. He wanted to encourage Wada to loosen up but he didn't want to lose control himself, so he had to go carefully. He'd seen men the worse for wear after drinking Shaitan's brew and he didn't want that to happen to him. He looked across at Ibrahim, sprawled beside him on the rather grimy cushions. One of them had to keep a clear head.

Wada tapped his nose, as if to say, 'If only you knew,' and drained the beaker. He moved as though to leave, adding, 'It's not without its excitement.'

'Not off already, friend, are you?' asked Talib. 'Here, have some more.'

Once again he filled Wada's beaker to the brim and motioned for the waiter to bring them another jarrah of wine.

'Well, if you insist. It's a long time since I've been in such convivial company,' he said, his words already taking on a bit of a slur.

'Good health,' Talib said, feigning to drink some more.

'And you, soldier. From one soldier to another.'

'But you aren't really a soldier now, are you?' he said, trying to provoke him again.

'Not a soldier? What do you think this is?' Wada said, pulling out his sword, embossed with the khalifa's emblem. He stood up, pulling himself to his full height, and mumbled, 'I've had to do things you wouldn't believe. You wouldn't believe.'

Talib tugged at Wada's cloak and said, 'Sit down and tell me then. What makes your job so much more exciting than mine?'

'You only have enemies out there,' he said, waving his sword wildly, as he almost fell onto the cushions. 'I have enemies everywhere. Even my masters could turn on me at any moment. I live in fear of my life,' he said, with a pathetic sob. The assumed courage turned to pathos in a matter of moments. 'You know your enemies. Mine are hidden. You have no idea what danger I face. No idea.'

Talib reached across and refilled his beaker 'We live in dangerous times, friend.'

Wada nodded his head, drunkenly. 'That is so true. I would have never got involved with all this if I'd known what was going to happen. I'm not a murderer, you know,' he said, leaning closer to Talib and breathing into his face. Even the copious amount of wine he'd drunk couldn't cover the loathsome smell of the man's halitosis. 'I've killed men of course. Every soldier has to kill. It's kill or be killed in the army, isn't it? But to murder an innocent man, no I couldn't do that.'

'Why, is someone accusing you of doing that?' asked Talib. 'Killing an innocent man? Who are you supposed to have killed? The khalifa's doctor?'

Ibrahim was keeping quiet and it was almost as if Wada had forgotten he was there.

'They will. They'll do worse than accuse me. If one day, you hear of my body being pulled out of the sea, like that old doctor—Allah rest his soul—you'll understand why I'm so frightened.'

'But you must have done something,' said Ibrahim. 'Was it to do with the wormwood?'

Wada stared at him through bloodshot eyes. 'All I did was buy it for him. That's all. It's not a crime to buy wormwood, is it?' He didn't wait for a reply but carried on rambling, as much to himself as to them, 'I bought it and I gave it to him. That's all I did. For the khalifa, he said.

Headaches. It was a cure that his family had used for centuries, but the royal physician wouldn't hear of it. Said it was dangerous. I believed him. I did. I believed him. These doctors don't know everything. They think they do. But they don't know everything.'

His voice trailed away. The wine was taking its toll and he was struggling to keep awake.

'So you believed him when he said he was trying to help the khalifa?' asked Talib.

'No reason not to. A personal servant. A personal servant to Yahya I. The khalifa. Been with him for years. What was I to think? I had no idea what he was going to do with it, did I? He wasn't a violent man. I'd known him a long time and I never saw him hurt anyone; he was almost like family to me. I never thought for one minute that he was going to use it to kill anyone. Not my fault what he used it for. Not my fault. How was I to know? Like family he was.'

'Who was that, then? Who was like family?' asked Talib, quietly. 'Who did you give the wormwood to? Did he use it to kill the khalifa?'

The man wasn't listening; the wine was making him maudlin. He continued with his ramblings, 'Beautiful girl. Even asked her father for her hand. Then the bloody prince saw her. Had to have her for his own, he did. As if he didn't have enough women already, wives and concubines. Why did he have to take my lovely Lubaba?' Another tear rolled down his grimy face. He wiped it away angrily. 'Never expected to see him again. Came as a shock it did, after all those years.'

'Who? Who were you surprised to see? The khalifa?'

Wada stared at him. 'No, not him.'

'Who then? Do you know who murdered the khalifa?' Talib asked gently.

But Wada was too deep in his cups. He tipped the dregs of the wine down his throat and slammed the beaker on the table, 'And that other one. Supposed to be loyal to the throne, he was. True and trusted. What a laugh. He's as crooked as anyone I know—and I've met a few thieves and cut-throats in my time.'

Wada paused while Talib poured more wine into the beaker, then resumed, 'I bet he got more for his part than I did. A handful of bloody silver, that's all I got. But I told him I wanted more. I wanted security for my old age. Pretended not to know what I was talking about, he did. But I wasn't going to be put off. I told him what I wanted. Not unreasonable. Not much to ask. He knew he had a lot to lose so he had to agree. That's how I got to be in the Palace Guards,' he said with a rather lop-sided smile. 'But that was a mistake. Big mistake. I should have asked for more money and just got out of here. I'm going to have to leave anyway. What's the point of waiting until they slit my throat and throw me in the sea as well. No, as soon as I get my month's pay, I'm out of here. Going to get a ship to the Maghreb, out of harm's way.'

'Well, one more for the road, in that case,' said Talib. He poured him a little more wine; Wada certainly had an enormous capacity for the stuff.

'So who gave the wormwood to the khalifa?' asked Ibrahim, holding out his own mug for a refill. 'Was it his servant?'

This time Talib made sure to pour him a small amount; he was going to have some explaining to do to Makoud if he caught them.

'What? I told you, all I did was buy the wormwood. I traipsed around for hours trying to find the bloody stuff, buying a bit here and a bit there. A right mean lot, you apothecaries. Took me hours to get what he'd asked for. But no, I didn't poison anyone. Do you think I'm stupid? Murder the khalifa?'

'But you said you spoke to someone. Someone who gave you a job in the Palace Guards. Who was it?' asked Talib. He was feeling impatient but he knew that if he tried to hurry Wada he might clam up altogether.

'Did I?' Wada looked at him suspiciously. 'Why are you asking me all these questions? Are you working for the muhtasib?'

'No, we're nothing to do with the law. You know who we are,' said Ibrahim.

'Ah, yes. You're the apothecary's son. You're going to be in big trouble when you get home, my lad,' he said, grinning and wagging his finger at him.

'So how did you get this nice cushy job of yours?' asked Talib. They were getting nowhere. Either he was very good at evading questions or they had overdone the wine. 'Who did you speak to? Was it Idris?'

'No, of course not. What you thought I went to the new khalifa? I'm not that foolhardy. He'd have had me executed for daring to speak to him. No I went to his lackey.'

'Ibn Baqanna?' asked Ibrahim in surprise.

'He's a clever lad, that one,' said Wada. He leaned back against the wall and shut his eyes. Talib thought he'd fallen asleep and was wondering whether to shake him, when suddenly he opened his eyes and said, 'I knew him in Sebta. Long time ago now. He's done very well for himself.'

It was hard to follow Wada's ramblings. Who was he talking about now?

'So it was ibn Baqanna who asked you to buy the wormwood? And you gave it to him?'

'No. It was my old friend. Said I'd be doing ibn Baqanna a favour if I bought it. Gave me a bag of silver for my pains. But that grand vizier is too bloody high and mighty now to have anything to do with me. Pretended he didn't know me.'

'Who is your old friend? asked Ibrahim, with a pronounced slurring to his words. 'And what did you do with the wormwood from our shop?'

'That lad has been drinking,' said Wada. 'I shall tell his father.'

'The wormwood, Wada?'

'I told you. I gave it to him for the khalifa's headaches. That's all I did. Like family he was to me.'

Talib could see that he wouldn't get much more out of Wada now the wine had got hold of him.

'A mistake. Bloody mistake. I should have asked for money. Got as far away as I could,' said Wada, peering into his empty beaker.

Talib poured the last of the wine into Wada's beaker and said, 'It's been nice talking to you, but we have to leave now. I need to get my friend sobered up before I take him home. Take care.'

'And you, soldier.'

Any moment now his head would fall forward and he'd be asleep. There he'd stay until morning or until the landlord threw him into the street. What would become of him? Talib couldn't make head nor tail of everything that Wada had said, but it did seem clear that his part in the conspiracy had been to buy the wormwood which he then gave to an old friend of his, and somehow ibn Baqanna was involved. He prayed Wada lived long enough to tell the quaid all he knew.

Talib pulled the tavern door shut behind them as he stepped out into the dark night.

'Aren't you going to arrest him?' asked Ibrahim. He stood facing into the wind, taking deep gulps of the salty breeze that came off the Middle Sea.

'I don't have the power to arrest him.'

He took Ibrahim's arm and began to walk back towards the apothecary's shop.

'But if he's in danger shouldn't we be protecting him?' asked Ibrahim, after they had been walking for a while.

Talib stopped and looked at him. 'You're right. If they managed to kill the physician then they'll want to kill Wada too. We'll take him home with us so he can sleep off the wine.'

'What will my father say? He's drunk. Baba doesn't approve of drunks.'

'We're not asking him to give him a job, only to let him stay until the morning. You and I can keep an eye on him. Where else could we take him? We'll have to risk it. Come on.'

They were walking by the harbour wall by then. It was a dark night with no moon; the only light came from the reflections on the water of the ships' lanterns bobbing up and down with the motion of the sea. All the harbour taverns were closed and in darkness.

'Stop. Who goes there?' demanded a deep voice. It was al-darrabun.

'As-salama alaykum.'

The night watchman held his lantern close to Ibrahim's face. 'What are you young fellows doing out at this hour? Hey, aren't you the apothecary's son?'

Ibrahim nodded, sheepishly.

'Looks like you should be in bed. And you too soldier.'

'We're on our way now,' said Talib.

'So what are we going to do?' asked Ibrahim once the darrabun had moved on.

'We'll go back and get him. Come on.'

'I doubt if he can walk,' said Ibrahim, who was staggering a little himself.

'Look, you stay here and I'll run back for him. You wouldn't be much use in that state anyway.'

Talib pulled his djellaba around him and headed back to where they'd left Wada. Everything was in darkness and the door of the tavern bolted by the time he arrived. He hammered on the door with his fists, hoping to rouse someone. At last he heard the bolts being pulled back and the door creaked ajar. 'What in the name of Allah do you want at this hour? Can't you see we're closed?' grunted the landlord, peering out at him.

'As-salama alaykum, friend. I'm looking for a man who was drinking in your tavern tonight,' said Talib.

'Well there's no-one here now except me and my wife. So bugger off.' The door slammed shut.

He thought about knocking on the door again, but what was the point? The man had no reason to lie to him. So what was he going to do now? They should never have left Wada in the tavern. That was the trouble with drinking wine; it stopped you thinking clearly. Now the man could be anywhere, although bearing in mind the state he was in when they left him, Talib doubted that he could have got very far.

Just at that moment he glimpsed a hooded figure moving in the dark alleyway.

'Wada, is that you?' Talib asked, stepping towards him. 'It's late, why don't you come home with me?'

Talib's training had stood him in good stead. It only took him an instant to recognise the flash of steel. Instantly he withdrew his own sword, moving forward to meet his opponent. This wasn't Wada. It was too tall for the old soldier. So who was it?

'Who are you?' he shouted, brandishing his sword and moving towards the cloaked figure but before he could reach him, the man had melted into the darkness. Talib cursed and retreated slowly. What was the point of chasing a shadow. He was convinced it wasn't Wada, but neither was it a soldier. A soldier would have taken the opportunity of surprise and attacked him, not hung back just watching. Lucky for him or he'd be lying in the alley with his head split open by now.

He sheathed his sword and retraced his steps to where he'd left Ibrahim, who was staring foolishly at a puddle of vomit at his feet.

'Feel better now?' asked Talib.

'Not really. Where's Wada? Did you find him?'

'No, I was too late. He's scarpered.'

'Probably sleeping in an alley somewhere,' said Ibrahim, wiping his mouth on the sleeve of his djellaba. 'So what do we do now?'

'There's not much we can do. We'll go home and tell your father what we've found out and tomorrow I'll go and see the quaid,' said Talib. 'By the way, I think we're being followed.'

'What?' Ibrahim spun round and peered down the gloomy alleyway behind them. 'What makes you say that?'

'There was someone hanging about outside the tavern, just now and when I challenged him, he ran off.' He decided not to mention the sword. Ibrahim was jittery enough as it was.

'Do you think it's the man who killed the khalifa's physician?'

'Who knows? But someone is aware that we're asking a lot of questions and doesn't like it. Is that ibn Baqanna or someone else?'

'You think it was ibn Baqanna?' asked Ibrahim, his eyes as wide as plates.

'No, I'm sure it wasn't him. He wouldn't be skulking around the alleys at this time of night. But he might have sent someone else.'

'So what should we do?'

'Nothing we can do except be careful. Two men are dead already. Whoever is doing this has nothing to lose. Come on, now, let's get you home to your father and then I can report back to the quaid.'

'But do you have enough to tell him? Wouldn't it be better if we tried to find this servant Wada was talking about, first?' asked Ibrahim. 'His old friend.'

'No. I can't enter the alcázar without permission. It's better if I speak to the quaid. He can handle it from there on. At least we know for sure now that Yahya I was murdered.'

'And according to Wada, ibn Baqanna is behind his death. But why? What did he have to gain? Could he have been acting on orders?' asked Ibrahim.

'For now, the important thing is to find the assassin. We know it has to be one of his servants, but which one?' said Talib, heaving a deep sigh. 'There are still too many questions and not enough answers. Until we have something more substantial they're not going to release him.'

CHAPTER 23

Aisha was apprehensive; she could feel the butterflies in her stomach just as when she'd had an exam at school, that same mixture of excitement and nerves, not knowing what she was going into but determined to see it through. Her father had told her about the proposal and she'd agreed to meet Bakr at his house that afternoon. He had asked to see her alone but her mother had insisted that she came along as chaperone. Now she trotted along beside her, chattering constantly about nothing in particular, a long stream of bagatelle that Aisha wasn't listening to; her mother always talked too much when she was nervous.

'Now, don't ask too many questions,' she instructed her. 'You don't want him to think you're being critical.'

'Yes, Mama.' Did her mother think she was still a child?

'And if he introduces you to his mother, be polite and behave modestly.'

Aisha choked back a laugh. Sometimes her mother was so ridiculous. Did she think she was going to storm into his house and behave like one of the khalifa's concubines?

'What is it, Aisha? It's nothing to laugh at. This is a wonderful chance for you and the children. You do realise that, don't you? Not many men would consider marrying a widow with two children. And a rich man, at that.'

'I know, Mama. But I haven't agreed to marry him yet. I hardly know him.' Again she smiled to herself. What would her mother say if she told her that she was more familiar with Bakr's right leg than his face.

'Is this his house?' Abal asked, her eyes growing round in amazement. 'It's very grand.'

'Well this is the address Baba gave us, so I suppose it must be.'

It was an impressive stone building with a decorated horse-shoe archway over the main entrance. A brass bell hung on the wall. She pulled the rope and waited for someone to answer. After a few minutes the door swung open and a young woman welcomed them with a broad smile. 'Ahlan, ahlan. You must be Aisha,' she said. 'Please come in, my brother is waiting for you.'

'Ahlan wa sahlan. Thank you.' Timidly she stepped into the hall and removed her shoes. Her mother's advice about modesty had been completely unnecessary; she was far too nervous to be anything else.

The house was as grand inside as out. They followed the young woman into a large, well furnished room and then through a doorway that led to an open patio, where winter jasmine was still flowering and pots of aloe vera displayed long reddish blooms. Lemon, orange and pomegranate trees stood in pots around the sides of the patio along with bushes of rosemary and thyme which perfumed the air with their sweet scent. In the centre of the open space was a round pond filled with goldfish and a fountain decorated in blue and yellow tiles. Bakr was seated by the fountain, feeding the fish. He looked up when he heard them approach and immediately rose to greet them, holding out his hands in welcome.

'As-salama alaykum, sayeda,' he said, addressing Aisha's mother. Then he turned to Aisha and said, 'I am so very happy that you have agreed to come and talk to me.'

'Wa alaykum e-salam, Bakr ibn Assam.' She lowered her eyes, not so much from modesty as to avoid looking into the ship builder's piercing black eyes which seemed capable of reading her innermost thoughts.

'Rayya, would you bring us some refreshment, please. As it's a lovely afternoon, we'll sit out here, if you like,' he said, looking at Aisha.

'That would be nice,' she said, her voice lacking any conviction. She felt annoyed with herself. There was no need to behave like a love-sick teenager; after all he was probably just as nervous as she was.

She sat down opposite the pond and watched the gold-fish; they were still expecting food and swam close to the surface, opening and closing their mouths in anticipation.

'Here. You can feed them some bread,' said Bakr. 'You need to crumble it quite finely, otherwise the greedy ones will try to swallow it whole and choke.' He crumbled a piece of dried bread and sprinkled it across the surface of the pond. Instantly the surface was broken by the excited movements of the hungry fish.

Aisha broke off a piece of the hard bread and crumbled it in her hand. 'Are they always this lively?' she asked as the fish immediately changed course to come to her side of the pond, now well aware of her presence.

'Always.'

Rayya returned with a tray laden with cakes, biscuits and dried fruit. Behind her came her younger sister, carry-ing a pot of tea and three glasses.

'This is my sister, Rusa,' Bakr said. 'Will you pour the tea please, Rusa.'

The girl smiled at them and began to pour out the scented tea. She handed a glass first to Abal, who seemed delighted by all around her. It won't be hard to convince her about this marriage, thought Aisha.

After they'd finished their refreshments and made some rather stilted conversation, Bakr said, 'Rayya why don't you show the sayeda our house and garden. If you would like to, that is?' He looked at Abal as he spoke.

'Yes, I'd love to see your beautiful house,' Aisha's mother replied.

While her mother was guided into the house by the two sisters, Aisha remained sitting opposite the ship builder.

'I thought it best if we spoke alone,' he said. 'I hope you don't mind.'

'No. I think it's best.' She waited, unsure of what to say next. There had been none of this awkwardness when she had married Daud. Both families knew that they wanted to marry and all that remained to be done was arrange the marriage contract.

Bakr seemed as unsure of what to say as she did, but at last he spoke, 'I have talked to your father and explained to him that I am looking for a wife, but I made it plain that I wanted to speak to you about it first. It seems that you and I are in similar situations. We have both been married and Allah has seen fit to take away those that we loved.'

She nodded. Baba had already told her that this man was a widower who had loved his wife very much.

'After my Juml died I was content to live alone and let my family take care of my children, but now I realise that I was being selfish. They need a mother and I need a wife.'

Still Aisha did not speak. Was that all she would be, someone to care for his children?

'But I realise that too would be selfish, if I only thought of my own happiness and not that of my bride.' He hesitated, unsure of how to go on.

Aisha waited a moment and then said, 'I too had given up any thoughts of marrying again. My husband and I were very much in love, and I must tell you that I love him still. He was not just my husband but my friend.' Her voice quavered as she spoke.

'And yet you have come here, today?'

'Yes. My father told me about you and your proposal. Like you, I feel that I am being selfish, wallowing in my grief. My children need the chance of a better life; they need a father. I know that you loved your wife, as I loved my husband, and I think that is the best recommendation for a contented marriage. If a person can love once, then they have the capacity to love again. Maybe that good fortune will be ours.'

The look he gave her told her everything; this was a man she could put her trust in.

'Tell me why you decided to speak to my father?' she asked. Her mother would have been horrified if she could hear her but she wanted to know if it was her he wanted or just any suitable woman.

He looked at her and smiled. 'When I saw you in your father's shop that day, I was struck by your beauty. In truth, I could not get your image out of my head. I thought if there was anyone who could make me happy, it had to be that angel of mercy.'

She laughed. 'That's what my father called me, isn't it? He's always calling me silly names. Well, you should know that I'm not really an angel at all, just a determined young woman and a loving mother. But if we do marry, I will do my best to make you happy.'

'Before you give me your final consent, I want you to meet my mother and all the women who live in this house. Also I think you should bring your children here to meet my son and daughter; I know they are younger but it would be nice for them to get to know each other and I too would like to meet them.'

She smiled at him and nodded.

'How many women do you have in this house?' she asked with a broad smile.

'Too many,' he said and laughed. 'Come I'll introduce you to my mother and grandmother.'

'Later will you show me the boat yard?' she asked.

At this request he first looked surprised, then pleased and said, 'Yes, of course. I'll take you there before you leave. It's very close.'

*

Bakr introduced her to all his family; at first his mother had viewed her and her mother with some suspicion but by the time they left she was happily chattering to Abal about the forthcoming wedding as though it was already arranged. The sisters were very interested in her, asking hundreds of questions about her family and life in Ardales; it seemed that they had all been very fond of Juml and her death had devastated not just Bakr but the whole family. If there was any cloud on the horizon it was that; would she ever be able to live up to Juml's memory? Did she want to?

They left her mother half-way through recounting the story of their journey to Malaqah while she and Bakr walked across the main street and down an alleyway that led to the ship yard.

'It's not really a place for women,' he said as they approached the entrance. 'People who work with ships and the sea are very superstitious; if a woman was to enter the yard itself they would consider that the ship would be jinxed. It would bring bad luck on it and everyone who sailed in it.'

'Oh, I didn't realise,' she said, feeling embarrassed. Why had she asked to see it anyway? 'I'm sorry. I was just interested to know where you worked. Let us go back.'

'Come as far as the entrance and you can see the extent of it, at least. It's much larger than in my father's day. I have doubled its size,' he said with some pride.

He led her to a huge rounded arch that rose above some heavy wooden gates. It was a larger version of the arch that covered the entrance to his house.

'From here you can see the domed roofs of the two ship building areas.' He pointed to an enormous building that lay between the road and the sea. 'Alongside that is an extensive dry dock, where the ships can be tested to see if they're watertight. But you can't see that from here, only if we go inside.' He looked at her, waiting for her reply.

'It's very impressive,' she said, 'But I think I've seen enough. It's time my mother and I went home.' She turned and headed back towards his house, only waiting for a train of camels to pass on their way to the market. One of them had dumped a pile of excrement in the street and the stench was unbearable.

His face had an expression halfway between relief and disappointment. Was he sorry she was leaving so soon? They walked back to his house in silence.

'I'll speak to my father tonight and you will have word of my decision by tomorrow morning,' Aisha said, when they arrived at the gate.

He nodded. 'If the house is too big for you, we can have a smaller house just for us and the children. There's no need for us to live with all of my family, you know. I would understand if you find them a bit overwhelming; I often do,' he said.

'Your house is lovely,' she said. 'And I like your family very much. Whether I decide to marry you or not, the decision will have nothing to do with your family; they are kind and generous people. I just need time to think about whether I could make you a good wife. Just let me have a few more hours to decide and then I will tell you.'

Disappointment was clearly etched on his face now. She felt her heart ache. He was a kind, affectionate man; she could see that from the way he talked to his sisters and his children. She would have a comfortable life as his wife and she had no doubt that he would make a good father to her children, but could she love him? Was it fair to marry him if she didn't love him?

He reached out and took her hand. 'Until tomorrow then, Aisha,' he said. 'May Allah help you to make a wise decision.'

He opened the door and waited until her mother appeared, but he said nothing more. Was he offended? He was the sort of man who usually got what he wanted; she could see that by the size of his business and the way his sisters ran around after him.

'There you are, Aisha. Come, my dear, it's time we went home. Thank you sayyad, for an enjoyable afternoon,' said her mother, bustling outside and taking her daughter's arm.

'The pleasure has been all ours, sayeda. Alla ysalmak.'

'Ma'a salama, Bakr. Until tomorrow,' Aisha replied.

'Until tomorrow.'

Once the door had closed behind him her mother started to question her, 'Well? When is the wedding? I hope you haven't left it too long. Summer would be good. That's the best time for a wedding. Your father and I were married in the summer. I remember it as though it were yesterday. I looked so lovely; you wouldn't think so to look at me now but I was a beautiful bride.'

Her mother continued in this vein all the way to their house, never waiting for an answer and barely taking in Aisha's thoughtful silence. At last, as they arrived at the door to the apothecary's shop, she said, 'Aisha, what's the matter? You don't seem at all excited about the prospect of getting married. What's wrong with you? Every young girl wants to get married.'

'I'm not a young girl, Mama. I'm a widow. I've done all that you have said already. Where is the excitement in it for me? And anyway I'm not sure there will be a wedding.'

With those words she walked into the shop and straight into the room where her children were playing. What would they think about Bakr and his family?

CHAPTER 24

Their commanding officer was one of the older, more experienced quaid's in the khalifa's army, a professional soldier who had risen through the ranks due to his bravery and his keen mind. They all said that he was the best tactician of all the commanders, only General Rashad surpassed him. The quaid pulled at his beard as he sat listening attentively to Talib's story.

'So soldier, you appear to have found a motive for the royal physician's murder. But where is this man, Wada, that you've told me so much about? I'd like to hear directly from him.'

'We can't find him, sayyad. I have searched the town and the barracks and there is no sign of him. When we spoke to him last night, he was in fear of his life. I think he may have left Malaqah.'

'Why do you think that? Maybe he's just in hiding.'

'He said that he regretted asking to be appointed to the Palace Guards. He felt he should have just demanded more money and disappeared.'

'Are you saying that the new grand vizier is involved in the death of Yahya I? And are you implying that the khalifa knew about this? You know that would be treason, don't you? Spreading malicious rumours about our Khalifa and Supreme Commander is punishable by death.'

'I'm not accusing the khalifa of anything, sayyad. I am just repeating what Wada told us.'

'Us? Who else was with you?'

'Umar's brother, sayyad. He came with me to make a positive identification of the man,' said Talib, his heart thumping. He'd sworn to himself that he wouldn't implicate Umar's family in this but now there was nothing he could do about it.

'I think you need to explain yourself, soldier,' the quaid said, frowning. 'How is Umar's brother involved with a man we now suspect as being connected to the death of Yahya I?'

With a sinking heart, Talib went through the details of Wada's visits to the apothecary.

'When they began to hear the rumours about Yahya's death, they told Umar about the wormwood. As you know, the royal physician backed up his suspicion that this was the poison used.'

'So Umar's father and brother were unwitting participants in the supposed murder of our ruler, is that what you're telling me?'

'Yes, sayyad.' What had he done? Did it really matter where the wormwood had been bought? It could have come from anywhere. He should never have said anything. 'Although Wada did mention that because nobody would sell him much, he had to go to other apothecaries as well.'

'I may need to speak to Umar's father.'

Talib said nothing.

'So, where do you think this man is now?' continued the quaid.

'I don't know, sayyad. When I questioned the landlord of the tavern he said Wada left right after us. He spoke of getting a ship to the Maghreb.'

The quaid turned to the nazir of Talib's squad and said, 'Arrange for men to search the port and question the harbour master. I want to know if any ship left for the Maghreb this morning and if anyone has seen a man of Wada's description.'

'Yes, sayyad,' said the nazir, bowing and leaving immediately. It was he who had insisted that Talib speak directly to the quaid.

'Now, let us consider this allegation by a man of dubious morals,' said the quaid. 'He says it was one of the khalifa's personal servants who put poison in the khalifa's food. Is that correct?'

'Yes, sayyad. Maybe the royal physician saw him do it. That's why he killed him.'

'Supposition, soldier. Why would a servant loyal to the throne suddenly decide to murder his master? There has to be a motive. Well, what do you say?'

'I think we have to find the servant and question him. I can't believe he murdered Yahya I for his own reasons; ibn Baqanna must have ordered him to do it. A servant in his position had nothing to gain and everything to lose.'

'As do you, soldier, and your friend Umar.'

'Sayyad?'

'We will continue to look into this matter. For your sake I hope we can find this Wada. As for the mysterious servant, I don't know what we can do. Palace servants are trusted men. However I will look into it.'

'And Umar? Can he come home now?'

'He will remain where he is until this is all sorted out. Just be happy that I'm not throwing you in gaol with him.'

'Yes, sayyad.' Talib knew not to say any more to the quaid, He was a fair man and if he said he'd look into it then he would. But that didn't mean that Talib had to stop.

*

At first Umar could see nothing, then as his eyes gradually became accustomed to the dark, he could make out his new home. Water dripped down stone walls and lay in fetid pools on the clay floor, and the only light came from a tiny slit window too high up for him to look through. But worse than that, worse than the pile of filthy straw in the corner that was supposed to be his bed; worse than the heavy iron bars that separated him from the rest of the world; worse than the rats that scuttled away to hide in the dark corners of the cell, was the stench of death and decay. People came in here to die. If they were lucky they died quickly, executed by a swift blow from a sword; if they were unlucky they rotted away in the cells, eaten with disease and despair, until death became a merciful release. If there was a hell, then this had to be it.

There was no point trying to speak to anyone. The soldiers had escorted him to the prison and then the aged gaoler had taken over. He might as well have been a prisoner himself with his ashen face, his stooped back and a cough that wracked his body continually; he spent almost as much time in that inhospitable place as the prisoners did. The only difference being that he was free to go home, if he had a home to go to.

Someone, somewhere, lost in the darkness of that netherworld, was moaning in pain, long drawn out gasps that spoke of anguish and hopelessness. Another was praying, desperately calling upon Allah to help him. In harsh, guttural tones another man called down all the calamities in the world to fall on the head of his enemies. Umar did not feel like praying and as far as he knew he had no enemies. If he ended his days in here it was through recklessness on his own part; he should never have gone to visit the physician. Why did he care if someone had murdered the khalifa? They were living in an age of treachery and duplicity; those who craved power would do anything to achieve it. Why on earth did he think that *he* could bring the murderer to justice? All he'd achieved was throw suspicion on himself. The only consolation that he had was that he hadn't told the quaid about his family's part in the investigation. At least they wouldn't be arrested.

He could hear heavy footsteps coming along the corridor. They stopped outside his door. Umar waited, scarcely daring to breathe. Who was it? What did they want? There was the sound of an iron key turning in the lock and the heavy door was pushed open.

The greasy white hair of his gaoler appeared around the door, then the old man pushed a clay bucket into the cell. 'If you need a piss, do it in here. I'm sick of cleaning up after you lazy scum. Understand?'

Not waiting for Umar to answer, he slammed the door shut and once more Umar was left alone. This was impossible. How could he hope to clear his name if he was shut up in here? Was Talib making any progress? He was only a young kid; would he have the guts to carry on without him? And what about his family? His heart sank when he thought of his mother; she would be wailing and crying but would she believe in his innocence? Would any of them? He felt himself sink into an abyss of self-pity and hopelessness.

They would never find out the truth about the killings and that would mean only one thing; he was never going to get out of here. Not alive anyway.

*

As Makoud listened to Talib, his feelings of helplessness and rage grew and grew. 'So he's still in the prison?' he asked.

'Yes, I'm afraid so. I spoke to our nazir but he said he could do nothing. Only the quaid could release him.'

'But you explained what that Wada person said?'

'Yes, but the quaid says it's only hearsay; he wants proof and until he has it, Umar has to stay in gaol.'

'How in the name of Allah are we going to get proof?' Makoud asked, putting his head in his hands. He had to do something. They couldn't leave Umar sitting in gaol, or worse. He stopped himself; he couldn't bear to think of what might happen to his son. What could they do to help him? He couldn't leave it to Talib and Ibrahim; they were both too young.

'Stay here, both of you,' he said to them. 'I'm going out for a bit. We'll talk more when I get back.'

He pulled on his djellaba and marched out of the house, leaving the two young men looking bewildered and the women of his household in tears. He had to speak to some-one who wasn't emotionally involved, someone who could help him keep a clear head, and that could only be his friend Avi.

As usual Avi was in his 'office' as he called the tiny room off the warehouse.

'Makoud?' he said, looking up from his accounts with a surprised expression on his face. 'What are you doing here at this hour?'

'I need to speak to you, Avi. Something terrible has happened.'

'Well come in. Come and tell me all about it,' he said. 'Can I get you anything? Some water? Some tea?'

'No, nothing. I just need to speak to someone. My head is going round in circles. I am so worried about Umar and I just don't know what to do.'

'Umar? What's happened to him? Come, sit down and take a deep breath. I've never seen you so distressed before.'

Makoud sat down beside his friend and began to tell him all that he knew about the khalifa's death and why Umar had become involved in trying to find out who was responsible. 'It's all my fault, you see. I should never have told him about that man buying the wormwood. I should have known what his reaction would be. He's always been one to jump in and try to find out the reason why. That was his favourite word when he was a child. Why? Why was the moon round? Why could camels walk such a long way without drinking any water? Why did the sun move across the sky? He can never just accept that some things just are.'

'So now he's in gaol?'

'Yes and I'm frightened he will never come out of there.'

Avi nodded, gravely. He sat there, tugging his beard and not speaking until Makoud said, 'What can I do? How do I find this Wada? He could be anywhere by now.'

'And the only person you have to turn to, is me? A Jew? I'm not sure I can be of any help, my friend. I know no-one at court. If you could get Umar out of the gaol then I could help you to hide him in Garnata. I have lots of friends in that city.'

'That's too dangerous. If we did that then he'd be a fugitive; he'd never be able to come home. No, we must prove his innocence.'

'But how? You need to find the man you're looking for. That's if he's still alive.'

'Yes, that's why I'm so afraid. If whoever is behind all this decides to kill Wada as well, then the only witness left will be Umar; they might try to kill him too.'

'What about your uncle, Rafiq? Didn't you tell me that he has some influence at court? Could he help?'

'That's a possibility. To be honest, I don't know who he knows there. It's years since he was a soldier and that was in Qurtubah. But it's worth a try. I'll send a message and ask him to come to Malaqah.'

'Yes, send a message by pigeon, don't bother with the barid; that takes weeks. And, in the meantime, I will speak to all the merchants and tell them to be on the lookout for this Wada. Tell me again what he looks like.'

After Makoud had described the man in as much detail as he could remember, he bade Avi farewell and headed back home. He dreaded going in and facing Basma; she had screamed and ranted at him all morning ever since she heard the news.

He opened the door to the shop; it was empty except for Aisha.

'What are you doing here?' he asked. 'Where's Ibrahim?'

'Ibrahim had to go out with Talib. I'm looking after the shop.'

'I told him to wait, here. I don't want to lose another son,' he snapped.

'He won't be long, Baba,' she said. He could see that she too had been crying.

'What is it, Aisha? Don't worry; we'll get Umar out of prison. He's always said that his quaid was a fair man; he'll soon realise that Umar never killed anyone,' he said, wishing he could believe his own words. 'Have you thought any more about what you'll tell Bakr? Will you marry him?'

'Oh, Baba, I can't talk about that now, not while Umar is sitting in some dungeon. I just can't. I'm sorry. I know I told him I would give him an answer today but don't ask me to think about marriage right now.'

'Of course not, my dear one,' he said, hugging his daughter to him. 'I'll explain to Bakr and if he is the man I think he is, then he'll understand.'

At that moment the door to the shop opened and in came Ibrahim and Talib, closely followed by Bakr.

'As-salama alaykum, ibn Ahmad,' said Bakr. 'I heard about your son, and I've come to see if I can do anything to help.'

Makoud saw him look across at Aisha and give a slight bow.

'Peace be upon you. Thank you, but there is little anyone can do unless we can find the man who was involved in poisoning the old khalifa.'

'You mean Wada?' asked Bakr. 'These lads have told me everything. I saw them asking questions down by the harbour. I have many contacts in the port; with your permission I will do what I can to find out about this man. If he has left by ship, I will know about it.'

'What if he crosses to the Maghreb further down the coast? At al-Jazira for example?' asked Talib.

'I'll send someone down there to make enquiries,' said Bakr. He looked at Aisha and smiled kindly, 'No need for tears, my dear. We will find him and get your brother released.'

'That is very kind of you, sayyad,' said Ibrahim as the ship builder went out, 'If we find out anything more, I'll let you know.'

'If only we could question the khalifa's servants' said Talib.

'No, you can't go accusing any of the servants without proof,' said Makoud. 'That would just put you in danger as well.'

'But we must find some way of identifying him,' said Ibrahim. 'One of them is the murderer.'

'On whose orders, though? That's the real question.'

'You think Idris I could be behind it? It's possible that ibn Baqanna was working alone.'

'Somehow I don't think so. If he's the murderer then why didn't he kill Wada? I'm sure he could have arranged that easily enough.'

'Maybe he will. Maybe Wada has been too wily for him up to now.'

'Wily? Not Wada. He's got too big a mouth on him.'

'Well where is he then?' asked Ibrahim. Makoud could see his son was becoming frustrated at their lack of progress.

'This is getting us nowhere,' said Makoud. 'Ibrahim, I want you to go to Ardales and speak to your great-uncle Rafiq. Ask him to come to Malaqah; we need his help.'

'But how can I go to Ardales, Baba? It will take days to walk there. Why don't you send a message by pigeon carrier?'

'No, I've thought of that; it's too risky. I don't want anyone to intercept the message. No, you must go in person.'

'Why not take my horse?' said Talib. 'While you're away, I'll ask the nazir to let me visit Umar. Then at least I'll be able to tell you if he's all right.'

'Very well. Ibrahim can you go right away?'

'Yes, Baba.'

Makoud waited until the two young men had left on their respective errands and then went through to his house to face the rest of his family.

*

He'd just sat down with a cup of hot mint tea when he heard the shop doorbell ring. He knew it would happen; it always did when he thought he'd escape upstairs for a few minutes.

'Don't throw it away,' he told Basma. 'I'll be right back.'

His wife scowled at him; she was still angry about Umar and believed it was all his fault that her son was in gaol.

'As-salama alaykum, friend,' he said to a man, who stood with his back to him, staring out into the street. 'What can I do for you?'

The man turned round and smiled. It was Abu al-Jabir's servant. 'I need something for my mistress. Since her father died, she is having trouble sleeping. I thought maybe some anise, or some sandalwood oil?' he said.

'A massage with sandalwood oil would be most relaxing for her,' said Makoud. He went to the cupboard and took out a small phial of the oil. 'You're the royal physician's servant aren't you?' he asked.

'I was. Poor man died. Murdered.'

'Yes, I heard. You were there, weren't you?'

'I was in the house, yes, but I didn't see what happened.'

'Oh, I thought I heard a young soldier had been arrested.'

'He has. He came to the house that night and threatened the good doctor.'

'But you didn't see him kill the physician?'

'Of course not. I would have done something to prevent it. What, you think I would have just stood there and let someone murder my master?'

'No, no, I didn't mean that at all. I just wondered if he was the only one who visited the doctor that evening?'

'The only one he didn't know.'

'So he did have another visitor then?'

'Only the servant who'd been looking after the khalifa when he was sick. He and abu al-Jabir became good friends; the doctor was at the palace so often he might as well have moved his bed there.'

'Apart from him and the soldier, no-one else visited him?'

'His daughter. But you're not suggesting she murdered him?'

Makoud laughed. 'Indeed not. So which servant was it? Taofik?'

'The masseuse? No. It was al-Azdi who looked after the khalifa. Never left his bedside, according to the doctor. Look, it's nice to stand here chatting with you, but I really have to go.'

'Of course, I'm sorry.' Makoud wrapped up the phial in a fig leaf and handed it to him. 'Please give this to the doctor's daughter, with my condolences. Her father was a fine man. It was a tragedy what happened to him,' he said.

'Thank you. I will pass on your message.

Makoud watched as the man left the shop and set off for home. His heart was racing. So it wasn't true. Umar wasn't the only person to visit the doctor that night; but he was the only one that nobody recognised. It had never occurred to either the servant or the daughter that their father's friend could have murdered him. He couldn't wait to tell Talib and Ibrahim what he'd found out.

CHAPTER 25

The nazir seemed genuinely concerned about Umar. There were only sixteen men in his squad; half of them new recruits like Talib and Umar, and he was responsible for turning them all from farm hands and schoolboys into fighting men. It was a job he took very seriously; if he failed then their chances of survival in battle were slim.

'I'm sorry, soldier. That's not possible. The prisoner is not allowed visitors,' he told Talib. 'I would lose my head if I was caught smuggling you in.'

'I won't be long. Let me have five minutes with him; that's all I ask. I just need to see that he's all right; his father is very worried about him.'

'So he should be. This is a serious matter.' The nazir hesitated and then said, 'Very well, but I'm coming with you. Maybe when you see inside the gaol you'll realise that this is no joking matter.'

What on earth gave the nazir the idea that Talib found it funny? He'd never been so worried in all his short life.

'Well come on, soldier. Let's get this over with,' said the nazir, striding off along the coracha, in the direction of the gaol.

At first the old gaoler was reluctant to let them in, but when the nazir told him it was imperative that they asked the prisoner some questions, he agreed, but made them leave all their weapons at the gate. As Talib stepped into the gloomy prison, he felt naked and vulnerable without his sword; fear gripped his heart and caused him to break into a cold sweat. The nazir was right; this was a serious matter. The walls seemed to crowd in on him and he could feel panic tighten his chest. If the nazir had not been there, he would have turned round at that very moment and run out of there. But he'd asked for this and now he'd have to see it through.

'How is the prisoner?' asked the nazir.

'How should I know? He's still eating and shitting, so I expect he's all right,' said the gaoler, coughing violently and then spitting onto the floor. 'It's my job to feed them and clean out their mess, not to ask them how they're feeling.' He banged on the door of a cell. 'You've got visitors,' he yelled and unlocked it.

The first thing that Talib noticed was the stench. It was unbearable.

'Umar? How are you, soldier?' asked the nazir, peering into the gloomy cell.

A figure in the corner moved towards them; it was Umar. He looked thin and his beard was long and unkempt but apart from that he seemed to be well.

'Sayyad, have you come to take me home?' Umar asked in a husky voice that didn't sound like his own. 'Have you got the proof to free me?'

'No, soldier, not yet. We're still searching for the man you spoke of but he seems to have disappeared.'

'I wanted to see you, Umar,' said Talib. 'We're all doing what we can to help you, but so far we have nothing to take to the quaid.'

'My parents?' Umar asked, his voice breaking with emotion.

'Your mother is distraught with grief and rage. She blames your father for it all, for bringing the family to Malaqah and for allowing you to join the army,' said Talib. 'But your father is determined to get you free. We are all doing everything we can.'

Umar collapsed onto the floor and moaned, 'So you have nothing. I'm never going to get out of here, am I? I didn't kill him,' he said looking up at the nazir in despair. 'I'm telling you; I didn't kill anyone.'

'Don't give up, Umar. We're doing everything we can. We're searching the ports and questioning all the sea captains but no-one has seen the man who bought the wormwood. Your father has even sent to Ardales for his uncle to come and help,' said Talib.

'What can he do?'

'Are you talking about the uncle who gave you that fine horse?' asked the nazir.

'Yes, Rafiq. But I can't see how he can help. He's an old man. He doesn't even know this city.'

'You never know. It's said that he is acquainted with General Rashad. Maybe he will speak to him,' he continued. 'But now we must go. Remember you're a soldier in the khalifa's army and more than that, a jinete. You were not born to die in a prison cell, but on the battle field. Keep that in mind.'

'Yes, sayyad.' Umar stood up and gave the nazir a short bow. 'Thank you for coming to see me.'

'Don't despair,' whispered Talib as he gave Umar a hug. 'We will get you out of here, somehow.' He wished he felt as confident as he sounded.

'Basil, how is she?' Umar asked.

'She is well; I exercise her every day.'

'Good. Give her a piece of sugar cane from time to time; she likes that,' he said, sadly. Being locked up was affecting him badly; he was no longer the ebullient young man he'd once been.

'Ma'a salama, Umar.' It was all Talib could do not to run out into the sunshine and leave the stink of that place behind him, but he held himself in control and walked calmly along the dank and dripping corridors behind the nazir.

Once they were outside, the nazir turned to him and said, 'Well soldier, you know what you have to do if you want to see your friend again. Find the culprits and bring them to the quaid. That is the only way we can get them to release our colleague. Take as much time as you need, but keep me informed of your progress.'

'Yes, sayyad.'

*

The others were concentrating their search on Wada, so Talib decided to go to the kitchens and see what he could learn about the khalifa's servants. He made straight to see the cook who'd been with them on that ill-fated mission to Qarmuña.

'As-salama alaykum, young lad. We've not seen you in a long time,' the cook said when he saw Talib. 'Where's that mate of yours?'

'Umar's in a spot of trouble,' Talib said. He then gave the cook a truncated version of the events that had led to Umar's arrest, carefully making sure not to mention their suspicions about the nature of the khalifa's death.

'What a lot of bullshit. That boy's no more capable of murdering anyone than I am,' he said with a scowl.

Not a very convincing argument, thought Talib, watching the cook bring his enormous cleaver down on the dead lamb that lay spread out on the kitchen table with a violence that threatened to split the table in two. The lamb, now separated from its head, was rapidly chopped up into manageable pieces. No, he certainly wouldn't want to cross this man; he was capable of anything.

'So what can I do for you?' the cook asked, putting the chunks of lamb into an enormous cooking vessel and lifting the carcass of another onto the table.

'I wondered if you knew what had happened to the old khalifa's servants when he died? Especially those that were close to him.'

'Can't say that I do. Probably been given other jobs in the palace or maybe they are serving Idris now. Why?'

'I'm just trying to find someone.'

'Do you have a name?'

Talib shook his head.

'Well, as I say, I can't remember anyone in particular.'

'Yes, you do,' said a skinny man, who was busy slicing vegetables and throwing them into the pot with the lamb. 'When we were in Qarmuña. There was that man who kept coming into the field kitchen and asking for stuff for the khalifa. Tea it was, mostly. That man drank a hell of a lot of tea.'

'Yes, you're right. A tall, wiry fellow. What was he called? Assid? Ahmed? No, Azdi, al-Azdi. I remember because I have a cousin with that name. He was from Qurtuba as well. He told us he was the khalifa's personal servant. Been with him for years, apparently. Seemed very proud of his position.'

'Do you know where he is now?' asked Talib.

'Not likely to be around here. Not now the khalifa is dead. Idris I has his own servants. Completely new household.'

'So what happens to the old servants? Do they just kick them out?'

'Well it depends. I think some of them, the more experienced and trusted ones, get reassigned to other people.'

'I know where he is,' said the skinny man. 'I heard some of the maids gossiping the other day. He's working for ibn Baqanna. The maids don't think a lot of the new grand vizier, a bit of a bully by all accounts.'

Talib felt his heart leap; at last they were getting closer. Could this be the servant that Wada was talking about?

'So what does he do for ibn Baqanna?' he asked.

'Same as he did for the khalifa, as far as I can see, personal manservant, but from what the women were saying, he does whatever the grand vizier wants him to do,' said the skinny man, taking a fistful of parsley and chopping it at a rapid rate before dropping it in the pot with the rest of the vegetables.

Talib felt his stomach rumble; the smell of the lamb was making him hungry.

'Why so many questions, lad?' asked the cook, lifting the lamb's bloody head and dropping it in a bucket.

'Just wondering how I could get to speak to him.'

'Forget that. The likes of you and I aren't allowed in the alcázar. Likely he spends all his time with the grand vizier.'

'But he must sleep and eat? Maybe I could speak to him then?'

'I know what you could do,' said the skinny man, who was by now very interested in Talib's problem. 'You could get one of the kitchen maids who take their food to them, to give him a message; she could pass it to him while he was eating and no-one would be any the wiser.'

'Get on with your work, you clown. You spend too much time listening to the story tellers, that's your problem,' said the cook, waving a knife at his assistant in what looked to Talib as a threatening manner. The skinny assistant just grinned at him and began chopping up dozens of cloves of garlic.

'You hungry, lad?' asked the cook. 'There's some churros if you'd like some.'

'I ought to go,' said Talib.

'Here, take a couple with you,' the cook said, handing him two freshly fried churros. 'And let us know what happens to that friend of yours.'

'I will. Ma'a salama.'

The skinny man followed him out of the kitchen. 'I can have a chat with the maids, see what they know about al-Azdi. If you want to know what's going on in this place you only have to ask the kitchen maids; they have a sixth sense when it comes to good gossip.' He grinned at him.

'I'd be grateful if you could,' Talib replied.

'Not a problem. I'd like to help Umar; he doesn't deserve to rot in prison for something he didn't do. Come by tomorrow or the next day and I'll tell you what I've found out.'

Talib felt a great deal more positive than he had for days, even though there was no way he could approach the grand vizier's new servant directly. He bit into the churros and let the sugary dough linger in his mouth for a moment before swallowing it. Even if he could speak to al-Azdi, what would he say? He couldn't accuse him of being the killer. What proof did he have? And what motive would a devoted servant have to kill his master anyway? It didn't make sense. Still it would be good to talk to him. If he was innocent, then he might want to help them find the real killer. And if he was guilty then maybe, just maybe, he'd give himself away. He'd wait to see what the under cook came up with.

*

It took Ibrahim all day and into the night to reach Ardales, with all the stops he had to make to allow the horse to eat and rest, but at last he reached his old home and headed straight for Rafiq's farm.

His great-uncle didn't take much convincing that he was needed in Malaqah; Ibrahim had the distinct feeling that the old man was tired of retirement and this summons was a welcome change to the monotony of the sleepy little stud farm.

As they rode back to Malaqah he told Rafiq all he knew about the circumstances which had led to Umar's imprisonment.

'I don't know what Makoud thinks I can do. Does he want me to help him break Umar out of prison? That's not going to be easy,' said Rafiq.

'No. Nothing like that.' Ibrahim laughed at the idea of his father and great-uncle breaking into the prison and fighting off the guards; his father had never seemed much of a fighting man to him and Rafiq was too old now for combat.

'So what then?'

'I don't know. Baba just told me to get you,' he replied, wondering why he'd been sent on this fool's errand.

They were making good time. Rafiq had given Ibrahim a fresh horse to ride and that meant that Talib's horse could just canter alongside them. Although he'd learnt to ride when he was younger—Rafiq had insisted that they all did, even Aisha—Ibrahim wasn't much interested in horses. Now he was beginning to realise just how hardy and brave these Arabian steeds were; they were perfectly adapted to travel long distances in hot climates and their physique was such that they could carry more weight than seemed possible.

'We should be in Malaqah by night-fall,' Rafiq said, as they reached the Guadalmedina river and began their descent towards the city. 'There's time for another stop.'

Ibrahim reined in his horse and jumped down. He tied the reins to a nearby tree and dropped down in the shade.

'Hey. This stop is supposed to be a rest for the horses. Not for you,' his great-uncle said. 'Take off her saddle and let her loose to graze. Then you can rest.'

Obediently Ibrahim did as he was told and watched as the mare wandered down to the riverbank but instead of drinking as he expected, she began to snort and paw the ground. The other two mares followed her to the water's edge, but they too held back and wouldn't drink. Something was making them nervous.

'What is it now?' said Ibrahim. He was desperate to just lie flat on the ground and let his aching limbs relax; it was years since he'd ridden anything like as far as this and his body felt as though it had been trampled by a herd of elephants.

'I expect something's polluted the water,' said Rafiq. 'We'll have to take them further upstream.'

'What sort of thing?' asked Ibrahim, reluctantly going across to see what was spooking their horses.

'Could be a dead goat. Horses are very particular. They don't like sharing their water with dead animals.'

'I'm not surprised. I wouldn't be keen to drink either if there was a dead goat floating in it.' He stopped. 'Or a dead man.'

'What?'

'There's a body in the river. It's caught up on those rocks. Look.'

A man's body was wedged between the far bank and a small rocky waterfall. His dirty white djubbah drifted in the current like a flag of surrender.

'We'd better pull him out. Probably some shepherd who slipped and cracked his head on that stone,' said Rafiq.

Together they waded through the icy river until they reached the body. Ibrahim had often seen the corpses of dead animals in the countryside—sheep, goats, sometimes rabbits half-eaten by buzzards and foxes, once a wild boar —but never a man. He was lying faced down, his hair floating in the water like tendrils of seaweed, his hands and arms spread out before him. Ibrahim stopped. His brain seemed to drain of blood; he was either going to faint or be sick.

'What a mess,' said Rafiq. 'Poor soul; he must have taken a pretty bad fall to cause all that damage to his head.' Gently he turned the body over. 'In the name of Allah, what's happened here? This was no accident. Look at him; he's unrecognisable.'

'It's Wada,' Ibrahim managed to say, his throat dry with fear.

'What? What did you say?'

'It's Wada. The man we're looking for.'

'How do you know? Even his own mother wouldn't recognise him with that face,' said Rafiq.

Ibrahim pointed to the man's right hand. Against the cold, white skin the blue tattoo of two crossed swords was clearly visible. Their search was over.

CHAPTER 26

Rafiq and Ibrahim stopped outside the apothecary's shop. They had wrapped Wada's body in a blanket and tied it to the back of Talib's horse.

'I'll wait here. Go inside and get your father,' said Rafiq.

Ibrahim was glad that his great-uncle was there; he could never have managed without him. His first instinct when he saw the body, even before he realised it was Wada, was to run away and leave it to the buzzards. He knew that was bad. Everyone deserved a proper burial. But the thought of touching it and trying to identify it, filled him with dread. Luckily Rafiq was not so squeamish. He had Wada's body out of the water and wrapped in a dry blanket before Ibrahim knew what was happening.

He opened the door carefully and looked into the shop; his father was serving a customer, a rather fat Jewish woman buying perfume.

'As-salama alaykum, my son. I'll be with you in a moment,' he said.

Once he'd finished and his contented customer had left, smelling strongly of Damask rose oil, he came outside to greet them. 'As-salama alaykum, and thank you for coming,' he said to Rafiq. 'Has Ibrahim explained our problem?'

'Yes, although I think to call it a problem underestimates the gravity of it, nephew.'

'Indeed. But why are we talking out here? Come inside. I will call Basma to make you some tea. You must be exhausted after your long journey.'

'Thank you, but we can't at the moment.' Rafiq pointed to the bundle on the back of Talib's mare. 'First I must take this to the quaid and then I must find Talib.'

'What is it?' asked Makoud, looking puzzled.

'It's him, Baba. We found him,' whispered Ibrahim. 'It's Wada.'

'You've killed him? He was the only one who could help Umar and you've killed him?'

'No, nephew. He was dead when we found him. Someone had smashed in his skull. We've just brought him back.'

'Are you sure it's him?'

'There's no doubt, Baba. He has the tattoo on his hand.'

'Oh no. I can't believe this is happening. What will Umar do now? They'll never let him go,' cried Makoud. Ibrahim had never seen his father so distraught. 'Maybe you're mistaken. Maybe it's not him. Remember what Talib said, lots of Christian soldiers have the same tattoo.'

'Baba. It's him. It's Wada. Someone killed him and left him in the mountains for the wolves to eat.'

'And they didn't make a very good job of it, which was lucky for us. We could have continued to scour the country for him for days and we'd never have found him. The violent storm we had two days ago must have washed his body into the main river and then he drifted downstream.'

'So he's not been dead very long?' asked Makoud.

'No, three days, four at the most.'

'He must have been killed the very same night we spoke to him,' said Ibrahim. 'Someone saw us talking to him in the tavern. Talib said that when he went back to look for Wada, somebody was lurking in the alleyway but it was too dark to see him clearly. He thought he was going to be attacked but in the end the man ran off.' He felt himself grow cold as he said it. Were he and Talib in danger?

'Stay here, Ibrahim. I'll find Talib and let him know about Wada. In the meantime, you be careful. Someone is going to a lot of trouble to get rid of any witnesses and as far as I can see that includes you, Talib and Umar.'

'We have to find the killer before he murders anyone else,' said Ibrahim.

'Yes, but not tonight. I'll bring Talib back here and we'll talk some more. We are up against a formidable foe and we need to be careful. All of us.'

'You're right. But I must let Bakr and Avi know we've found Wada; they've been making enquiries amongst the merchants and the seamen,' said Makoud.

'Avi I've heard you speak of often, but Bakr? Who is he?' asked Rafiq.

'He wants to marry Aisha,' said Ibrahim in an offhand way.

He saw Rafiq's eyebrows shoot up in surprise. 'Well that's interesting. You must tell me more about this man when I return this evening.'

*

Talib couldn't get the skinny man's original suggestion out of his mind. He may have said it in jest and it may have been quickly dismissed by the cook, but nevertheless it had the makings of a good plan. If he could get a message to al-Azdi and tempt him to come out of the alcázar then they could kidnap him and question him. And if the maids knew of any reason in his past why he might have had a reason to poison the khalifa then that would prove he had motive. At the very least they could prove to the quaid that he was a suspect, even if they couldn't get him to confess.

He wondered if Ibrahim had returned with his great-uncle. Personally he couldn't see what the old man would be able to do to help but Umar's father seemed to have great faith in his influence. Maybe he was just clutching at straws but the way things were at the moment, any assistance was welcome.

There's someone here to see you, Talib,' said one of the soldiers.

'Who is it?'

'He didn't give a name but he said it's important.'

Talib buckled on his sword and put his cloak around his shoulders; he didn't go anywhere nowadays without a weapon.

'Yes?' he said, stepping out of the Dar al-Jund and looking at the grey-haired old man who was holding Talib's horse by the reins; there was what looked like a body slung across her back. 'You wanted to speak to me?'

'I'm Umar's great-uncle,' said Rafiq.

'As-salama alaykum, sayyad. I am pleased to meet you. But where is Ibrahim? Is he all right?'

'Ibrahim is with his father. I have come to tell you he's back in Malaqah and wants to speak to you this evening. Can you get away?'

'Yes, that's no problem,' Talib said, greatly relieved that nothing had happened to Ibrahim. 'But was it necessary to come yourself? A message would have been enough.'

'We've found the man you were looking for, Talib,' said Rafiq.

'That's wonderful news. Where is he?'

Rafiq placed his hand on the bundle slung across his horse. 'No, it's not wonderful,' he said. 'Wada's dead. But at least we know that there's no point chasing all over the country looking for him, now.'

Talib listened as he explained how they had found him, quite by chance, and now Rafiq wanted to hand his body over to the quaid. 'Are you sure that's him?' he asked, pointing to the body.

Rafiq pulled back the blanket so that Wada's right hand hung down. 'Is that the tattoo you saw?' he asked.

'It looks like it. Let me see his face.'

'You won't recognise him from his face; it's been beaten to a pulp.'

Talib noticed the dark brown stain on the blanket which at first he thought was dirt but now could see was dried blood.

'Are you sure it's him?' he repeated. 'It could be any Christian soldier.'

'Bit of a coincidence, don't you think?' said Rafiq. 'He disappears after speaking to you and Ibrahim and then a body with the same tattoo and the head caved in, turns up a dozen Arab miles from Malaqah. I'd say it was him.'

'Was he wearing the uniform of the Palace Guards?' asked Talib.

'No. In fact he was wearing only a thin tunic and an old djellaba. It was as if someone had stolen his clothes. Even his boots. But whether it's him or not, I'd like to get rid of this corpse as soon as possible. It's starting to stink. It's time he was in the ground,' said Rafiq.

'Of course.' Talib hesitated. Who should he speak to? They could take the body to the muhtasib but then they would have to explain how they knew who he was. The muhtasib might even arrest them. 'I'll speak to our nazir. He'll know what to do. Just wait here; I won't be a minute,' he said and rushed back into the Dar al-Jund to find the nazir.

Two witnesses were now dead and another in gaol, falsely accused of murder; this was getting out of hand. Was the murderer following them? Did he know they were investigating the khalifa's death? If so, then they were all in danger. Now he was certain that the man lurking in the shadows outside the tavern that night was the man they were after.

A few minutes later he rejoined Rafiq who was waiting patiently with the horses.

'You're sure it's the same man?' the nazir asked, as he followed Talib outside.

'Yes, sayyad. May I introduce you to Umar's great-uncle Captain Rafiq ibn Makoud.'

'As-salama alaykum, yes, we met before, when you brought Umar his magnificent horse.'

Rafiq nodded in recognition and dismounted. 'Wa alaykum e-salam, 'he replied. 'This time I have brought you the body of a man we think is the palace guard, Wada. I have no other name for him but I believe he can be identified by the tattoo on his right hand. I found this man when I was on my way to Malaqah to visit my nephew.' Talib noticed he didn't mention Ibrahim had been with him.

The nazir pulled back the blanket and gave a shudder. 'Well he's dead all right. What a mess. Someone didn't want him to be recognised, did they?'

'We think he'd been stripped of his uniform,' said Talib.

'That could have been bandits,' said Rafiq. 'I don't know if it was an attempt to hide his identity, but it's a possibility.'

'That's the problem; there are too many possibilities. What we need is proof if we are to get Umar out of gaol,' said the nazir. 'Well, leave this with me. I will speak to the quaid and see what he says.'

'The body?' asked Rafiq.

'Yes, that too. I will have it buried, once the quaid has seen it.' He hesitated. 'This Wada wasn't a Muslim, was he?'

'No, sayyad. He was a Christian, but not a very religious one, I believe,' said Talib.

'Good. So we know what to do with the body.' He signalled for one of his squad to come over. 'Help this soldier take the body into the Dar al-Jund.'

As Talib and the soldier lifted the body down from Talib's horse, the nazir turned to Rafiq and asked, 'Will you be staying in Malaqah for some time?'

'Yes, I will be at my nephew's house until this matter is resolved.'

'Good. I will contact you there. I'm sure the quaid will want to speak to you in person.'

'Ma'a salama,' Rafiq said, mounting his horse once more and turning in the direction of the city.

*

Aisha can't stop thinking about Bakr. She was so surprised to see him come into the shop and say he wanted to help Umar; she thought that when he knew her brother was in prison he would no longer want anything to do with her but he seemed as anxious to prove Umar's innocence as they did. She had liked his family, especially his children. It was sad that they had lost their mother at such a young age and that poor little Naila had never known her mother at all; that must be awful, to not have even a single memory of your mother. She sighed when she thought how her own little Imran had never had a chance to know his father

When all this was behind them and Umar was safe, she would seriously consider Bakr's offer; she could do so much worse and it would be good for her children to have a father again.

She could hear voices in the shop, so she crept down the stairs to see if there was any news. Her father was talking to Rafiq and Bakr while Talib and Ibrahim listened intently.

'Baba, do you have news? Has anything happened?' she asked, knowing that in the circumstances, her father would forgive the interruption.

'Aisha, my child, come here. Bakr was just about to tell us what he's been able to find out.'

Bakr smiled at her and said, 'As-salama alaykum, Aisha.'

'Wa alaykum e-salam, ibn Assam,' she said, demurely. For the first time she felt shy in his presence; maybe it was because Baba and great-uncle Rafiq were looking at her and smiling—in their minds they had her married already.

Bakr turned back to the men and said, 'From what you've told me, I now understand why nobody in any of the ports had seen anything of Wada; he was laying low. He never left the city.'

'So that night, he either decided to go north and his killer followed him or he was murdered when he left the tavern and the assassin took his body into the mountains to dispose of it,' said Rafiq.

'Yes,' said Talib and told them about the hooded figure outside the tavern. 'I should have chased after him.'

'It could have been anyone,' said Rafiq. 'And he might not have been alone. You did well to scare him off.'

'Either way, nobody had seen Wada down at the harbour,' continued Bakr, 'Although he was known by quite a few of the seamen, none of them thought him capable of murder but they were all agreed on how avaricious he was; they said he would do almost anything for a handful of silver. So, as I've said, I found out nothing new about him but my enquiries were not entirely useless. The captain of a qarib, whom I have known for many years, tells me that he has been told to take a very important passenger to Sebta.'

'And?'

'He doesn't know the name of the passenger, but he has been told to sail at night and keep close to the coast.'

'So who do you think it is?' asked Makoud. 'And what has it to with us?'

'Maybe nothing at all, but the order came from the grand vizier, ibn Baqanna.'

'The captain thought it was very strange that they were ordered to travel at night; the coast is rocky and difficult to navigate in the dark. The journey would be much safer and faster by day.'

'So he is smuggling someone out of Malaqah; someone who knows too much?'

'Why not kill him?'

'Because he's useful to him,' said Aisha, without thinking.

Bakr smiled at her and said, 'Yes, indeed. It's someone he wants to keep alive but he doesn't want him talking to anyone.'

'So when is the captain picking up this mysterious passenger?' asked Makoud.

'Tomorrow night, as soon as the sun goes down.'

'I know who it is,' said Talib. 'It's al-Azdi. It has to be. He's ibn Baqanna's servant now. But why is he sending him to Sebta?'

'So he doesn't talk. Once they've dealt with Umar, they'll bring him back to Malaqah,' said Rafiq.

Aisha felt faint when she heard his words. This was no game; her brother's life was at stake.

'It has to be more than that,' she said. 'He's only a servant. I can't imagine the grand vizier protecting him. No, he's sending him to Sebta for a reason.'

'To murder someone else?' said Talib.

'That's where Idris I's young nephews are. He sent them there after their father died,' said Makoud.

'So you think he intends to assassinate them?' asked Ibrahim. 'Is that why he wants it kept quiet?'

'Hey. Slow down. We're getting carried away with theories. What we need is some facts,' said Rafiq. 'First of all, why would he want to murder the khalifa's nephews? What's his motive?'

'Hassan will inherit the throne when he comes of age. His uncle Idris is only khalifa until then,' said Makoud. He smiled. 'One of the advantages of being the closest apothecary to the alcazaba is that I hear all the gossip.'

'So what else do the gossips say?' asked Rafiq.

'They say that it was really ibn Baqanna's idea to send the previous grand vizier to Sebta with the children, so that he could replace him. They say he is a devious man and the khalifa does nothing without his advice. Apparently they were very close when Idris was governor of Sebta.'

'So you think the khalifa knows about this as well?' asked Rafiq.

Makoud threw his hands in the air and said, 'No. No. I'm not saying that, ammu. I pray to Allah that the khalifa is not involved in a plot to murder his own nephews. That would be too terrible.'

'What a short memory you have, Makoud. Worse things than that happened in Qurtuba, when you were a lad.'

'Maybe. But that was civil war. We are at peace now, and this is Malaqah. I don't think the khalifa is capable of murdering children.'

'But his grand vizier is?'

'Oh, I don't know. Maybe. Like you said, this is all supposition.'

'Tomorrow the quaid wants to speak to us; we are to go to the Dar al-Jund after morning prayers,' said Rafiq. 'We will tell him all we know.'

'Do you want me to come?' asked Bakr.

'No, I think it's best if he doesn't know that you're involved, in case it all goes wrong. And you too, Ibrahim, stay here and look after the shop for your father. Talib, Makoud and I will go. I think we have enough information now to persuade him that Umar is not involved in this. I hope so, anyway.'

Aisha saw her brother turn away to hide his disappointment. But ammu was right; if things went wrong they didn't want Ibrahim involved as well.

'What about al-Azdi? Will you tell the quaid of our suspicions?' asked Bakr.

'Yes. I will suggest he sends some men along to investigate. I'm sure they can come up with some pretext. Rumours of smuggling or pirates. There are plenty of excuses for boarding a suspicious looking vessel, and leaving after sunset is suspicious in itself.'

'Take care. There's a dangerous killer out there and he won't stop until he has got rid of all the witnesses,' said Bakr. 'Now I must get back home, my sisters will be wondering where I am. Good luck tomorrow. If you need any more help, just come to the shipyard. And if you want to speak to the captain, I can take you to him.'

'Thank you, Bakr. You are a good man to take so much trouble to help our family,' said Makoud, embracing him.

'I hope one day, your family will be mine too,' he replied, smiling at Aisha. 'Ma'a salama, my friend.'

Aisha felt her heart race when she heard his words.

CHAPTER 27

Makoud had hardly slept all night, unlike his uncle who had snored happily in the next room until the call of the imam had eventually woken him from his deep sleep. Now they were standing by the Boveda Gate, waiting for Talib; it was shortly after sunrise and already the sun was staining the clouds a deep pink. He rubbed his hands together to warm them.

'Are you sure we're doing the right thing, ammu?' asked Makoud. 'What if the quaid doesn't believe us? He might think we're all involved in the conspiracy.'

'He might but then he'd need proof. I can't see him arresting a retired soldier and a successful apothecary, can you? What reason do we have to lie to him?'

'To free Umar?'

'Well there is that, but I have the feeling that the quaid is not planning to make a scapegoat of Umar; he just wants enough proof so that he can release him without breaking the law. At the moment all we have is a number of damning coincidences; not least of which is that al-Azdi was in the royal physician's house the night he was murdered. Personally that would be enough for me, but I think the quaid would prefer a confession.'

'I can't see that happening.'

'Ah, here is our young soldier. As-salama alaykum, Talib.'

'Wa alaykum e-salam, sayyad. I've spoken to the nazir and he says he will accompany us to the quaid,' said Talib, chewing his bottom lip, nervously.

'Very well, lead the way, lad,' said Rafiq. Makoud was pleased that his uncle had slipped so easily into the role of leader; he would know how to talk to these men much better than he could. He spoke their language.

To be honest, Makoud was rather overwhelmed by the alcazaba. He lived in its shadow but he'd never entered inside; now he could see what an impenetrable fortress it really was. There were soldiers stationed along the ramparts and at every gate, others training on the parade ground and everywhere he looked there were the armaments of war. They followed Talib through the twisting passages of the alcazaba, then climbed up the coracha and into the Jbel-Faro where the nazir was waiting for them. Makoud looked around him; it was impressive. From the walls of the fortress he could see far into the distance in all directions; any enemy would be spotted long before they arrived at the gates. And as below, there were armed soldiers everywhere and even more evidence of the strength of their army; a great wooden trebuchet stood in the corner by the gate, alongside giant cauldrons, battering rams, wooden ladders for scaling walls. The sound of the blacksmith's hammer rang out across the fortress, as he forged and repaired horseshoes, swords, daggers, lances, knives, arrow heads, shields, weapons and much more. Reluctantly Makoud dragged his attention away from all the activity, from the saddlers, the grooms, from the forge belching black smoke into the air, and turned to greet the nazir.

'Sayyad, this is Umar's father,' said Talib.

'As-salama alaykum, sayyad,' said Makoud, wondering if that was the right way to address his son's commander.

'And his great-uncle you have already met.'

'Yes, indeed. Thank you for coming here today. The quaid inspected the corpse you brought yesterday and agrees that it could well be the body of the man you were looking for.'

'Good. I hope someone's buried it by now,' said Rafiq.

'Yes, we handed it over to a Christian priest to deal with. But I hear you come with more news.'

'Yes, but not proof. Not yet,' said Rafiq. He began to tell the nazir about their suspicions.

'So you don't know for certain who the man is that will be slipping out of Malaqah under cover of darkness?' the nazir asked, stroking his beard and looking from one to the other.

'No, but it could be al-Azdi. After all it was ibn Baqanna who paid for the qarib. Why would he do that?' said Talib. 'If he was going to Sebta himself, he would go in daylight on the royal caravel and not slip away like a common thief.'

'Why indeed, soldier. It is a mystery as you rightly say.'

'And now we know that al-Azdi was with the royal physician the night he was murdered. His servant saw him but didn't think it important enough to tell us.'

'Interesting. So the evidence is mounting but is it enough?' he pulled at his beard, then said, 'Well now let's go and speak to the quaid. He's expecting us and he doesn't like to be kept waiting.'

*

Makoud had already decided that it was better to let Rafiq speak first and wasn't surprised when the quaid ignored him and Talib and directed all his questions to the old soldier.

'As-salama alaykum, soldier. Your reputation precedes you.' he said, embracing Rafiq like a long-lost friend. 'Your successes in battle are well known; even our young officers know your name. And to think I have the opportunity to meet you in person.'

'I was lucky to survive, sayyad. There were many who didn't,' said Rafiq. 'Civil war is brutal.'

'True. Now tell me, what have you found out?' asked the quaid, getting straight to the point.

Makoud listened while Rafiq went through everything they knew. When it was all laid out it didn't seem enough to convince the quaid of Umar's innocence. He felt his heart sink; they were never going to get his son released.

'So you see, sayyad, when you ask yourself the motive behind these killings it all goes back to the death of Yahya I,' Rafiq continued. 'The question is, who wanted him dead? When we know that we will know who was behind the death of the royal physician and a man whose only crime as far as we can see, was buying the poison that may have killed the khalifa. Now we have the possibility of another crime being committed. What if it was al-Azdi who poisoned the khalifa? On whose orders did he commit this crime? And did the doctor suspect him? Is that why he was killed? And is he the mysterious passenger leaving Malaqah tonight? If he is, then why is he being sent to Sebta? Is it for his own safety? Would a grand vizier go to all that bother for a slave? It seems strange to me. Or, and this is more worrying, is it to commit another crime?'

The quaid said nothing at first then he stood up and began to pace around the room. He looked very concerned. 'I understand your logic, Captain ibn Makoud, but there are too many probabilities in your story. I can't release Umar on the strength of probabilities. If you had brought me Wada alive, instead of dead, we could have questioned him. As for the physician, we only have Umar's word for his story and that has been discredited by the man's daughter. I agree that the fact that al-Azdi was also present that night, shines a different light on events, but it still isn't proof that he killed him. You see my predicament. There are no witnesses to any of these murders.'

'But there is still al-Azdi. You could question him,' said Talib.

The quaid looked at him and said, 'Yes, but on what grounds? Bring me at least some motive for his crimes and I will question him. In the meantime get me more information about the whereabouts of this qarib and I will send some men to investigate. If they find that al-Azdi is aboard I will give them orders to arrest him.' He paused and tugged at his beard in frustration. 'You realise that I can't confront the khalifa or his grand vizier about this directly? At least not until we know that neither of them are involved.'

Rafiq nodded. 'Yes, I know that, but I'm sure if we can get al-Azdi to talk to us, we will convince you that Umar is innocent.'

'Bring me something more substantial and I will do all I can to get your nephew released,' the quaid said, standing up. The meeting was over.

The despondent trio made their way back towards the Boveda Gate, but before they had gone very far, the skinny under cook came hurrying towards them.

'Talib, Talib, a moment,' he called.'

'What is it? Have you found out something?' asked Talib, motioning for the others to wait.

'I don't know if it's of any use, but yes, the serving maids had a lot to say about your friend al-Azdi.'

'Tell me.'

'Not here. I'll meet you outside in a few minutes. Wait for me by the apothecary's shop.'

'That's convenient,' said Makoud, with a smile. 'I take it he doesn't know I am the apothecary.'

Talib shook his head.

'What does he want?' asked Rafiq.

'It sounds as though he has some news about al-Azdi's past. I thought it might strengthen our case if we knew a bit more about this man. Is he the sort of man who would murder a khalifa? And if so, why? There has to be a reason. Maybe our friend has found our motive for us.'

'So who is this friend of yours?' asked Makoud.

Talib was slightly embarrassed to admit that he didn't actually know his name, but that they had got to know him when they were part of the campaign against Qarmuña. 'He works in the kitchens,' he said.

'Can we trust him?' asked Rafiq.

'I think so. As much as we can trust anyone at the moment.'

They had barely reached the shop when the under cook reappeared, looking hot and slightly agitated.

'Can we go in the shop?' he asked, looking behind him.

'Of course. Come in,' said Makoud, locking the door once they were all inside. 'Please sit down. I will ask my wife to bring us some tea.'

'No, no. Nothing for me, thank you. I will just tell you what I've found out and then I must go, before I am missed,' said the under cook.

'Well?' asked Talib, looking anxiously at the man. What had he uncovered?

'As I said, I don't know if it's of any use, but I thought it strange. Al-Azdi served the old khalifa for many years, since he was a young lad. He started working for him during a campaign near Qurtubah—Yahya was only a prince at that time, and quite an arrogant one, by all accounts—when al-Azdi, his sister and a dozen other people from his village were enlisted to work in the royal household as servants.'

'That's not unusual,' said Rafiq.

'No, I agree. But al-Azdi's sister was very beautiful and when the prince saw her, he wanted her for his harem.'

'Again, that's the sort of thing that often happens.'

'But his sister was about to be married that very week. The bride price had been paid, the wedding arranged, the guests invited. All this was explained to the prince but he wouldn't listen; he was determined to have her.'

'And you think that's sufficient reason for al-Azdi to poison the khalifa?' asked Ibrahim, who had joined the little group.

'Maybe not on its own, but what happened later gave him reason.' They all stared at the assistant chef, waiting to hear what came next. 'When the campaign ended, instead of taking her back to his harem, he threw her out. Told her to go back to her fiancé. The poor girl was so humiliated that she hung herself.'

'By the love of Allah, that is a terrible story,' said Makoud. 'Suicide is strictly forbidden; it means she will be barred from Paradise for all eternity. No wonder her brother was upset.'

'Whether that means he wanted to get his revenge on Yahya, or not, I don't know,' said the under cook. 'But I thought you'd like to know.'

'Indeed. Thank you, friend. This might be just what was missing from our puzzle,' said Talib.

'I hope this helps to get Umar released. Now I must go. Let me know what happens with your investigation; I promised the kitchen maids that I'd tell them what you find out. Oh, and by the way, one of them has said she would be happy to take a note to al-Azdi for you.'

'If our suspicions are right, there won't be any need for that, but thank you anyway,' said Talib.

Makoud unlocked the door and the man slipped out into the street and hurried back to the alcazaba.

'Well,' said Rafiq. 'That's very interesting. So our suspect does have a motive, after all.'

'Yes, but why wait all these years to do anything about it?' asked Makoud.

'Because someone paid him to do it. The money alone was probably not enough to make al-Azdi murder his master, but coupled with the hunger for revenge that has been growing inside him all these years, it was just what he'd been waiting for.'

'Revenge? Of course. There is nothing more powerful than the thirst for revenge,' said Rafiq.

'So, do you think that whoever is behind this, knew about al-Azdi's sister?' asked Ibrahim.

'If he did, then it narrows it down to only a few people. It's not the sort of thing that families talk about.'

'His brother probably knew. They were very close when they were younger, so they say,' said Talib.

'It would be interesting to know who was on that campaign with them,' said Rafiq. 'I'll see what I can find out.'

'And who was the girl's fiancé? Maybe it was Wada,' said Ibrahim.

'He did ramble on about some woman he was going to marry. You think that's his connection to al-Azdi?' asked Talib.

'Could be. So what do we do now?' asked Ibrahim.

'You can open up the shop,' said his father. 'We need to talk to Bakr's friend, the captain.

*

Bakr was in the shipyard working on his new plans when they arrived. Immediately he sprang up and went to greet them.

'As-salama alaykum, friends,' said Bakr. 'So what did the quaid say?'

'He'll send some men to see if it's al-Azdi on the ship, tonight,' said Talib, excitedly.

'Can you give us the exact location?' asked Rafiq.

'I'll speak to the captain, right away.' He rolled up his plans and tied them up with a piece of twine. 'You come with me, soldier and then you can take the information straight back to your commander, and make sure he knows that the captain is not involved in anything underhand. My reputation will be destroyed if they arrest him.' He pulled his djellaba around his shoulders and said to Rafiq, 'Let me know what the outcome is. I hope he's the man you're after.'

Talib looked at Rafiq. 'What will you do now?' he asked.

'I'll go back to Makoud and wait. What else can we do?'

Talib felt disappointed; he'd hoped they would at least go along and see al-Azdi being arrested.

'Come on soldier, I've got a lot of work to get through today,' said Bakr.

Talib followed him out of the shipyard and along the beach towards the harbour. The man they were looking for was sitting with a group of fishermen, mending their nets. One of the fishermen, a young lad, looked up at him and said, 'Hey, aren't you Umar's friend?'

'Yes,' said Talib. 'Who are you?'

'I'm Dirar, his youngest brother. Do you have any news of him?'

Talib shook his head. 'Not yet. Sorry.'

'It's a shameful business,' muttered his companion. 'Locking up a young soldier like that. Just looking for someone to pin it on. They don't care who killed that doctor as long as they have someone to blame.'

The other fishermen nodded in agreement.

'Did you want me?' asked the sea captain, looking at Bakr.

'Yes, can we have a word?'

'Sorry mates, I'll have to leave your delightful company,' the captain said with a grin. 'I've got work to do.'

While he and Bakr walked along the jetty, Talib squatted down beside Dirar. 'We think we know who killed the royal physician, but it's just a question of proving it,' he whispered. 'Once we have proof, your brother will be free.'

'Is there anything I can do to help?' Dirar asked.

'Maybe there is. Will you be working tonight?'

'Yes, I go out with the fishing boats every night. Why?'

'What time is that?'

'Usually quite late. A couple of hours after sunset, I guess.'

'Very well, I'll meet you down here at dusk. Don't tell your father.'

'All right. But why?'

'You'll find out later. Now I must go.' Talib got up and moved away from the fisherman just before Bakr returned.

'Come on, soldier,' he said, striding back towards his shipyard, with Talib hurrying behind him.

As soon as they were out of earshot of the fishermen, Bakr said, 'The captain has been instructed to moor the boat in the estuary of the Guadalhorce. The passenger will arrive immediately after the sun sets, and the captain's to sail south along the coast and take him to Sebta. Then he is to return, and to mention it to no-one.'

'Does he know who the passenger is, yet?'

'No. Now you know what you have to say to the quaid?'

Talib nodded.

'And don't forget about telling him that his soldiers mustn't arrest the captain. He is innocent in all this.'

'I won't forget.'

'Right. Get along with you. Let me know how it goes.'

'I will, Bakr. Thanks for your help.'

An unease was growing in Talib's mind. Wada was dead, murdered before he could incriminate anyone. If al-Azdi really was involved then he was in danger too. The quaid was sending armed soldiers to arrest him tonight, but what if one of them were to kill him. He could say it had been unavoidable, that al-Azdi was trying to escape; no-one would ever know for sure what had happened in the dark.

Talib had to make sure that al-Azdi was taken alive so that he could be questioned.

CHAPTER 28

The next morning Aisha decided to go and visit Rebekah; she was feeling guilty that she had stayed away from the family for so long. The foolishness with Gideon had left her embarrassed to face them but she missed their company. When she looked back at that visit to the Jewish cemetery, she couldn't believe that she had acted so rashly; she could see more clearly than ever that she had never loved Gideon. It was her loneliness that had prompted her to act so imprudently. Now it was time to reach out to them again and to hope that they had forgiven her. Sara's wedding was in a few weeks' time and would be a good opportunity to reinforce their friendship. She had been working on a wedding gift for her and now it was almost complete.

'Are we going to see aunty Sara again?' asked Maryam.

'Yes, sweetheart. It's time we went to visit them.'

'Yes, we promised to help with sewing the squares.'

'Well maybe we can do that today,' she said knocking on the gates.

When Musif opened them, there was a look of surprise on his face. 'As-salama alaykum, sayeda. We haven't seen you, in a long time,' he said with a welcoming smile and no hint that he knew what had passed between her and the eldest son of the house. 'The ladies are sitting in the garden, as usual. Would you like me to call them?'

'No thank you, Musif, I'll make my own way there.'

Maryam was already running ahead of her and before she arrived she could hear the warm welcome her daughter was receiving. As she turned off the path, she saw Rebekah hugging Maryam and kissing her.

'Aisha, how lovely to see you. I thought you'd forgotten your friends; it's been such a long time,' she said.

They all got up to greet her and bombarded her with questions:

'How is Umar?'

'Has he been released yet?'

'What have you been doing with yourself?'

'How is his poor mother?'

Eventually Rebekah interrupted them to say, 'Enough, let our dear friend sit down and rest. She will tell us all about her brother in her own time.'

'I wish I had some good news to tell you, but so far nothing has changed. My great-uncle has come from Ardales to help secure his release, but so far has had no success,' said Aisha, her eyes filling with tears.

'Oh, my dear girl, I'm sure it will all work out. So what about you? What have you been doing with yourself?'

'Mama has a suitor,' called Maryam, who was supposed to be playing with the children but didn't like to miss out on the adults' conversation.

'What?' shrieked Sara. 'Is that true? Tell us all about him. What is he like?'

'Is he good looking?' asked one of the younger sisters.

Aisha felt herself blushing. She'd had no intention of talking about Bakr but now she had no option; they would be offended if she didn't tell them at least something about him.

'Yes, it is true but nothing has been decided yet.'

'Have you been to his home? Have you met his family?'

'Well, yes.'

'And has he spoken to your father?' asked Rebekah.

'He has. But Baba says it's my decision.'

'And you don't like him?'

'He's old and ugly,' said the young sister, looking distinctly disappointed.

'Well no, he's not really that old, but he is older than me. And he isn't ugly,' she said, surprising herself at the strength of feeling with which she gave her answer.

'Is he rich?' asked the young girl.

'I don't know. He owns a shipyard at the port and a big house, so I don't think he's poor.'

'It sounds as though you quite like him,' said Rebekah.

'I told Baba that I can't consider marriage while Umar is still in prison. He understands that. He says that Bakr is in no hurry.'

'Well, he sounds a very considerate man,' said Rebekah. 'But I wouldn't leave him waiting about too long. There'll be plenty of fathers looking for a man like that for their daughters.'

Sara was staring at her with a big smile on her face. 'Wouldn't it be lovely if we were to get married at the same time?' she said.

'Don't be silly, Sara. You'll be marrying in a synagogue,' said her sister.

'I know that, but how nice it would be if we were both married.'

Aisha had stopped listening to their chatter. She was thinking of Bakr and what Rebekah had said. The thought of him choosing someone else to marry bothered her.

CHAPTER 29

Just before the sun disappeared over the horizon, Dirar and Talib were crouched down in the reeds at the mouth of the Guadalhorce. A flock of flamingoes flew over, heading for an inland salt lake; the sinking sun caught their pink plumage as they passed, making it glow brighter than ever against the darkening sky. Suddenly a black-headed duck splashed down onto the water close by Talib, startling him; the duck gave him one look and paddled away.

The captain had sailed the qarib right into the estuary and moored it close to the bank. Talib could see him walking about the deck of the ship, waiting for his passenger. The vessel had a single mast and its sail was still furled; it was going to take him some time to set sail when the passenger arrived, leaving plenty of opportunity to intercept him. Talib noticed a movement on the opposite bank; two soldiers were crouched down in a grove of sugarcane. Were they all the quaid had sent? Surely not. And so far there was no sign of the mysterious passenger. Had something gone wrong? Had Bakr misunderstood?

'I can hear horses,' said Dirar. 'Someone is coming.'

They crept closer to the qarib, keeping low among the reeds. Talib could see that the soldiers had also heard the horses. He waited, hardly daring to breathe.

Three horsemen came into view. They pulled up along-side the qarib and one of them started to talk to the captain. Then he leaned down and gave the captain a leather pouch which he examined carefully and then slipped into his pocket; it probably contained his payment. Meanwhile one of the others dismounted; he was a tall man, who stood head and shoulders above the rest. Talib felt his heart begin to race. Was this al-Azdi? It had to be.

He nudged Dirar and whispered, 'That's him. I'm sure it is.'

'So what do we do?'

'Let's see what the soldiers do, first.'

The tall man climbed on board the qarib and while his companions rode away, the captain began preparations to set sail. As one of the sailors began to unfurl the sail, Talib and Dirar crept closer to the qarib; they wanted to be able to jump aboard if al-Azdi tried to escape.

Suddenly the two soldiers broke their cover and ran to-wards the ship.

'Stop. We have orders to search this ship for illegal car-go,' one of them shouted, clambering aboard. 'Bring all your men up here on deck. And put your weapons down where we can see them.' He pointed at the tall man. 'You too.'

The qarib only had a handful of crew members and it didn't take long to line them up in front of the soldiers. Tal-ib kept his eyes on the man they thought was al-Azdi; he was edging his way to the back of the ship.

'What are you looking for?' asked the captain.

'We'll know when we see it,' said one of the soldiers.

They began moving among the men on the deck, peer-ing at them and questioning them.

'Why don't they arrest him?' asked Dirar. 'What are they waiting for?'

Talib was asking himself the same question. As each minute went by, al-Azdi was edging closer and closer to the back of the ship; any moment now he would make a run for it, and if he got into that dense grove of sugarcane they'd never find him. Talib pulled out his sword and whispered, 'Come on. We've got to stop him.'

Dirar picked up a stout stick and together they crept closer to the ship; soon they were right against the bow. If he jumped off, they would have him.

'I think we need to look below deck,' said one of the soldiers.

'But there's nothing there,' said the captain, obviously confused at the soldiers' attitude. 'Everyone's here, on deck.'

This was al-Azdi's opportunity; with the soldiers out of sight, he leapt over the side of the qarib but instead of landing in shallow water, he landed almost on top of Talib and Dirar.

Immediately Talib's sword was at his throat. 'You're under arrest,' he said, certain this was the man whom Wada had told them about.

'What the hell are you doing, you miserable little boy? Get out of my way,' the man snarled at Talib, stepping towards him, a dagger in his hand and his arm raised to strike.

But before he could do so, a look of astonishment came over his face and he collapsed at Talib's feet. Dirar was standing behind him, a big grin on his face. 'That felt good,' he said, swinging the stick. 'I hope I haven't killed him.'

'I hope so too. Quick, we must tie him up before he comes round.' Talib pulled off his leather belt and tied al-Azdi's arms behind his back with it.

'What are you up to?' asked the captain, leaning over the side of the ship.

'We've got him. He was trying to escape. Will you call the soldiers,' said Dirar.

The captain hesitated a minute then said, 'No, lad. I'm not sure that's a good idea. I can't say I trust those two. They were looking everywhere but where they were supposed to; I think they wanted him to get away. You get him out of here and I'll keep them busy. Here, Farid, give them a hand.'

One of the sailors jumped into the water beside them and dragged al-Azdi's body further up onto the bank, out of sight of the qarib. He then took off his scarf and tied it tightly round al-Azdi's mouth. 'You got a horse?' he asked.

'Yes,' said Talib, relieved that he'd brought his mare with him.

'Well, wait here until the soldiers have gone and then sling him on the back of your horse and take him wherever it is you're planning on taking him. And I should tie his feet together, too. He seems a slippery customer to me.'

'I will. Dirar give me your belt.' He pulled the leather belt as tightly as he could around the man's ankles and propped him up. 'You keep an eye on him. I'm going to see what the soldiers are doing.'

He crept back to the water's edge and lay there, half-submerged until he heard the soldiers ride away. Moments later the qarib set sail, heading back for the open sea and Sebta.

'They've gone,' he whispered to Dirar. 'I'll get the horse and we can take him back to Malaqah.'

'But what will we do with him? The soldiers were supposed to arrest him; that's what you said. Why didn't they?' asked Dirar, greatly confused.

'I don't know. All I know is that it was a good job we went along to check on them otherwise he'd have got away. But the question is, who gave them their orders?'

'The quaid?'

'I don't think so, but then I don't know who we can trust anymore. I'll take him back to the Dar al-Jund and you run home and tell Rafiq what has happened.'

'Wouldn't it be safer to take him to our house?'

'I couldn't put your family in danger like that; we don't know who's behind this. No, I will have to trust the nazir; I'm certain there's no-one in our squad who would betray us. I'll come and see you later.'

CHAPTER 30

Umar stared at a tiny patch of sunlight on the wall of his cell; it would not be there for long. Soon the sun would pass overhead and no more rays of sunshine would be able to enter the dark hole that had become his home; he would be left with the uniform gloom that was the only distinction he had between day and night. He had lost track of how long he'd been in there. Was it days? Weeks? Months? He had no idea. At first he'd started scratching a mark on the cell wall for each day that passed, but then he stopped. It did nothing to hearten him when he felt the line of scratches grow longer and yet still there was no news. They had forgotten him. They had been unable to prove his innocence and so he was now doomed to spend the rest of his days in this infernal stinking cell. He no longer prayed to Allah. What was the point? He wasn't listening to him. He was neither going to save him nor take him to paradise; he had left him to rot in hell. What had he done to deserve it? All he'd wanted was for the truth to come out. Surely Allah would understand that? Allah knew he was innocent. But even as he thought it, he knew that innocence was no safeguard against evil. Didn't innocent children die? Some too young to have even had bad thoughts. They died in the moment they were born, they died of plague and sickness, they died of hunger and they died when barbaric soldiers slaughtered them. If Allah wouldn't save them then why would he save Umar?

At night he slept fitfully but when he did, his sleep was filled with dreams, images of Ardales, of when he was a young boy, of playing in the fields with his brothers and Daud. Sometimes Daud came alone and talked to him, just like he used to do; he told him to be strong. He told him that paradise was not ready for him yet; he told him not to give up the will to live, and when Umar woke the next morning, for a brief space of time, he felt stronger. He felt that his life was not over and he would survive this. But as the day moved on and the gloom turned to blackness, when the stench of despair again filled his nostrils, that fleeting hope slipped through his fingers and he was once more trapped in a black hole.

What was happening? Where were his family? Were they safe? Had anyone found out about the wormwood and his father's involvement? Would he ever get out of here? Questions ran round and round in his head like demented bees. If only someone would come and answer them.

He heard the gaoler's slow, heavy steps come along the passage, the pauses as he stopped at each cell and the rattle of his keys as he unlocked each cell door to push in the inmate's meal. He counted them aloud, so that he could hear the sound of his own voice, 'One, two, three, four, five, six, seven.' He stopped. It was his turn. The door creaked as it swung open and his plate of greasy food was pushed inside. 'Hello,' he called. 'Have you any news for me? Has the quaid sent word about my release? When am I getting out of here?' His voice grew shrill and suddenly he was banging on the door like a madman, his food scattered over the filthy floor. 'Let me out of here. Let me out,' he screamed.

But the gaoler's only response was to lock the door and continue delivering the food to the other inmates.

'Shut up, you madman. You're never getting out of here. None of us are. The only place you're going is to meet your executioner. If you're lucky,' shouted the man in the next cell.

Umar collapsed on the floor and wept. It was true. When was he going to accept it?

*

Talib had thrown a blanket over the unconscious al-Azdi, so that nobody could identify him. He walked his horse calmly into the alcazaba, steadying the swaying body with his hand.

'As-salama alaykum, Talib,' said the sentry on the main gate, a young recruit who had enlisted at the same time as Umar and Talib. 'How are things going in the jinetes?'

Talib kept walking, as he replied, 'Good. I'm enjoying it. And you?'

'Yes. Bit boring this guard duty, though. Nothing seems to happen. What's that you've got there?'

'This? Nothing really. Just a drunk soldier I'm taking back to the squad. Can't stop to chat because I'm late already.' At that moment al-Azdi let out a loud groan.

The sentry grinned, 'Sounds like he's waking up.'

'Yes, and I don't want to face him alone. He's an ugly brute when he's got a hangover.'

'Maybe we can meet up one evening?' suggested the sentry.

'Yes, good idea. Compare notes, like.'

'Yes. Ma'a salama.' Someone else was approaching the gate and the sentry had no more time for gossip.

Talib's heart was racing but he continued to walk at the same, measured pace until he was round the corner and out of sight, then he leapt up behind al-Azdi and cantered along the coracha and into the Dar al-Jund. By now, al-Azdi was squirming and trying to free himself from his bonds. Talib was tempted to give him another bang on the head, to quieten him down, but he didn't want to end up accidentally killing him, so he just swore at him and threatened to cut off one of his hands if he didn't shut up. It worked and his prisoner lay quiet.

'Have you seen the nazir?' he asked one of the soldiers in his squad.

'He's in the stables.'

Talib dismounted and led his horse through the Dar al-Jund to the stables. Sure enough, there was the nazir, brushing his grey mare.

'As-salama alaykum, soldier. What have you there?' he called, putting away his curry brush and walking towards him. 'Have you heard the news? The man you were after has escaped. The soldiers failed to arrest him. Personally I can't understand how six armed men failed to arrest one servant, unless he was pre-warned that they were coming.'

'Six men? Sayyad, I need to talk to you. It's urgent.'

'Very well. Speak up, soldier.'

Talib explained the events of that evening and how only two soldiers had been there, and they had made no attempt to apprehend ibn Baqanna's servant.

'So, you think they were ordered to let him escape?'

'I do. And why were there only two of them? We never go out in twos; there's always at least six of us to make an arrest.'

'But I myself, heard the quaid give the order for six men to go. Someone must have countermanded it.' The nazir, stroked his beard. 'This is not good. If someone higher than the quaid is countermanding his orders then we will get nowhere with this investigation.'

Al-Azdi, who no doubt could hear their conversation, began to squirm and groan. The nazir pulled the blanket off the wriggling figure, then looked at Talib. 'Well?'

'We couldn't let him escape. We would never have caught him again,' said Talib. 'I've brought him to you, because I don't know where else to take him.'

'I don't know whether to congratulate you, soldier, or to curse you. If this man is being protected then it could mean the end of our careers at the least, or two more dead bodies at the worst.'

'I thought you could explain to the quaid and then he could question him,' said Talib, hoping he wasn't in too much trouble.

'Well we can't leave him here, in the open. Bring him into a stall and we'll tie him up properly. Then I'll go and talk to the quaid.'

Talib did as he said and once the prisoner was securely bound and gagged, he turned to the nazir and asked, 'What do you want me to do now?'

'Stay here and make sure no-one comes in to see him. Cover him over with that blanket again, to keep him from prying eyes. I will be back directly. If we're lucky, the quaid will question him this very night.'

Once the nazir had left, Talib closed the stable door and sat with his back against the wall, his eyes on the still figure in the corner. He had gone very quiet. What was he thinking now? He'd expected his patron to prevent his arrest but thanks to Talib's foresight the plan hadn't gone as expected. Was he expecting a rescue attempt? Talib shivered. If there was one, then they would have no hesitation in killing Talib. He drew his sword and held it across his chest. For a moment he wished Umar was there to help him. Instead, he was alone, doing this for his friend.

The quaid looked distinctly unhappy when Talib and the nazir led al-Azdi into his quarters. They sat him on the ground and untied the gag in his mouth.

'Is this who I think it is?' he said before turning to the servant and asking, 'What is your name?'

The man remained silent, sullenly looking straight in front of him.

The quaid tried a different approach. 'You look as though you've been in the wars,' he said pointing to the enormous bruise on his face and the streak of blood across his head. 'Do you want to tell me what happened?'

Al-Azdi wasn't at all as Talib had imagined. He was lean and wiry, and much taller than the average Berber—this he already knew—but his head was completely shaved and there was not a hair on his body; he wore only a simple white tunic and djellaba, and a gold ring hung from his right ear lobe. It was unusual for the palace servants to be clean shaven, unless they were eunuchs. Was this a disguise?

Still there was no answer from their prisoner; each question was received with the same stubborn silence.

'My men tell me you resisted arrest. Is that correct?' the quaid asked.

At last he looked at the quaid and snarled, 'They kidnapped me. Snatched me off that ship. My passage was paid and now the ship has sailed without me. Who's going to refund my money? Not that greedy captain. It's him you should be arresting. Not me.'

'Well, so you *can* speak,' said the quaid.

The man stared at him then spat on the floor.

'So you'd paid for your passage, did you? Where were you going, exactly?'

Al-Azdi seemed to have decided that he'd said enough and resumed staring ahead of him, his mouth clamped shut.

'Very well, if you're not going to speak to me, then I will have to answer my own questions. First of all, your name is al-Azdi and you were a personal servant to Khalifa Yahya I for many years, a trusted man who was closer to him than any of the other servants.'

Talib saw a flicker of surprise in the man's eyes. So his disguise hadn't worked that well.

'And I think you were on that ship to avoid being arrested for poisoning your master, the khalifa.'

The man's face remained impassive.

'But, we have been asking ourselves, why would a loyal and trusted servant do such a thing?'

The quaid waited for some response from the captive, but al-Azdi remained steadfastly looking at the wall in front of him, deaf to his questions.

'Then we learnt about the sad tale of his beautiful sister and we understood,' the quaid continued.

At this the prisoner turned and looked directly at the quaid. The surprise which had clearly shown on his face when he heard the quaid's words, had quickly turned to hate.

'You see we know all about your motive for poisoning Yahya I and for murdering the royal physician—a man who thought you were his friend—and even the hapless Wada. You couldn't leave any witnesses. But you know something, my good man, this all seems far too complicated for a simple man like you. You could have murdered the khalifa and then disappeared. You could have returned to your old home outside Qurtuba and nobody would have been any the wiser. The royal physician was too frightened to say anything. And who would have believed Wada? It would have remained a sad, but not unexpected death. I ask myself why you didn't do that. Why did you stay and murder two more men? I can only come up with one answer. You were obeying orders. Someone else is behind all this. Now I want you to tell me who it is. And quickly, because my patience is wearing thin.'

'I have nothing to say,' al-Azdi replied.

'Silence will not help you. We know that you committed these murders and for that you will be executed.'

It seemed that nothing would induce the prisoner to confess.

The quaid, always a good tactician had one more card to play. 'I have heard that you work for ibn Baqanna now. Maybe I should be talking to him?'

At last he received a response.

'Yes, I am the servant of the grand vizier but I will say nothing until I have seen him,' the man said and then shut his lips again in a tight line.

So that was it. They were not going to get anything more out of him without the help of the grand vizier.

'May I suggest something, quaid?' Talib said, hesitantly.

'What is it, soldier?'

'We haven't properly identified him yet. Maybe we should get someone who knows al-Azdi to confirm that it's him?

The quaid looked at the nazir and raised his eyebrows. 'You're right, soldier. Who do you suggest?'

'I know that the kitchen staff are acquainted with him. Perhaps one of them could help us?'

'Very well. Go now and see who you can find at this unearthly hour.'

Talib saluted and hurried out of the room.

'In the meantime, take him to a cell and lock him up,' the quaid ordered the soldiers standing behind him.

Al-Azdi didn't struggle as they pulled him to his feet, and walked calmly out of the room, his head held high, as if he knew there was nobody who could touch him.

Once they had gone, the quaid turned to the nazir and said, 'We need the help of someone with more authority. Tomorrow I will speak to General Rashad.'

'You're not going to speak to the grand vizier?' asked the nazir.

'No. Not yet. I don't want anyone spiriting him away before we can get him to confess all that he knows. Thanks to your prompt action, soldier, we have him locked up, and the grand vizier, if he is involved, will think his servant is on his way to Sebta.'

'But what about Umar?' asked Talib. 'Can he be released now?'

'Patience, soldier. Let's see what the general has to say. He may be able to get something out of that assassin without involving ibn Baqanna. But as far as I'm concerned, it is as clear as a mountain stream that that man is guilty.

However, while Umar is still in gaol, he is out of harm's way. No, we can't let him out, yet.'

*

It didn't take Talib long to reach the kitchens. The head cook was nowhere to be seen but the friendly under cook was busy preparing a huge pot of soup.

'Hello there,' he said, with a cheery grin.

'As-salama alaykum, friend. I need your help' Talib said.

'Again? What is it this time? Haven't you got that soldier released yet?'

'No, but thanks to you, it shouldn't be long now. I just need you to do me one more favour,' said Talib, helping himself to a purple carrot.

'Very well. If I can help, I will.'

'We think we've caught al-Azdi attempting to escape to Sebta, but as none of us has ever seen him, and he's refusing to talk, we need you to identify him.'

'What's he look like, this bloke you've caught?'

'He's very tall, taller than me and thin. Even thinner than you are.'

The under cook looked down at his stomach and said, 'I'm not thin. I'm just not fat.'

'Well, whatever you say. He's tall and thin. He's shaved his head and beard and wears a single earring. Is that him?'

'Doesn't sound like him. Yes, the al-Azdi I know is tall and a bit on the skinny side but he has a long beard. Very proud of his beard he is.'

'Will you come anyway and see if you recognise him. He has to be the murderer; he has motive and opportunity. The only question is, whether he is capable of murder?'

'Oh, yes. He's capable of murdering the khalifa. He gave the appearance of being a loyal servant but according to the maids, he really hated him. Very well. Just give me a minute to finish this soup and I'll come with you.'

He tossed a handful of garlic cloves into the pot, gave it a quick stir and said to the scullion boy, 'You keep an eye on that pot. If I find it's boiled over while I'm away, you'll be in trouble. And give it a stir from time to time.'

'Yes, Mali,' said the boy.

Mali. So that was the under cook's name. He waited while Mali removed his greasy overall and put on a clean djellaba and then said, 'He's in gaol. Just follow me. It won't take long.'

Mali didn't look too happy at the mention of the prison, but nevertheless he followed Talib across the parade ground and down to the forbidding dungeons. The nazir was waiting outside for them.

'This is Mali,' said Talib. 'He can identify al-Azdi for us.'

'Good. Follow me and don't say anything. I will do all the talking,' said the nazir.

Talib took a deep breath before ducking low to get through the main gate. It was just as before but that didn't make it any better; he still felt his heart begin to race and once again the walls seem to be closing in on him.'

'What's the matter, soldier?' asked the nazir. 'Don't fancy spending a few nights in here?' He chuckled.

Talib said nothing and followed behind Mali, who seemed impervious to the putrid smell and the cold, dank atmosphere in the dungeon.

'This is the one you want, I think, 'said the gaoler. 'Came in, just a short while ago. Hasn't got much to say for himself. Do you want to go inside?' he asked, producing a huge iron key.

'No, that won't be necessary,' said the nazir. He turned to Mali. 'So, can you identify this man?'

Mali approached the bars and peered inside. The man was squatting at the back of his cell and his head was covered by the hood of his djellaba.

'It's difficult to tell from here,' he said. 'We need more light.'

'Gaoler. Give me your lamp,' said the nazir. 'And you, stand up so we can see you.'

The man in the cell didn't move.

'Very well, in that case, I will have to make you,' said the nazir and taking the lamp from the gaoler, he unlocked the cell and went inside. 'Mali, come in here and tell me if this is the servant named al-Azdi.'

The under cook entered the cell and peered at the unmoving figure on the ground. Cautiously he stretched his hand out and pulled the hood off the man's head. His bald head gleamed in the light of the oil lamp.

'Well, the al-Azdi I met had a thick head of hair and a long beard,' he said. 'But, I'm pretty sure it's the same man. One thing I do remember about him is that he had a gold tooth; it was at the top and very obvious when he smiled.'

'Well I don't think he's going to be doing much smiling for a while,' said the nazir and roughly pulled the man's head back. He stuck his fingers inside his lips and lifted them back to reveal the gold tooth. 'So it's him.?

'Yes, I'm sure it's al-Azdi,' said Mali.

At last the man turned to look at them and the look he gave Mali was of pure hate. This was a man who could keep a grudge for years and then act on it. It didn't surprise Talib that he was capable of killing the old khalifa.

CHAPTER 31

That morning Makoud was up earlier than usual; he'd washed, said the morning prayers and already breakfasted by the time Dirar arrived home.

'Have you heard, Baba?' his son asked, as soon as he came through the door. He looked a mess; his djellaba was torn and stained with mud.

'Heard what, boy? And why are you in such a state? I know yours is not the cleanest of jobs, but you don't usually come home looking as though you've been dragged along the riverbed.'

'So you haven't heard?' Dirar said with a huge grin.

He was beginning to annoy him. 'Obviously not. Are you going to tell me whatever this news is, or am I going to have to shake it out of you?'

'We got him, Baba. That al-Azdi bloke. We got him.'

'What do you mean, we? When did you become involved in all this?'

'The soldier friend of Umar, he asked me to help him.' Makoud listened to his excited son as he related what had happened and how he had saved Talib. 'And now he's in gaol, I think. Anyway, Talib took him straight to the Dar al-Jund. He said I had to go back to work.'

'Well, you have had a busy night,' said Makoud, sitting down and smiling at his young son. 'But more importantly, did you bring any decent fish home with you?'

'We were out after tuna last night, but only caught one, a big one. We did catch plenty of mackerel, though. I've brought you some for lunch.' He dropped his basket on the table; inside lay six gleaming fat fish.

'Well done, on both counts, lad. A good night's work.'

'You've heard?' said Rafiq, joining them on the patio. 'Has there been any more news from Talib?'

Makoud shook his head. 'Do you think he'll talk? That al-Azdi.'

'I doubt it. Unless they torture him.'

Makoud saw his son's eyes widen in horror. 'Would they do that?' he asked.

'It's been known,' said Rafiq. 'But men will say anything under torture. It's not the best way of getting to the truth. I think I'll go and see General Rashad, myself.'

'Do you know the general?' Dirar asked, obviously impressed at his great-uncle's connections.

'From way back.' He picked up an orange and began to peel it. 'He's the only one who is able to give the order to release Umar. If he can't help us, then I don't know what else we can do. It would be very risky to take our suspicions to the khalifa. And as for ibn Baqanna, well he's involved somehow; we just don't know exactly how, yet.'

'Surely we have enough evidence now?' said Makoud. Was his lovely son destined to rot in gaol for the rest of his life? No, he wouldn't allow it. 'Do you want me to come with you?'

'Yes. You're an upstanding member of the community, a well-regarded apothecary. If nothing else, it will show what a solid, Muslim background the boy has,' said Rafiq, throwing the orange peel into the pot. 'Good for the soil,' he added, looking at Dirar and winking.

'Wait while I tell Ibrahim to look after the shop and then we'll go,' Makoud said. He doubted whether it would make a grain of difference if he went or not, but at least he'd feel he was doing something to help. Hanging about the shop was driving him mad. He could barely concentrate on his work and where he was normally very patient with his female customers, who would spend hours deliberating over which perfume to choose, he now found himself pushing them into making a decision whether it was right or not, and had even suggested irritably to one dithering woman that she might find what she wanted from another apothecary.

'Good luck, Baba,' said Dirar, giving his father an unexpected hug.

*

Uncle and nephew walked up to the Boveda Gate together. There was no problem gaining access to the alcazaba this time; the sentry recognised Rafiq straight away.

'As-salama alaykum, sayyad. Back again?'

'Yes, soldier. Our work's not done yet.'

As they stepped once more into the fortress, Rafiq whispered, 'We'll go straight to the quaid first, to see what's been happening. I only want to see the general as a last resort.'

Makoud nodded. As before he was feeling intimidated by the strong military presence that was always on display. 'Isn't that the quaid over there?' he said.

The quaid was coming from the direction of the dungeons and he looked furious. A soldier was almost running to keep up with him and was obviously trying to tell him something.

'Ah, Captain,' he said, when he saw Rafiq approaching. 'Just the man I need. This whole case is making me very angry. Come with me. We must speak to General Rashad, at once.'

'As-salama alaykum, quaid. What's happened?' Rafiq asked, walking beside him. 'Has something happened to the prisoner?'

'He's dead.'

At those words, Makoud thought he'd pass out. In the name of Allah, surely his beloved Umar hadn't died. Not when they were so close to getting him released. He let out a groan of despair.

He felt Rafiq's hand on his arm, 'Courage, nephew. I think he's talking about the other prisoner,' he whispered.

Al-Azdi had been killed? That was almost as bad. There were no witnesses left now. It all depended on General Rashad. Would he believe them when they told him of Umar's innocence?

'We've come to see the general,' said the quaid to the guard outside the general's quarters.

'Who wants to see him?'

'You know very well, you stupid man. Just tell him I'm here.'

'Wait here.'

'Officious bastard,' the quaid swore under his breath.

Almost immediately the guard returned and asked them to follow him. The general was a big, burly man, of a similar age to his uncle and with a short grey beard. He stared at them through bright blue eyes, before saying, 'Ahlan, quaid. I see you have brought some visitors with you, one of whom I know very well.'

'Yes, General.'

The deputy head of the army got up and embraced Rafiq. 'As-salama alaykum, dear friend. What can I do for you? Or have you just come to sell me another excellent but over priced horse?'

'Wa alaykum e-salam, General. No, I'm not horse trading today. I come on a much more important matter, a family matter.'

'Please sit down, all of you,' said the general, looking at Makoud, curiously.

'This is my nephew, General. He is an apothecary. You will understand why he is here when we explain why we need your help.' He and the quaid then proceeded to tell the general about their original suspicion about the khalifa's death and the subsequent deaths of all the witnesses.

The general listened carefully and then turned to Makoud and said, 'I take it this man, Wada, bought the wormwood from your shop?'

Makoud felt his stomach hit the floor. 'Yes, General,' he managed to answer. 'But I didn't know he was going to give it to the khalifa. It's not illegal to sell wormwood.'

'Don't worry. I just want all the facts before I decide what to do. So, it was your son who was accused of murdering the royal physician, by the man's daughter?'

Makoud nodded, miserably. 'He didn't do it. He's not a murderer.'

'But he had a sword at the man's throat?'

'I believe so.'

'Mmn. And the other witnesses?'

'The man Wada was murdered,' said Rafiq. 'He was found in the Guadalhorce river, but after he'd confessed to one of your soldiers.'

'Yes, you said. And Umar was in prison at the time?'

'Yes, General,' said the quaid. 'He couldn't have murdered him.'

'What interests me is the man who's said to have administered the poison to the khalifa; why was he trying to leave the country? Why was he going to Sebta?' asked General Rashad.

'We have an idea, General, but I'm beginning to think that it is dangerous to even speak of it,' said Rafiq.

'One minute.' The general turned to the two soldiers standing by the door and said, 'Leave us alone for now. I will send for you when I need you.'

The soldiers saluted and left. Only Makoud, Rafiq, the quaid and the general remained in the room.

'Now you may speak freely,' he said. 'Before we go any further, I think I need to question this prisoner, al-Azdi, at once.'

'I have just been to the gaol to collect him but I was too late. The prisoner is dead. His throat was cut sometime last night. The gaoler has no idea who got in, nor how they managed to kill a prisoner in a locked cell,' said the quaid.

'Where is he? The gaoler?'

'I have had him removed from his post for now. I will question him later, but I'm sure nothing will come of it. I expect he was asleep. Somehow the assailant persuaded al-Azdi to approach the door of his cell and then he reached in and cut his throat. There was blood on the bars.'

'It was probably someone he knew,' added Rafiq. 'Someone he trusted.'

'I can see the motive for the deaths of the royal surgeon, Wada and this al-Azdi, but if they are all linked to the death of the khalifa, what was the motive for his death? Khalifas live very short lives as it is, especially when they are always waging wars against their neighbours. What was so important that he had to be killed then?' asked General Rashad.

'And who would benefit?' added Rafiq. He looked behind him to make sure that the soldiers had not returned.

'The obvious man is the khalifa's brother Idris, but they were devoted to each other,' said General Rashad.

'So everyone says, but he sent his nephews to Sebta,' said the quaid.

'Yes, but that wasn't his idea. No, I'm beginning to see who could be behind all this, a man I've had some suspicions about for some time. I began to wonder what he was up to, when he arranged to have my good friend, Labib, moved to Sebta to look after Idris I's nephews. He was a lowly official in Sebta, a backwater of the kingdom and he wanted more. He wanted to come to Malaqah and not just that, he wanted to be part of the royal court. Since he has been the grand vizier I have seen first hand how power-hungry he is. He gave no thought to those children and their mother when he advised Idris to banish them. I admit I fear for their safety when the time comes for Hassan to take up his inheritance.'

'Ibn Baqanna?' asked Rafiq. 'We know that al-Azdi worked for him. That much he did confess.'

The general nodded. 'Now he is untouchable. It seems very plain to me that he wanted someone who was close to the khalifa and he knew that al-Azdi could be easily manipulated because of what happened to his sister.'

'But how did he know about it?' asked Makoud.

'He was there on that campaign; he was Prince Yahya's advisor at the time. He would have known Wada too; he was the girl's fiancé.'

'So that is what links them all together?'

'Yes. He didn't have to get his hands dirty when he had two vengeful men ready to do it for him.'

'So, ibn Baqanna gave the orders and al-Azdi did the killing?'

'It looks very much like that but unless we have solid proof that he gave the order to poison Yahya, we can do nothing. We can't even go to Idris I in case he's involved, although I doubt that he would commit such a crime against his own brother. However I don't want to risk it. I'm sorry but I think this case is now closed. All the witnesses are dead.'

'So who has murdered al-Azdi?'

The general shrugged his shoulders. 'It wouldn't be hard for ibn Baqanna to find someone to slit the man's throat for a purse full of silver. I'm sorry but there is nothing more we can do.'

'No,' groaned Makoud. 'It's so unjust. My son will die in the dungeons of the alcazaba that he swore to defend and there is nothing we can do to help him?'

General Rashad looked at him and said, 'Let me finish, my good apothecary. Although we cannot bring the culprit to justice, that doesn't mean that we cannot release someone who has no motive for the murders, who had no access to the khalifa, and was in prison when at least two of the murders were committed. But before I release him, I would like to speak to this young soldier. Wait here.' He went to the door and said to the soldiers, 'Bring me the prisoner Umar ibn Makoud.

Then he turned to Rafiq and said, 'While we wait for the young man, tell me about life in Ardales, Rafiq. Are you not tired of living in retirement yet?'

*

When the soldiers eventually came back with Umar, Makoud had difficulty in recognising this undernourished, filthy figure as his son. The soldiers had made some attempt to clean him up—probably by pouring a bucket of water over his head—and one of them had found some boots for him. His hair hung in a tangled mass about his shoulders and he stared around the room as if he were in a dream. Perhaps he was; perhaps he didn't realise what was happening to him.

'Umar,' he said, moving towards him. 'Umar, it's me, Baba.'

He felt Rafiq's restraining hand on his arm.

'Are you the prisoner, Umar ibn Makoud?' asked General Rashad.

Umar looked at him blankly then nodded.

'Your quaid, your friends and your family have been continuing with the unwise investigation that you began into Khalifa Yahya I's death. I say unwise because it is an investigation that was doomed to failure from the start and has caused three more deaths in the process. I realise you are a loyal soldier and your actions were prompted through wanting justice for the khalifa. However justice cannot always be served, especially when the crime committed stems from very powerful people; that is something you have learned the hard way, soldier.'

Umar continued to stare at the general as if he were talking to them all and not addressing him personally. Makoud saw him glance around the room, as though trying to work out where he was. The light appeared to be bothering his eyes and more than once he raised his hand to shield them.

'I have heard all the evidence in this case and come to a conclusion. For a start, it didn't make sense for you to murder your prime witness in this charade, so I cannot see any motive for you to kill the royal physician. The only witnesses to your presence at the house of the physician were his daughter and his servant and neither of them saw you kill him. All we have in fact is her accusation. The accusation of a young woman grieving for her father and looking for someone to blame. The quaid has questioned the servant again and the man admits that the good doctor had another visitor, someone he knew, after both you and his daughter had left. Al-Azdi, a man he saw regularly and regarded as a trusted friend. So I am not going to charge you with the murder of Abu al-Jabir. Dismissed. You are free to go.'

At first Umar didn't move; he seemed bewildered.

'Have you gone deaf now? Dismissed, I said. The case is closed.'

'But…'

'You heard General Rashad. It is closed. The truth is never likely to come out. But we must move on and I want you to do that as well,' said the quaid.

'Yes, sayyad. Thank you sayyad.'

Makoud couldn't contain himself any longer; he rushed forward and threw his arms around Umar and hugged him.

'Baba. Can I go home now?'

'Yes, son. We're going home.'

*

Naja al-Siqlabi had just finished giving the princes Hasan and ben-Yahya their Arabic lessons when the messenger arrived. He had been staring out across the patio to the Middle Sea and wondering why the man he was supposed to meet last night had never arrived.

'Sayyad, may I speak to you?' the man said, removing his hood and bowing before the ex-slave.

'Who are you and what do you want?' snapped Naja. He was feeling irritable. He'd waited until almost dawn for the man to arrive and as a consequence, had little sleep. He'd considered cancelling the princes' morning lesson, but he knew Queen Fatima would not have approved; she was determined to give her sons the best preparation possible for their future roles as khalifa. And dereliction of duty would be a poor example on his part. It was pointless anyway; the boys were poor students. All they could think about was learning to become warriors. Both their mother and he had told them that a ruler needed more than just strength to rule a country, but they were both so young they thought they had all the time in the world for such things as mathematics and Arabic. Well not if Malaqah's new grand vizier had anything to do with it.

'I have a message for you from my master, ibn Baqanna,' the messenger said, bowing again. 'It is important and I am to give it to you personally.'

'Very well, hand it over.'

He took the carefully rolled parchment and thrust it into the pocket of his djellabah.

'Is there a reply, sayyad?' asked the messenger. He was a scruffy looking man, who was staring at Naja as though his life depended on it. He smiled to himself. Knowing ibn Baqanna, it probably did.

'I'll let you know when I've read it, idiot.' He turned to the young slave who had shown the messenger in, and said,

'Take him to the kitchens and tell the cook to give him some food. He looks as though he hasn't eaten for days.' His old friend ibn Baqanna was not known for his generosity to his servants but he could at least feed them. Being an ex-slave himself, Naja knew what it was like to go without food.

'Right, now where were we?' he asked the two princes. 'Ah, yes. Mathematics.'

'But I thought we'd finished,' said ben-Yahya, giving his tutor a woeful look. He certainly had a better head for figures than his brother.

'Well today you're lucky. We are finished. Run along, the imam is waiting to see how much you have learnt of the Quran since yesterday.' He saw the boys look at each other and grimace.

'Ma'a salama, sayyad,' they chorussed and hurried across the patio towards the mosque where the imam was waiting.

Once they were out of sight, Naja sat down in the school room and pulled out the parchment. What was it that was so important that ibn Baqanna would risk sending him a personal message? He read it carefully. It was brief and to the point.

'*Naja al-Siqlabi,*

The man you were supposed to meet at the harbour has been arrested. It is known that he is my servant, therefore it is too risky to go ahead with our plans at the moment. Do nothing until you hear from me again. I will take care of things here.'

It was unsigned. 'Our plans' Naja snarled to himself. Since when were they 'our plans? This had all been ibn Baqanna's great idea to gain power and wealth for both of them. Now while Baqanna had achieved the wealth and power he craved, Naja was stuck here in Sebta, tutoring two dunderheads. He threw the parchment down in annoyance. So Baqanna was taking care of things, was he? He knew what that meant and it didn't bode well for his unlucky servant.

CHAPTER 32

Talib was getting his horse saddled ready for the evening exercise ride when Umar returned to the Dar al-Jund.

'How are you?' he asked. 'Are you back at work already?'

'Yes. Rafiq said if I didn't get back straight away, I'd never do it. Wait until I get Basil ready and we'll ride together,' said Umar.

He slipped the harness over Basil's nose and tied it in place. The mare nuzzled him affectionately, wanting some attention, so he pulled an apple from the pocket of his tunic and offered it to her.

'Good girl, Basil,' he whispered. 'Good girl.' He stroked her black mane and as he did so, he began to feel the tensions of the last few weeks drift away from him. Weeks? It felt more like years. How could he explain that to Talib? He didn't want anyone to know how it had almost destroyed him in there. Even now, he could hardly bear to think back to his imprisonment. What had been worse? Was it the loneliness, with no-one to talk to except a few madmen the other side of the cell walls? Was it the filth? The hunger? No, it had been the loss of his faith. When he'd stopped praying then he'd really felt alone and abandoned; that's when despair became his constant companion. Since he'd been released he couldn't face going to the mosque—he was sure the imam would know that he'd stopped believing in Allah—instead he prayed at home with his family. Gently he placed a quilted mat onto Basil's back and then lifted the saddle into place. Once she was ready he led her down the coracha and out into the main street. He was desperate to get away from the confines of the city and just ride, to fool the wind in his face and Basil beneath him.

'Well?' asked Talib.

'Later, my friend. We'll talk later. For now, I need to clear my head. Let's just ride.'

They trotted across the Fortified Bridge and into the suburbs, then let the horses have their heads; they cantered down onto the shore, following their daily exercise route. He dug his heels into Basil's flanks and felt her come to life beneath him. As one they galloped down the beach, the wind blowing his long hair back from his face, his lungs hungrily breathing in the salty air. He was alive. They were not going to execute him after all. And he was free. Until the moment of his release he hadn't fully appreciated just how dangerous his predicament had been. The quaid was a meticulous man and luckily for Umar, not one to make snap judgements, otherwise he'd have been summarily executed weeks ago. He urged Basil on, her hooves pounding through the smooth sand, sending it flying up behind them.

By the time they reached the rocky outcrop which marked the end of their exercise area, his heart was pounding and he could feel the adrenalin racing through his body. There was nothing so invigorating as riding along the beach. He slowed his mare to a walk and waited for Talib to catch him up.

'You should give her her head a bit more, Talib,' he said. 'She's not giving it everything. Don't be frightened of her. She knows what she's doing.'

Talib patted his horse's neck and smiled. 'I know. It's good to have you back, Umar.'

*

Aisha was sitting in the sand watching Maryam playing by the water's edge. She could see the soldier's exercising their horses as they did every evening when the sun began its descent; it was a wonderful sight to see the horses galloping along the sand, silhouetted against the reddening sky, their manes flying and their hooves creating a small sandstorm in their wake. The sun's rays, although weak, were still warm and she began to feel drowsy. She lay back, resting her head on Imran's shawl. Her baby son was happily digging his hands into the soft sand and letting it fall all over him, chuckling to himself every time it cascaded through his chubby fingers. She felt she should stop him, clean him up and set off for home, but she hadn't the heart to do so; today for the first time in a long while she felt at peace. Her brother was safe and sound, riding his beloved Basil along with all the other jinetes, and for once she felt she had a future to look forward to. As they had been doing for some weeks now, her thoughts turned again to Bakr; he was a good, kind man and he wanted to marry her. She had considered his proposal objectively, reflecting on what it would mean, not just for her, but also for her children. Only one question remained unanswered. Would she be able to love him as he loved her? She couldn't imagine a marriage without love, although she knew that there were many such unions. It was a question that came to her every time she saw him. Now at last she felt she had her answer; when she'd seen how concerned he was about helping her brother, she knew she could grow to love him. What she was beginning to feel for him was not the passion that she had felt for Daud, but a more mature longing to be part of his life, to share his world, to be a mother to his children. She would never stop loving Daud, but now she felt her heart was big enough to love someone else as well.

GLOSSARY

Al-Andalus the Islamic name given to Moorish Spain
Alboran Sea the part of the Mediterranean near Malaga
Alcaiceria textile workplace, especially silk
Alfarero potter
Al-Jazira the city of Algeciras
Ahlan welcome
Ahlan wa sahlan. the reply to welcome
Alla ysalmak response to goodbye
ammu uncle
Arab mile between 1.8 and 2 kilometres
As-salama alaykum Hello
Atarazanas shipyards
Baba father
Barid postal service
Barrio district
Calendula used as a disinfectant
Churros a sweet fried batter
Dar al-Jund soldiers' quarters
al-Darrabun night watchman
Dirhams silver units of currency
Dinars gold unit of currency
Djubbah a simple tunic
Djellaba a hooded cloak
Djinn a mythical being from the spirit world
Garnata the city of Granada
Hammudid dynasty rulers in al-Andalus 1016 AD - 1056 AD
Iddah period of mourning: four months and ten days
Imam holy man
Insha'Allah God willing

Isbiliya the city of Seville

Jebel al-Tarik Gibraltar

Jarrah jug

Jihad holy war

Jinete horseman

Ma'a salama goodbye

Maghreb the region of North West Africa bordering the Mediterranean Sea

Malaqah the city of Malaga

Medina a town

Middle Sea one of the names for the Mediterranean

Muhtasib officer in charge of municipal police

Naquib officer in charge of a contingent of up to 2,000 men

Nazir sergeant in charge of a squad of 16 men

Omayyads the rulers of al-Andalus 970 AD - 1031 AD

Qadi religious judge

Qarib a wooden ship, strong enough to go out into the ocean but also close inland

Qarmuña the city of Carmona

Quaid officer in charge of a corps of up to 10,000 men

Quran the central religious holy book of Islam

Qurtubah the city of Córdoba

Puerta gate

Saqaliba a slave from northern and eastern Europe

Sayyad master or sir

Sayeda madam

Seedo nickname for Grandfather

Sea of Darkness one of the names for the Atlantic Ocean

Sebta the town of Ceuta in North Africa

Shaitan the Devil

Shatrang check-board banner

Souk market

Taifa an independent Muslim-ruled principality
Teta nickname for grandmother
Wa alaykum e-salam Peace be upon you
Zenana the innermost apartments where the women live

The Apothecary

AUTHOR'S NOTE

Many of the Moorish names used in this book are long and easy to confuse with each other, as certain names keep being repeated. The names I have used are all prior to 1600 AD and follow prescribed naming practices.

Arab name elements fall into five main categories. For simplification I have used only two of them. An ISM, which is a personal name, given at birth, such as Makoud, followed by a NASAB which tells you which family they belong to, such as ibn Ahmad (son of Ahmad) or Aisha bint Makoud (Aisha daughter of Makoud). With members of the royal family you will see that the names can be very long, such as Yahya ibn Ali ibn Hammud al Mutali (Yahya son of Ali son of Hammud al Mutali). It was not considered polite to call older people by their ISM.

It was customary for one of the male children in an Arab family to be called after his grandfather.

The wrestling match I have described is what is known as Canarian wrestling. Recent research shows that this type of wrestling was performed by the original people of the Canary Islands, the Guanches, who have been proved to have been of North African origin and closely related to the Berber people. As a large percentage of the population of al-Andalus were Berbers, it is quite likely that this was the type of wrestling that the soldiers did as a form of daily exercise in al-Andalus.

CPSIA information can be obtained
at www.ICGtesting.com
Printed in the USA
BVHW041043050121
597035BV00010B/541